Matthew Crow was born and raised in Newcastle. Having worked as a freelance journalist since his teens he has contributed to a number of publications including the *Independent on Sunday* and the *Observer*. He has written two novels for adults. The second, *My Dearest Jonah*, was nominated for the Dylan Thomas Prize. His first YA novel, *In Bloom*, was much loved and much praised.

ATOM

First published in Great Britain in 2017 by Atom

1 3 5 7 9 10 8 6 4 2

A CIP catalogue record for this book
is available from the British Library.

ISBN 978-1-4721-1420-4

Typeset by M Rules
Printed and bound in Great Britain
by CPI Group (UK) Ltd, Croydon CR0 4YY

Papers used by Atom are from well-managed forests
and other responsible sources.

MIX
Paper from
responsible sources
FSC® C104740

Atom
An imprint of
Little, Brown Book Group
Carmelite House
50 Victoria Embankment
London EC4Y 0DZ

An Hachette UK Company
www.hachette.co.uk

www.atombooks.co.uk

ANOTHER PLACE

MATTHEW CROW

PART ONE

Searching for Sarah

1

The Summer It Rained

I got out of hospital the summer they were looking for Sarah.

The summer I got better, then worse, then better again.

The never-ending summer.

The blink and you'll miss it summer.

They showed where I lived on television.

It was the day that they found the hairclip in the wastepipe leading to Hook's Scar. A helicopter caught a glimpse of our chimney as it sliced through Shetland Avenue and across the promenade towards the beach.

'I live there,' I said in the common room. It was fifteen minutes until the start of my last group, and there were only three of us on the sofas.

Lou said that she had lost her virginity between some bins behind Jumping Jacks nightclub. Samantha said it looked rubbish. Ginny asked whether Sarah was at my school. When I told her she was in my year she asked me if I knew who'd taken her. I said I didn't know and that she could have just run away for all anybody knew. Samantha said it wouldn't be on the news

3

if she wasn't dead already and then Ginny started crying and left the room.

In truth I knew it would be bad.

Sarah had the kind of beauty that forced you to look, but a manner that caused you to turn away fast. She didn't seem like the type of girl who simply wandered off and got lost. She seemed like the type of girl that was taken.

I had known her in secret, which was the way she seemed to form all of her acquaintances; and in fragments, the only way she would give of herself – sharp pieces picked from the whole, doled out necessarily and sparingly to those who cared enough to make an effort.

'We're the same, you and me,' she'd said quietly on one of our last nights together on the beach. 'I mean we're different, and all that. But deep down we're the same.' She had mused, sat there draining the last of her vodka as the tide pulled in. 'We're just two different types of fucked,' she concluded.

I began to think about her more and more during those last days on the unit. In a strange way it was nice, after weeks of focusing solely on myself, to be reminded that I was not the only part of the world that needed fixing. The longer she was missing, the further away she seemed to get, the less I was able to focus on anything else, to the point that her recovery became my mission. As if by solving the mystery of Sarah I could solve the mystery of myself.

In the run up to my release I had been given a notebook to fill out.

'Baby steps, Claudette,' Doctor Warren had informed me, handing the notepad across to me with a plastic biro. 'Set small goals that you can easily achieve, and a large goal to work towards.'

4

'Do I have to show this to anybody?' I had asked, and he smiled as he shook his head.

'It is for you and you only,' he said. 'It may seem silly, but try it. You'd be amazed at how much you are able to achieve once you set your mind to it.'

That night I had done as instructed. I picked easy tasks to adhere to on a day by day basis, and weekly goals that didn't seem entirely unachievable.

Towards the back of the small notepad was a page headlined in an insistent font: A LONG TERM GOAL I WILL WORK TOWARDS, it said in block letters, underlined and exclaimed.

It was here that I wrote my goal for the summer. A goal I would only share with those whose involvement helped my mission. The last secret between me and the friend I had known only at night.

That summer I would find Sarah Banks.

Jimmy was the nurse on guard that day. He looked up from his crossword and squinted over the rim of his glasses at the television, where a camera now panned over the main stretch of the beach.

'The first place we ever took our Sonny for a walk after he was born, along that promenade,' he said. 'We found a fiver in the shingles that day and bought some chips. Good day.' He smiled and returned to his puzzles.

I stared at the footage on screen. Across the sand, dark patches wound in and out of one another from where the search party had combed the stretch from the lighthouse, past the pier, all the way towards the power station. The camera showed all of the places I knew; the ice-cream shop and the amusement arcade, and the other ice-cream shop and the other amusement arcade.

Leaflets showing Sarah's face lined the faded boards that surrounded the Mariners' development.

Missing
Have You Seen This Girl?
Call This Number

Her image was multiplied, over and over again, like a morbid Warhol painting on the development that never really was.

The Mariners had started life as a dance hall. Then, after various and fleeting stints as a disco, a roller-rink and an indoor market respectively, it was shut down, boarded up and eventually bought by a developer to be turned into: 'Quality One Two and Three Bedroom Apartments: City Style, Coastal Views.'

The company responsible had made a big deal of holding town meetings with a view to getting everybody on board. They promised to employ local tradesman. They swore to retain the character of the building. 'Maintain the best and strengthen the rest', said the flyers that came through the door, before planning permission had been granted.

The development had made its way as far as the scaffolding stages before money ran dry and the Mariners was abandoned to rats and squatters.

Mostly the closed-down shops up there on television just looked embarrassed. When I was a little girl the promenade was the brightest, busiest thing in the world. There were people. There were sounds and open signs and coloured lights in the dark.

Dad was on the Street Wise team then: a group of locals who

met up after work in hi-vis jackets, armed with bin liners and litter pickers, to clear the beach.

Sometimes he'd take me when after-school club had been cancelled.

'Come on,' he'd say, putting his jacket on me. 'We're going on a treasure hunt. Biggest bag wins.'

We never did find any treasure. I'd get to the end of the beach, all clean and shiny again, and look forlorn at our notable lack of jewels and coins.

'Well, there's always next time,' Dad would say, handing me fifty pence and a wink for my efforts.

Once the rot set in there was no stopping it. Each day another shop was boarded up. Weeds grew from cracked windows and the crowds grew less and less. It was the same with me. Sometimes I'd look back at old photographs and try to pinpoint the exact moment I broke; when the world changed colour and suddenly I was different. There was no single moment. It was a gradual change, like a cloud moving across a picnic. If you lined up the photographs of Dad and me, from baby to adolescent, you could see it happening. Beside him stood a girl whose eyes grew sadder and more terrified with each extra inch she grew, as though the more she saw the more she realised there was to be utterly frightened of. More to be bemused by. More not to understand.

'Ever get the feeling you're on a sinking ship?' Dad once chuckled sadly as we walked home from the bus stop one evening to find that his second favourite sandwich shop – Goodfillers, with the logo of the French stick wearing a tuxedo – had been boarded up. He still hadn't fully recovered from the loss of Pita Pan, and would struggle to find solace in the substitute offerings of Lord of the Fries.

7

I didn't say anything and I suppose I didn't have to, because Dad just put his arm around me and held me tight as we walked the rest of the way home.

The day Sarah disappeared I had been in the hospital three weeks and four days. It would be another three days before Dad came to pick me up.

I was unsticking the photographs from above my bed when Violet came in to check on my packing progress. I'd arrived at hospital in the same torn school uniform that they'd found me in. The rest of my clothes had appeared during the first few days, when I slept right through the chemical fog administered by kindly nurses. Occasionally I'd lift my arm as a tourniquet was tightened and blood samples were taken to check that my cocktail of narcotics weren't doing more harm than good. But mostly I slept.

Dad had driven up every day, or so I was told. He had left clothes, which were folded and put into drawers for me, and photographs which I had to stick to the walls with chewing gum. Safety pins were a no-no. I suppose even Blu Tack could be lethal if you ingested enough.

Violet was tall and oblong with a hairdo that looked as though it had been built from Lego. She wore hiking boots and wax jackets everywhere she went, summer or winter, as if she thought she might be required to conquer a sudden precipice in the middle of Tesco. Violet was not a doctor or a nurse or anything that seemed to grant you letters after your name. She called herself a counsellor and mostly chatted about your day, before scurrying off to make notes and show them to the doctors in charge. If the hospital were a prison, Violet would have been shivved for snitching long before now.

Fortunately it wasn't a prison. Despite the bars on the windows and the skeleton keys and the occasional forcible restraints. And Violet was sweet and kind and often brought distracting chocolates, so nobody ever thought to attack her for her treachery.

'How you feeling?' she asked, walking straight into my room.

'I don't really know,' I said as I scrunched the last of my underwear into a bag. 'Good, I suppose. *Positive.*'

Violet turned to check that we were alone for a moment then lowered her voice.

'It's me you're speaking to now, Claudette. Don't feel the need to use therapy talk. You can feel however you feel, in whatever words you like. I don't mind. You've done well. You've earned your right to simply not know at times.' She leaned over the bed, holding out an open bag of sweets.

I smiled and rummaged in the bag.

'Scared, a bit,' I said, swallowing a plastic-y tasting blackcurrant cube. 'Well, apprehensive more than anything.'

'You're bound to be scared. I'm nervous coming back to work after taking a long weekend. Four weeks is a long time, Claudette.'

'Ever started a long weekend the way I started my stint here?' I said, and Violet laughed as she shook her head. She had read my notes, I knew. So was aware of the state I'd been left in by the time I was admitted. Depression and I had been on speaking terms for some time by that point. I may not have always understood its rules, but its rhythms I had grown to recognise. And yet the white-hot snap of mania had come at me quickly and without warning. It was as though all of a sudden my body and mind could only recognise extremes; that unless I felt everything then I would feel nothing at all. And so I pushed harder and harder until I guess I just gave out.

'You're a good person, Claudette, and a smart girl. You've come far and you'll go farther,' she said with a knowing nod.

I think in Violet's head she was the type of figure they'd make a film out of one day. The one person who got through to the seemingly unfixable head-case. The truth was, most of the other girls spent all their time in rec making fun of her. But to me she seemed sweet, in a sad sort of way.

I nodded appreciatively and Violet gave me a special sort of wink.

She placed the half tube of sweets on my bedspread as she left me in peace. 'For the energy,' she said. 'Nice to see your appetite hasn't dipped.' She smiled and left me in peace.

The room was stripped of my things. It no longer belonged to me and I no longer belonged to it. I felt my body begin to shake as I picked up my bag. Because for all my bravado, it had suddenly dawned on me just how clueless I was about whatever came next. For as long as I could remember my life had belonged to a condition that had taken me down. But everybody knows how to break. There were films about girls unravelling and boys exploding. Every other song seemed to be about Losing Your Mind or Going Under to a place where there was no light. There was a point of reference for coming apart. I'd been gifted a condition that had its own aesthetic. But putting myself back together? That was something that nobody showed you how to do. There was no framework. No well-trodden footpath.

We break suddenly.

We break spectacularly.

But to rebuild takes time and effort. It is a skill set none of us are born with.

Without realising it we spend half our lives being shown how to come apart. But putting ourselves back together? That was the great unknown.

I felt like a blank page.

And I was terrified.

2

Gee, But It's Great To Be Back Home!

'All set then?'

Dad greeted me at the front desk, where he stood with Violet. He had worn his best shirt and was carrying keys to a borrowed car.

'Just about,' I said, taking my package from Violet.

'These will last you the first few weeks,' she said. 'And remember you're not in this on your own. We're only ever a phone call away. You've got your first appointment with the counsellor set up for next week.'

'Oh yes,' Dad interjected. 'We've been well drilled.'

'Then that's you.' Violet beamed. 'Well done, Claudette, you've come on leaps and bounds. We're all very proud of you.'

Dad and I went out to the car.

'So ... how's your day been?' he said, with a deadpan look that I couldn't help but smile at.

'Well, the hotel wasn't up to much.'

'Out of ten?'

'A low six if anything.'

'This simply won't do,' he said. His tone was light but his

voice weak and scratched. I could tell he had been crying. 'Set spell-check to livid! To TripAdvisor forthwith!' He opened my door, taking my hand to guide me into the front passenger seat.

'I'm not glass, Dad,' I said, shattering the wry jollity somewhat.

'No . . .' he said. 'No . . . But precious cargo is precious cargo. You're my pension, Claudette Flint. I intend to maintain you the way I never could my savings account.'

'Don't worry big man, I'll see you right,' I said.

Dad chuckled, but after a while he sighed and his eyes softened. For the last month I'd been relearning how to cope on neutral. I wasn't ready to test myself against extreme emotional duress, especially not with the man I loved the most.

'I missed you,' he said with such quiet sincerity that it hit my stomach like a wrecking ball.

I leant out of the car window as he shut the door and squeezed his hand.

'So did I.'

We drove home in silence, getting used to sharing space.

'Well, I'll put the kettle on then,' Dad said as I dragged my bag into my room and shut the door behind me.

The window had been replaced with new glass. Double glazed this time. With a security sticker still stuck to the bottom right hand corner. I unpicked the clear plastic as the radiator clicked and clanked, before omitting a gentle hum of warmth that seeped up towards my wrists.

I left my bag on the floor and lay back on my bed. There was a bare patch on the far wall where the blood must have been particularly stubborn. Memories of the day leading up to the hospital came in dribs and drabs. I felt the glass shatter against

13

my hands; felt the sharp edges slicing cleanly at my skin. I remember walking as though my life depended on it. Dripping blood all the way to school. I remember standing at the gates. I remember a fuss around me and then ... nothing.

The thought of Dad hunched on his knees, bleaching my blood from the paintwork, made my stomach tighten and knot.

The thoughts became loud but then settled as my phone alarm buzzed against my leg to remind me to dose up. Fluoxetine made me nauseous if I took it before lunchtime, I had found, but without my morning ritual with the pensioner's pill divider Dad had bought me, I needed some form of reminder or I'd forget altogether.

I turned off the alarm while I fished a tampon from my bag, securing my gum in its wrapper before washing down three tablets with a flat bottle of Coke that stood guard beside my bed.

Being back home still didn't feel quite right. Or rather it felt like only half of me had returned. That the rest of me – the part that had been jettisoned to make room for the mania that had taken the steering wheel in those last weeks – was still out there somewhere, lost and homesick. I didn't feel quite whole. The memories still burned bright behind my sockets, so I scrunched my eyes together tightly and tried an exercise that they taught in one of our group sessions. Whenever you feel bad about your actions during an episode you think to yourself, *When I'm In Control I* ... and then go through the good things that you've done for people.

When I'm In Control I ... help with the vacuuming.

When I'm In Control I ... leave Dad's dinner in the oven if he's on night shift.

When I'm In Control I ... spend time with Dad even though I'd rather be in my room.

14

When I'm In Control . . .

A gentle knock on the door interrupted my exercise.

'Yeah, I'll be through in a second,' I said, translating the sound of the knock into the question I knew it was.

'I forgot to get biscuits,' Dad said through the door. 'Shall I pop out and get some?'

'I'll go,' I said, opening the door. Dad had one tea towel draped across his shoulder and another pressing inside of a World's Best Dad mug.

(When I'm In Control . . . I buy cheap card-shop mugs, because I know that the sentiment implied will mean more than the five ninety nine it cost me.)

'I don't mind,' he said, trying to stifle his concern with selflessness.

'Dad, I'll go. I need some air. That hospital was always too warm. The air was stagnant.'

'You watch how you go,' Dad said eventually, quietly resigned to having lost this battle. 'Do you need any money?'

'Nah, I'm liquid,' I yelled, tucking the spare key into my jeans pocket as I slammed the front door behind me.

A man I didn't recognise stood at the counter as a beeping door announced my arrival. He was talking to Mrs Nesbitt, who ran the shop. Their voices dipped as I made my way past sanitary-wear towards the biscuit section of the aisle. Out of eyesight, Mrs Nesbitt said something and the man let out a short, sharp laugh.

'Not in our day, eh?' he said as he made his way towards the door which beeped again as it closed behind him.

I took the biscuits to the counter and held them out to be scanned.

'Claudette, isn't it?' Mrs Nesbitt asked. She had lived in the area for longer than most of the architecture and knew everybody's business. Feigning ignorance over a detail as pivotal as your name was simply one of many power moves in her armoury.

'That's me,' I said, pressing the biscuits towards her.

'Hmmm,' she said uncertainly, locking me in her suspicious glare as she carried out the meagre transaction. 'I'm keeping an eye on you, mind,' she said as I opened the door to leave, though her tone implied more warning than concern. 'You just be careful.'

I walked the long way home, across the grass banks that separated the beach from the high street, to avoid a camera crew in the alleyway that I'd normally have cut through.

Sarah seemed only to travel via backstreets. She had an encyclopaedic knowledge of the town's veins and arteries, and could take you wherever you wanted to go without being seen. It was a habit that had rubbed off on me to a degree, but out of curiosity more than necessity. The effort Sarah often put into disappearing made me realise that more often than not she was hiding from something. She just never said what, exactly.

Across the beach there were white tents erected where evidence had been found. Metal poles with Do Not Cross tape marked out square sections of sand. And men in overalls placed dug-up treasures into marked plastic bags. Cameras dotted the lower promenade as a dozen or so presenters all found different ways to tell the world that nobody knew anything.

Ross Lions stood on the upper promenade. He was throwing chips towards the mawkish reporters in a bid to make seagulls attack.

'Got you!' he yelled, as a gull the size of a shire horse

bumbled its way towards the high heel of a presenter, causing her to dance on the spot as it fussed over the soggy chip.

I'd almost passed unnoticed when Ross's voice snagged behind me.

'Claudette Flint!' he yelled, as I turned slowly to meet his gaze. 'I didn't think you were coming back.'

'I nearly didn't,' I said.

'You coming down here then?'

I shook my head and held up the biscuits.

'Got my morning all planned out, thanks,' I said, and Ross nodded, the bravado slipping from his face.

'You all right though?' he asked. Ross was an idiot. But somewhere, hidden deep, was a genuine human being.

'Yeah,' I said, nodding as I turned to leave. 'Thanks. Are you?'

He shrugged. 'Never better,' he said as he returned to tormenting the camera crews.

Ross had been the first boy I ever kissed.

When we were eleven we'd play Chicken on the road behind our flat. One person would stand on the white lines as a car came towards them, and stare it down until they got scared and jumped out of the way. The winner was the person that avoided death by the narrowest margin. One by one the boys would stand there snarling at oncoming vans and cars. The girls would sit quietly and watch, rapt with admiration, until our number was up and we were called home for tea.

One night Ross and I were the last ones standing.

'I've got to be home,' he'd said as the evening became inky and chilled.

'But I haven't had my turn yet,' I said, standing up and making my way towards the kerb.

'Girls can't play,' he said as I walked into the middle of the empty road and closed my eyes.

For a while it was still and quiet. There was nothing but the sound of waves lapping in the distance.

It came gradually at first. I didn't open my eyes. I just let the sound of the engine grow louder and louder until it blocked out everything else around me. I spread out my arms and tightened my eyes until I felt a yank on my right arm and the whoosh of the car speeding past us as a horn blared out and faded into the distance.

Ross had hauled me onto the kerb with such force that I'd rolled underneath him. I opened my eyes as his lips touched mine and his tongue scraping across my top row of teeth.

'Gross,' I said, pushing him off me as I sat up.

'Better than being run over.'

'Says you,' I said. 'Does this mean I win?' I stared at the scorched tyre marks where the car had tried to swerve.

Ross stood up and shook his head.

'Don't tell anybody,' he said

'That I beat you?'

'That we kissed.'

'Why not?' I asked.

'Because you're strange. If you say anything I'll tell them you're lying.'

And with that he ran off towards the bus stop.

The promenade's lawns were strewn across with takeaway wrappers, tin cans and the odd used condom. The concrete waves of the skate park lay silent and empty and in the distance a helicopter chopped the air into bullets of sound that carried on the wind.

All of the benches facing the sea were memories. Each one held a plaque covered in grime. They said things like: **Mary's Seat, Who Loved The View**, or, **In Memory of Charles, Forever At Sea**. It was sweet. And slightly comical. These benches would bear a very different sentiment when my friends and I started dying. They would say things like: **In Memory of Paul, Who First Fingered Charlotte Here After the Sea Cadets Disco**, or, **Forever Aaron, Who Vomited Two Bottles of Lambrini and Half a Doner Kebab All Over This Very Bench**.

Each seat was covered in bird shit except for one. It was here that Mr Fitzpatrick sat.

Mr Fitzpatrick was nobody's dad, though he paid particular cantankerous interest in us all when we were growing up. No ball bounced in the back lane without a yelled warning from him that people were trying to sleep.

'You've a whole beach out there, why you making a fuss in a dirty old lane?' he'd yell.

Silence was what he demanded. And more often than not it was what he got.

Our parents had warned us about Mr Fitzpatrick.

'Just do as he says,' they told us. 'He's old and he's got nobody else,' they'd say.

'Mr Fitzpatrick likes things just so.'

That was at first, before he shifted for most of our parents from being a curmudgeonly nuisance to being an active figure of hate.

Before long his disdain became more problematic.

There would be knocks on the door as apologetic police explained that they were being forced to respond to reports of antisocial behaviour in the form of ball games and hopscotch. Phone calls from Social Services after Mr Fitzpatrick had declared that any children allowed to play out that late were surely victims of neglect.

Our parents weren't so keen to accommodate his quest for quiet after that.

The funny thing was that, save the odd night-shift worker, almost nobody slept through the day except for Mr Fitzpatrick himself. A few years later, when I first stopped sleeping, I'd watch him leave his house in the dead of night. Stare at him in the yellow glow of the street lamps, tracing the path of his long shadow until he was out of sight.

Then as I got older and started sneaking out at night myself, I would follow him. Even when my brain felt like a den of spiders I could focus on one individual task if I concentrated hard enough. In the daytime it varied. But at night-time it was always Mr Fitzpatrick.

I'd follow him from a safe distance, watch him winding his way down to the beach in the dark. He'd scurry and shuffle, the way men who wear flat caps do, stopping dead where the sand grew cold. Then it was as though he was reborn. His posture would change. He'd straighten up and puff out his chest. His worn-down hump would disappear and he'd look out, framed by moonlight, whispering to the waves as they dragged farther and farther out.

I walked over to the bench and sat down beside him. He didn't look at me. At first it was as though he didn't even register my presence. He just carried on staring out at the waves, oblivious to the flickering police tape and slamming van doors from which made-up ladies with microphones emerged.

'You're the one with the funny name,' he said in a voice that sounded like a question and an accusation all at once.

'Depends on your sense of humour I suppose,' I said. He surprised me by chuckling to himself, and I felt a brief rush of pride, having elicited an emotion from the man we used to joke was made of stone.

'Are you well?' he said eventually, as two gulls landed unsteadily on the water.

'No,' I said, still staring straight ahead. 'But I'm better.'

'Better than what?' he asked

'Better than I was.'

'It's a start, I suppose,' he said, slowly standing up.

'I suppose it is,' I said. For there was nothing else I could think to say to him. Mr Fitzpatrick had never spoken this much to me ever, or anyone else for that matter. Spoken *at* them, yes. But a two-way conversation was not usually his style.

'Well, it was nice speaking with you,' he said with a faint hint of surprise as he stood up and collected himself, shuffling off towards the wires and the cameras in the distance. 'And I'm glad to see you're on the mend,' he added, but was gone before I'd had a chance to ask why exactly he seemed to care.

There was a chill and a shadow as I readied myself to make my own way home.

'All right,' came a voice from behind, deep and certain.

The shadow moved to my right before Dan Vesper's shape filled my view.

Dan had never exactly gone to our school, but everyone there seemed to know someone who knew someone who knew him. He ran a dance night at the biggest club in town but most of his income seemed to come from business conducted in alleyways and car parks. Occasionally Sarah would climb into his car after school, though nobody ever saw exactly where the pair of them went together, or where it was that she got out. He was what they described as the darkness on the edge of town. The one and only time I'd mentioned his name to Sarah she had blanched.

One afternoon, staring out the window in double maths, I saw her leave school early. She climbed into Dan's car before disappearing into the grey afternoon.

Later that night, walking home from Donna's, I noticed her sitting in the skate park on the crest of a concrete wave, alone but for a Staffordshire terrier resting sleepily across her thighs.

'Where did you get him?' I asked, trying my hardest to hide my fears. I always had been the opposite of an animal person. The notion of trusting a beast not to turn and devour you at whim never quite sat comfortably with me.

Sarah looked up. She seemed sadder than usual. Not quite broken. But her fight had gone.

'He was lost,' she said quietly, looking down at the dog with a mother's love. 'And he found me, *actually*. He won't hurt you.' She was almost defensive, catching my apprehension.

'You can't know that.'

Sarah shrugged.

'Anyway, at least he's warm,' she said, slipping a hand beneath the beast's chin.

'Do you have somewhere to go?' I asked eventually, steeling my nerves and moving closer to the strange, dangerous pair. Sarah looked up at me then away again with a sneer.

'I can go wherever I like,' she said bluntly; the weight of the day rested heavy on her shoulders as she sat slumped, absorbing the animal warmth.

'Come on,' I said, placing my hand on her shoulder which flinched at the touch. 'My dad works nights. You can stay at mine.'

As we undressed for bed that evening I noticed bruises on her wrists and teasing her inner thighs.

'Did Dan do that to you?' I asked as we climbed into bed and lay rigid, neither of us used to the shape of another body beside us.

'Do what?' she asked, her face turning cold as she turned to the wall and flicked off the lamp, disguising her fear.

'Sarah, you have to say if something's wrong,' I whispered, despite there being nobody else in the house. The darkness demanded a hushed reverence. 'I can help, but not if you don't talk.'

Sarah sighed and rolled back, staring up at the black canvas of the ceiling.

'I can help myself,' she said flatly, like a mantra grown stale. 'And if you really want to help then you'll keep your mouth shut.'

She fell quiet, then said, 'Does Dan ever talk to you?'

Her voice was smaller than I was used to. I shook my head no and felt her body relax, as much as it ever did.

'Good. But if he ever does, don't say you know me, OK?'

I didn't respond.

'*OK*?' she said again, like a parent drumming safety lessons into a child.

'All right, Sarah, I won't,' I agreed and I felt her nod her head beside me.

'And don't ever tell him where I am,' she whispered. 'Even if you know.'

'I won't.'

'Good,' she said, her breath growing heavy as sleep came at her hard. 'Thank you, Claudette,' she said, almost on a whisper, before one final sigh carried her into a dream.

When I woke up the next morning she was gone. Within a week she had disappeared completely.

I had no evidence connecting our conversation that night to the fact of Sarah's disappearance , but somewhere deep down I knew that wherever Sarah was, she was there because of Dan. Just being in his presence made me feel vulnerable. Even his niceties felt barbed.

'Hello,' I said, and went to stand up, though Dan managed to sit next to me in a way which suggested I would leave only at his say-so.

'Are you who I think you are?' he asked and I felt myself blush. His tracksuit was a dark blue and zipped up towards his chin, so that only the bare essential flesh was exposed to the world. Every part of him that could have been made secret was.

'I don't know who you think I am,' I said as calmly as I could manage. Scanning the green as subtly as I could, I realised that there was nobody else in sight. I was alone and Dan was sat next to me. I did not know much about him but I knew that nothing he did was without reason. Our meeting had not simply been chance.

He thought for a moment and slid closer to me.

'I'm Dan. And you're Claudette,' he said as a statement of fact. Even had it not been my name, in that moment I would have conceded. 'Whole world's going mad and yet you're the one they locked up. Funny, isn't it?'

'I suppose when you look at it that way,' I tried, so keen to stand up.

'You work at the chemist, don't you?' he asked, scanning the horizon behind me.

'I doubt I do any more.'

'How are you for money?' he asked and I felt my legs begin to twitch with cold and nerves.

'Fine, in so much as I have none.'

Dan laughed and slid from the seat, crouching down in front of me to meet my eyes direct.

'Take my number,' he said, pulling a pen from the back pocket of his jeans. I handed him my phone but he waved it aside and took my wrist in his hand, pushing up my sleeve to the elbow before scratching his digits into the soft underside of my arm. 'There now,' he said, 'if you ever need anything you call me. Any time of the day. Any time of the night.'

I smiled and nodded, pulling my sleeve back down and wrapping the cuff tight in my fist, sealing his details away from sight.

'Look after yourself, Claudette,' he said as he went on his way. 'And if you can't then I can. Don't be a stranger.'

When I got home, Dad was trying – and failing – to hide his anxiety.

'You were a while,' he said, as he ran a tea towel around the inside of a cup.

For some reason walking back through the door a second time felt different. Not perfect, by any stretch of the imagination. But right. Seeing Dad there, in the living room, looking slightly worried, slightly relieved, like he always did and like he always no doubt would, made me feel anchored in a way my first return simply hadn't. Dad was right where he was supposed to be. And in that moment so was I.

'What was that for?' Dad asked with a smile, as I kissed his cheek on my way into the kitchen.

'Nothing,' I said, opening the biscuits as I went. 'I'm just pleased to be home, that's all.'

3

Troubled Waters

After I'd been in hospital for a few days and the tablets had kicked in, Dr Weston asked me for one happy memory. Nothing grand. Nothing life-changing. Just something that I couldn't help but remember fondly.

I struggled at first. I ummed and aahed for a while until I settled on the only thing I could bring to mind: the sound of Dad cleaning the flat.

Where we lived everybody listened to the radio. Not Dad. He listened to records. Every Sunday he would play the album *Bridge Over Troubled Water* on repeat until it was time to serve dinner. I never complained. I liked it. It was different and it was special and it was ours.

His routine was as unchanging as the tracklist. Before long I started associating certain sets of lyrics with certain activities. 'Bridge over Troubled Water' was the sound of the vacuum cord being rolled up and the Hoover being returned to its mantle in the back cupboard. 'Cecilia' was the rubbing of red eyes, as dust was swept from the skirting boards. Dad would yell about 'words he'd never heard in the Bible' as he slashed and salted the Sunday roast, before slamming it in the oven.

This was my happy memory; my safe place. These were the sounds and the routines that I'd touch like landmarks in the dark to remind myself of where I was.

Sometimes, when I was well enough, I'd help with the chores, and find myself singing along with Dad at the top of my voice. The music and lyrics were so perfect, so beautiful, that they felt like a gift that had been prepared especially for us. And then, other times, when depression came in its molasses wave, I'd lie in bed and feel the words cut and jeer, as if they'd been written only to highlight my shortcomings to the world at large, like graffiti on a school locker.

... Half of the time we're gone but we don't know where,
Half of the time we're gone but we don't know where ...

Even though it wasn't Sunday I woke to the sound of the Hoover grinding to a halt just as the violins were kicking in and the last verse was warbling to a climax. There was a thud and a thump and a muttered swear word as Dad's head hit the low beam of the cupboard. Then blissful silence until a faint knock at my door.

'Good morning, sunshine,' Dad said as he opened up a narrow crack in the door.

I groaned. I was awake but not quite yet ready to admit as much.

'Can I make you some breakfast?' he asked. 'Full English? Continental?'

'Not just yet,' I said, bleary. 'I'll be up in a second'

'And then we'll go for a walk?' he tried, leaning further into my room.

I rolled onto my back and breathed in deeply. I hadn't the heart to tell Dad that all I really wanted was to spend the day in my own bed, reading passages from books, half-heartedly masturbating and picking at junk food. After six weeks, the luxury of a closable door and no appointments to attend was one I was keen to revel in.

'Sounds great,' I found myself saying, despite having had every intention to come up with some unarguable excuse.

'Then that's that. Breakfast will be served in the living room, on account of the *Frasier* repeat that's about to start. Goodbye.' He closed the door and shuffled into the kitchen.

I turned on the TV in my room and adjusted the aerial. The static burred angrily as the image formed on screen, and suddenly I found myself staring at the school playing field while a woman's voice gave it a narrative.

'Sixteen-year-old Sarah Banks was last seen over six days ago when she failed to return home to the Riverdean Care Home where she has been living for the past three years. Since then search parties have combed the local area but police are said to be no further forward in their investigations . . .'

The voiceover continued as the camera panned between shots. They showed the beach and the arcade. They showed the road leading to Riverdean, and then zoomed out on a map. There was a red circle outside of school where Sarah should have caught the bus, and an outline around the town showing the boundaries of the search party. Then her school picture appeared. She looked beautiful in a hurried sort of way, like she always did. Her foundation not quite rubbed in, her eyeliner not quite un-smudged. More than anything I was surprised that she'd been in school long enough to queue for the photographer. Sarah's flexi-time approach to her education was a running joke.

She popped in when she felt like it, and other than that she did whatever it was she did all day. For someone so notorious, she could slip through the cracks like nobody else. Only this time her absence was national news.

I heard her voice in my mind, deep and rich. Heard her speaking quietly, the way she did sometimes as she and I sat together on the beach at night. Never intentionally, of course. Because Mr Fitzpatrick wasn't the only one I'd see on my mid-night walks. Sometimes Sarah would be there, too. Sometimes she'd ignore me. Sometimes we'd sit together. Often we would talk.

'You're all right, you,' she said to me on one of the last nights we'd spoken. 'You're not like other people.'

'I wish I was,' I said, taking a sip form the squat bottle of vodka she'd plucked from her backpack.

'Why? Everyone else is a mess. You're just a different type of mess. At least yours has a name. Everyone knows what depression is. They've got tablets for it and everything.'

'It has many names,' I said, squinting past the sting of the vodka. 'None of them complimentary.'

'You see things and you don't look away.' She took a bigger swig of vodka than I could ever manage. 'Most people won't do that. They look away. Pretend they can't see what's happening. Not you though. You stare right at it. It's like you see more than anyone else and it drives you crazy.'

'Like, I see you?'

'Like, you see everything. Maybe that's it.' She stood up. 'Maybe you're the sane one and it's the rest of the world that's mad.'

'Even if that's true it leaves me in the same position, doesn't it?' I'd said.

Sarah chucked her bottle into the sea and thought about what I'd said.

'Oh yeah,' she said, and laughed. But kindly, not with cruelty. 'I suppose it does. Either way you're screwed, eh?'

Dad and I walked down to the beach and across the sand. School still hadn't broken up. Other than clusters of policemen the beach was largely empty, save for the odd midday dog-walker and lunch-break jogger.

We walked as far as we could before coming to the second pier, by which point I felt that I had more than fulfilled not only my duties as a daughter but also as a functioning human being.

Dad had other ideas.

'Let's walk along to the lighthouse,' he said. Then, sensing my disdain, added, 'Come on, it's not much further. Plus if we make it back in one piece I'll buy us doughnuts on the way home.'

'I'm tired,' I said, half-heartedly. I was tired all the time so it was hardly a revelation, but still I thought it might buy me some leeway.

'I know. But it's just one foot in front of the other. We'll be home before you know it.'

'If we skipped the lighthouse we'd be home twenty minutes sooner,' I said.

'There's that can-do attitude I love,' Dad said, placing his arm around my shoulder and leading me to the edge of the stone walkway.

We were the only ones at the end of the far pier. We walked around the huge base of the lighthouse, staring out to sea. To our right the first pier was empty, save for a family scattering ashes into the water below. We sat on a bench facing back towards land. In the small bay at the mouth of the estuary a team of policemen were mounting inflatable speedboats. It was where we used to play as children. The beach was for tourists. The estuary was for us locals – murky, and hidden from the main stretch, it was the camouflage we needed for all manner of anti-social behaviour.

Some of the policemen were dressed in uniform. Others in diving gear. Great oxygen tanks were strapped to their backs as they perched awkwardly on the edge of the boats, holding on until it was time to jump.

They pushed out and began slowly moving away from the shore. The boats chugged gently forward. Behind them water sliced like pages of an opening book. They reached the middle of the estuary before the men in wetsuits leant back and disappeared beneath the surface.

'Have the police been to the house yet?' I asked as the engines were killed and the water around them returned to the flat glass sheet it had been before they disturbed it.

'Only on the first day,' he said, squinting to get a better look. 'The usual – had I seen anything, noticed anything different in our garden or on my way to work. Nothing worth worrying about. Did you know her well?' he asked.

I shrugged. I knew Sarah better than most, in some ways. In other ways I didn't know her at all. She was a mystery long before she disappeared.

'She was in my class. When she actually turned up,' I said. 'But we ran in different circles.'

'Poor girl,' Dad said quietly.

'She had secrets,' I said. 'Not that I know what they were. Not really. I suppose she was just never in one place long enough to become a whole.'

'She was certainly here long enough to become known. Everybody seemed to know her name,' he said and I shrugged.

'That's not the same as knowing a person though, is it?' I said almost angrily and Dad shook his head in agreement as I went on. 'People had an idea about Sarah they built around some of the things she did. But they didn't ever try to get to know her as a person.' I thought of the hard, kind friend I had made over the weeks before she had disappeared.

'It's sad.' It was clear he was ready for a different subject. 'Anyway, enough of all that,' he said, quieter this time. 'I want to know how *you* are.'

I breathed in and thought for a moment.

'I don't know,' I said, making to stand up as Dad gently put his hand on my shoulder, guiding me back to my seat.

'Yes, you do,' he said, pulling me tighter to him. 'You know exactly how it feels. And you're a smart girl. *Tell me.*'

'How can I explain something I don't understand though?' I asked.

'You don't need to be able to understand it. But talk. Just talk, that's all I ask. Because the only thing that breaks my heart more than hearing how unwell you are is the thought that you're keeping it locked up inside of you. Keeping it to yourself when I can carry some of it. Not as much as I'd like, but some.'

'I'm sick of talking,' I said, 'it doesn't help.'

'It does. You just need the benefit of hindsight to realise that. It's *not* talking that causes the most harm. And I don't mean brushing it off or turning it into a punchline. That's all well and good just to cope, but it won't get you better. It's the hiding that causes the blockage that leads to the rupture.'

'I know,' I said, 'it's just ... I never know exactly what it is you want me to say?' I said, wiping a tear from my eye and clearing my throat. 'Depression came along and was awful but I learned how to cope with that, sort of. But the mania – that really frightened me, Dad.' My throat tightened as my hands began to shake. 'I was so scared. I felt like I was trapped inside myself. I don't understand how something that exists inside of me can become bigger than I am? It doesn't make sense. And it scares me. It scares me now, knowing it. It scares me not understanding. And I just can't get better because . . . ' I said before my voice cut out and I took a moment to catch my breath.

'Because why?' Dad asked, gripping my hand tightly, urging me to go on.

'Because it's still there. Waiting. It's going to come back.'

'But you're stronger than you think you are, Claudette. You've beaten it once. You can do it again.'

'Yeah but I don't want to have to be,' I said through tears, as Dad tightened his arm around my waist. 'Can you imagine how exhausting it is putting yourself back together knowing full well that you'll break again? Can you? I mean, really? Because it's hard, Dad, it's really, really hard. And sometimes I don't think I'm strong enough. And sometimes I do. And other times, the hardest times, I'm just so fucking miserable that I wonder why I'm even bothering.'

This time it was Dad's turn to wipe a tear.

'You're bothering because you're worth it,' Dad said sternly. 'You are the strongest, bravest person I know. And the world is lucky to have you in it, no matter how unkind it can sometimes seem. Don't ever forget that. Life is chaos for us all, Claudette,' he said, unwrapping himself from me as we stood up to leave. 'The more you try to make sense of it the deeper you'll go until it's drowning you. The trick is to let yourself move with the current. It'll take you where you need to be eventually.'

'But what if I don't always like the direction it's headed in?' I asked.

'Then you're human.'

'I object.'

'Overruled,' he said quietly, kissing my head.

I put a song on repeat so that within three plays it would become white noise and sat cross-legged on my bed, staring at my open notebook. I could hear Dr Weston's voice in my mind as he handed it to me.

'The idea is that we begin not only to understand the limits of our own abilities, but also consider the relation of cause and effect,' he'd told me, as he tapped his pen on his knee. 'The effort we put in is often in direct correlation with the outcomes we observe.'

When I'd asked him where the Chaos Theory fit into all of this – that a butterfly could flap its wings in one country and cause a hurricane in another – Dr Weston said that it didn't. And that this was an example of allowing our mind to become troubled by issues unrelated to the task at hand.

'Zoom in, Claudette. Focus on the here and now. You'll be amazed at how much you can achieve if you focus on each small task one at a time.'

'Look after the pennies and the pounds will see to themselves?' I offered and Dr Weston had nodded.

'Quite. What I've noticed about you is that you zoom out and out. Forever looking for context and meaning in some grander sense. Each task becomes swamped by such a gargantuan frame that it becomes wholly unmanageable. Look closer, Claudette. You're an exceptionally capable young woman, when you let yourself be.'

I returned to the notebook. On the first page in large letters was a headline:

EVERY DAY I WILL . . . it said hopefully.

Out of desperation, and having long since learned how to answer the way people like to hear, I had scribbled:

Wake up at the same time.

The small-scale demand had been repeated several times, too, as if it knew I had not been trying.

EVERY DAY I WILL . . .

Make my bed, I had written beneath it.

Routine. Commitment. Just what they want to hear.

EVERY DAY I WILL . . .

Leave the house.

EVERY DAY I WILL . . .

Read one chapter of a book for pleasure, as well as for education.

Beneath this, when my mind had begun to wander, my answers became less helpful and more outright crass.

EVERY DAY I WILL . . .

Do some kinky hand or mouth stuff with a stranger.

EVERY DAY I WILL . . .

Mention the negative effects of my chosen birth control measures to my dad.

EVERY DAY I WILL . . .

Deface some public property with politically charged graffiti.

EVERY DAY I WILL . . .

Write an anonymous confession letter to the police.

I smiled at my own dumb sense of humour as I tore out the page and scrunched it into a small ball. Humour, no matter how morbid, was a variable that the road to recovery simply could not take. Dr Weston once told me that counselling was no place for jokes.

Section Two of the Goals Book was where the heat was really on.

The same demanding font yelled out in caps lock:

EACH WEEK I SHALL . . .

Read an entire book, I had written first, cheating slightly by simply cobbling together the outcome of my daily aim's efforts added together. (*Cause and effect*, I wrote in the margins, along with a smug smiley face.)

EACH WEEK I SHALL . . .

Perform an act of kindness for a friend, relative or neighbour.

Because fuck it, why not.

EACH WEEK I SHALL . . .

Do something I have never done before.

Pleasingly vague.

There's a saying that madness is doing the same thing over and over again and expecting a different result. I don't know what I expected from my lists as I flicked back and forth between the pages, but I was certain that the sight of it was enough to make anybody crazy. I felt nothing as I stared at the list of activities I had set myself – the achingly dull touchstones of a normal life. And, more to the point, nothing was exactly what I expected to achieve.

It's unusual to be bored and exhausted all at once, but as I looked down at my life on a page that's exactly how I felt.

The only slight shiver of excitement came when I reached the back of the book once more.

MY LONG TERM GOAL IS . . .

To find Sarah Banks.

To my surprise Ross had replied almost immediately to my text. Sometimes, in the flat, the sound of our upstairs neighbours made me feel like I had been buried alive. That afternoon, thoughts of Sarah and Dan were like scorpions that had made their way into my cruel coffin. I needed to get out of the house. I needed to get out of my *self*. And in Ross I recognised an acquaintance who would be able to fill me in on gossip without the need to ask me if I'm feeling OK and other dumb questions like that. I texted back and within five minutes I was out the door.

I found him sitting on the ground, propped against the barrier of the promenade, holding a cigarette in one hand and feeding scraps of chips to a lost dog with the other. I smiled when I saw him and remembered Sarah's summation of him.

'Ross is backwards,' she'd said warmly one night. We were playing a game whereby we'd list the boys in our school one by one, and either describe the ways in which we would have sex with them, or how we would destroy them completely. Sarah's disdain for the male population was fierce. She probably had her reasons, but the vitriol was no less shocking. Ross, however, seemed to be a rare chink in her armour.

'It's like he got confused, and instead of being embarrassed about what a dickhead he is, he's embarrassed about the fact that he's actually a good person. He hides the wrong bits.'

I gently ribbed her for having a weak spot for the gawky troublemaker. Then it dawned on me.

'You like him, don't you?' I was genuinely curious.

She had smiled and then frowned, looking far into the distance.

'Ross is all right. He knows half the shit I get up to and he still likes me. That takes a lot.' She sighed sadly, lying back in the cold sand. 'But if he knew the other half, he'd probably kill me.'

37

Ross clocked me and stood up quickly, causing the kitten to dart beneath an ice-cream van.

'Sarah used to do that,' I said.

For a girl who always seemed to be in such a hurry, I never once saw Sarah pass an animal without stopping to admire it. She'd draw warm purrs from skittish alley cats in the dead of night, running a finger behind their ear, or waylay hungry hounds on a midnight prowl, offering old crisps from the depths of her bag.

'Do what?' he asked, blushing at having been caught red handed in an act of kindness. 'And anyway how would you know?'

'Here,' I said, handing Ross a half-drunk bottle of Coke and ignoring his question.

'It's flat,' he said, as he downed the dregs in one go.

'Sorry,' I said.

We sat in silence for a moment.

'Town's pretty mental right now,' I noted dumbly as groups of police held micro-conversations on the beach below.

'You'd know,' Ross said, and I smiled.

'Ha ha,' I said. 'Sarah liked you, you know?' Ross stiffened.

'What did she say?' he asked, taking me aback with the urgency in his voice.

'Nothing. God, only good things. She liked you,' I said, 'she said you were a good person, that you liked her and that that was no easy task in itself.' I rolled my eyes. 'Calm down.'

Ross shook his head and looked sadly to the beach below.

'Yeah well, either way she's gone. And she's never coming back.'

As the police made their way from the beach back into the vans in the car park Ross and I skimmed over the type of mind-less small talk I'd been craving.

'Is anyone at yours at the moment?' he asked eventually, looking up like a lost child.

'Dad's home,' I said, a little too quickly. Ross had been persona non grata at the Flint household since he took it upon himself to initiate a food fight at my sixth birthday party. 'Why? You want to jump my bones?'

Ross smiled and grimaced.

'You wish. I need a shower, that's all.'

My heart sank. Ross's family arrangement or lack thereof never failed to fascinate me. His dad had never been a feature in his life growing up and by all accounts he'd been only a passing figure in Ross's mum's life too. Not that she was the maternal type, preferring to leave Ross in the care of various aunties, uncles and neighbours as she went from one doomed romance to the next.

'He's on nights,' I said. 'I'll text you later. You can use the facilities but only if you wash and go. No messing about. He'd have a shit-fit if he found out I'd let you in the house when he was out.'

Ross thought and nodded.

'Cheers, Claudette.'

I began readying myself to leave. 'Thanks for the chat, Ross.'

He glared at the horizon like he was challenging the oncoming dusk; daring the dark in a fight he could never win.

'Didn't have much choice, did I?' he said with a shrug.

'Aren't you going to ask how I am? Tell me you're here if I need you?' I said sarcastically.

'Fuck off,' he said shaking his head kindly. 'I can see you're fine.'

'I'm never going to be fine,' I said with a half-smile.

'Then I'm never going to waste my time and ask then,' he said, pulling anther sad roll-up from his pocket and attempting to spark its tip with a dying lighter.

'Good,' I said, and flicked his head as I stood up and made my way back across the green. 'Because I wouldn't tell you anyway.'

4

The French Resistance

My mum came from Normandy and left me with her name. My dad hails from Tyneside and bequeathed unto me his eczema. Neither heritage added to my overall school experience.

At first I was simply the French girl.

Claudette.

Courgette.

Regret.

Gannet.

My only saving grace was that it wasn't the easiest word to rhyme. In that respect I fared better than Brady Tucker. But it was still different and foreign, still felt *wrong* on young, dumb tongues that spat it out – '*Claudette*' – in a pitch and tone that was an insult in itself.

When I started losing patches of myself in a fine white mist of dead skin, I became 'Frosty The Snowman' (wherever she goes the blizzard will blow!)

Then I started scratching, bringing blood weeping to the surface of the cracks like ravines of lava, and I acquired the tag 'Freddy Krueger'.

By the time the scratching became cutting I was already known as 'Psycho'.

On my good days I'd convince myself it was a compliment in a roundabout way. It suggested a uniqueness and originality.

On my bad days I was so convinced I had died that the sound of most words fell off me like spit down a window. Abandon hope all ye who insult; for she feels not their intended blow.

I'm not sure which of my parents I have to thank for the crazy in me.

Maybe it was one of the few things Mum left behind after she fled, along with a gap on the road where the car should have been and a hurriedly written apology.

Maybe it was Dad. The way Grandma used to shift her many, many china figurines throughout the day to mirror the journey of the sun suggested an obsessional streak in that side of the family that went beyond liking things Just So.

Or maybe I was just plain old broken.

I woke up the next morning and the sheets were pink with smears of blood. I'd been scratching in the night and my right arm felt raw and exposed. Even the gentle breeze from my window felt like a sandstorm that would flay me alive.

I smeared a glob of Savlon across my skin and felt it change from cold to scalding in seconds. 'Can I come in?' Dad asked from the other side of the door.

He seemed to have a sixth sense for my waking hours. It was like the moment I moved a muscle he knew it and was right there, poised for interaction. I had tried on several occasions to explain to Dad that even when I'm well, I come to morning like a weighted corpse reaches surface. It's slow and ugly. It's

42

normally pushing lunchtime before I am ready to even feign civility.

'Nnnnngh,' I said as the door opened.

'Hello love,' he said, holding a duster, 'how you feeling?'

'Tired,' I said.

'But it's morning,' Dad added.

'I'm edgy like that,' I said, sitting up in bed.

'What would you like for breakfast today?' he asked. 'I could make something.'

I thought for a moment; from the floor my Book of Aims stared up expectantly at me.

'No,' I said. 'I'm going to have breakfast in a café today. I'll take a book.'

'Oh,' Dad said and smiled. ' . . . *tres chic*. Let me know if you want any company then.'

The café was too warm and the queue too long. The menu had changed since I'd been in hospital and the music on the loud-speaker was quick and jaunty. A niggling anxiety grew in my chest. Suddenly the task of breakfast seemed insurmountable so I slipped out and to the benches on the lawns, where I sat with my head between my legs, clawing for breath.

I tried counting to ten.

I made it to five.

I pulled back another long sweet breath and felt myself begin to calm.

I counted to ten.

I breathed out.

I breathed in.

I breathed out.

'Hello,' said a voice, interrupting my ritual. 'Are you OK?'

43

A woman in a suit, holding a polystyrene cup, had sat beside me while I had been reacquainting myself with basic respiration. I did not know who she was and I did not particularly care to find out.

'I thought I was going to have to call an ambulance for a second,' she said as she sipped her tea.

'I'm fine. I have asthma,' I said quickly, rather than the truth. Something about panic attacks seemed to fascinate a certain sort of person. Maybe they thought it spoke to a delicate, artistic temperament; a tragic poetry of the lungs. Whatever it was, often it meant they wanted to delve into great detail. Which is the last thing you want when you're hyperventilating, if ever.

Asthma was a safer bet. Nobody ever wanted to talk about asthma. It was like saying you had stew for dinner. People accepted it and moved on.

'You just seem a bit out of sorts,' she said, refusing to drop it.

She smiled and sighed and took another sip from her tea. Blotches of bright-red lipstick thickened around the rim of the cup, as though she was disintegrating slowly from the face down.

'Must be a weird time, what with that girl disappearing ...' she said. 'Sarah, was it?'

'It still is, as far as anybody knows,' I said and went to stand up.

'Did you know her?' the woman asked, throwing her half empty cup into the bin and following me across the links.

'As much as anyone.' I shrugged.

'And what was she like?'

'She was like a sixteen-year-old girl. I have to go home.'

'You know we would pay, if you had any stories ...' the lady said, handing me a business card from a newspaper. The

44

thought of giving Sarah's story away made me feel uneasy. The thought of selling her secrets made my insides roar.

'Oh, gross,' I said, picking up my pace. 'I'm not talking to you.'

'We're here to help.'

'If you wanted to help then you wouldn't be here,' I said, trying to shake her off.

'My name's Nancy. You're . . . Claudette, aren't you?'

This stopped me in my tracks. There is something about a stranger using your name that makes your blood run cold, even for a split second.

'How do you know that?'

'I know everything,' the woman said with a smile.

'If that was true then you wouldn't need these,' I said, holding up her business card before slipping it into my back pocket.

'You've been off school for a while, haven't you? Having a little rest.'

'I was admitted to a psychiatric hospital with bipolar one,' I said.

'Crikey, you cut to the chase, don't you. I was trying to be polite.'

'Piss off,' I said, walking away from her, fast.

'No harm done,' Nancy called out, 'I'll be here. If you ever do want a chat. About anything. Nothing. No detail too small. I'll be here.'

I ploughed on, her voice receding into the distance.

'How was your morning constitutional?' Dad said as I made my way back inside the house and slammed the door behind me.

'Collecting friends and memories wherever I go.'

'Classic Claudette,' Dad said, bringing me into a hug in the middle of the front room. 'You're shaking,' he said, holding me tighter. 'Did something happen?'

'I just bumped into someone from school in the café,' I lied. Something from the back of the flat made a clanking noise and caused my bones to stiffen. 'What's that?' I asked.

'Ah, and there you were thinking your morning couldn't get any better,' Dad said.

My stomach dropped.

'Donna's in the kitchen. I didn't know you'd be back so soon. She came to see you and I offered her a cup of tea, and well, you know . . .'

'*Oh, Dad, no . . .*' I whispered.

'I can get rid of her if you like?' Dad said. 'I can say you're not up to it, or I can simply assassinate her. Whichever you feel would cause the least amount of social awkwardness.'

He gave me a proud smile when I told him I'd see her despite my misgivings.

'I'm promising nothing,' I said, eager to curb his enthusiasm. 'And you'd better keep an eye on her through your crosshairs. I may yet signal for rescue.'

'For you, my girl, anything,' he said.

We sat in my room mostly in silence.

'Would you like some music on?' Donna asked me.

I said not, and that if I did I would put it on myself. Donna looked like she was going to burst into tears, which was not her style.

'I'm trying,' she said. 'This is weird for me too.'

'I'm sorry,' I said, and meant it. 'I really am. It's not you. It's just . . . I've had a pretty odd few weeks.' We both laughed awkwardly.

Donna was the tallest girl in our year and the first to get tits. She was pretty enough to sit with the popular girls, which she did for a while, but too smart to be drawn into the viper pit of their conversations. So for a long time she just sat, mute, at the edge of the table, staring out at the dinner hall longingly, like an owl in a battery farm.

It was only when Mrs Swift separated the popular girls in Biology that Donna was sat next to me and we became fast friends.

'What was it like? Hospital I mean,' Donna asked, as she pretended to scan the posters on my wall that she'd seen hundreds of times before

'It was . . . helpful,' I said. 'I mean, I don't feel like I want to explode any more. So it worked in that respect. Now I just feel plain old depressed.'

'Were you frightened?'

'At times.'

'Are you . . . *better*?'

'For now,' I said.

'They tried to give me tablets once,' she said, 'after Dad died, when I was off school.' Donna looked at me hopefully.

'Donna, don't.'

'What?' she said. 'I'm just saying, you're not alone.'

'God, please Donna, not you too,' I said, sitting up. 'I know. OK. I know. But something shitty happened to you and you felt bad about it. I'm not saying it wasn't awful but it wasn't some lifelong condition you had. It was a perfectly reasonable human response. What happened to you and what I'm like . . . it's not the same.'

'I was only trying to help,' she said softly and then hardened. 'And don't do that. Don't make out like you're the only person this has ever happened to. Why do you always have to be the one?' she said, angry now. 'Why does your pain have to be the pain we all worry about? The one we all have to make space for? When most people feel like shit they just get on with it. Life's hard and it happens to us all, *Claudette*. You're nothing special.'

She lay back down.

She was right and I knew it. Having spent four weeks in hospital focused on nobody but myself I was finding it hard to relearn the to-and-fro of life outside. I had to remind myself that not every moment of every day was geared towards me and my recovery; that I had to share the stage with others.

'I'm sorry,' I said after a pained minute and Donna shrugged, clearly still pissed off. 'I missed you,' I tried eventually.

'I didn't miss you,' she said, still raw but acting a little more indignant than she really was.

'I'm sorry about what I said. The thing about depression is it makes you self-obsessed,' I told her. 'I'm trying.'

'Hmm,' she said, *'very,'* in a waspish, camp voice, mimicking the favourite comeback of our history teacher, Miss Dent.

It made me glad that it had been Donna that visited first, before anybody else. We'd known each other long enough to have a shorthand that could diffuse almost any awkwardness. Certain phrases, even a look if timed just right, could lead us into hysterics that bemused anyone and everyone else. With Donna there was always an off button, always a quick escape from a sticky situation. And I loved her for it.

We both took a moment to catch our breath from laughing.

'What have people at school been saying?' I asked.

I lay my head in Donna's groin as she dragged her fingers from my scalp towards the tips of my hair.

'Oh, not much. I don't think many people noticed. It's GCSE season. It's all revision timetable this and coursework that.'

'Really?' I asked, momentarily forgetting that the whole town seemed to know where I'd been. Donna fixed me a pitiful look.

'Of course not,' she said with a roll of her eyes as I dug my elbow into her leg. 'Sorry, but what do you expect? You had a breakdown in the middle of lunch.'

'I'd thought at least with Sarah gone they'd have switched their attention.'

'Turns out Year Eleven have mastered the art of multitasking.'

I felt myself wither.

'Who cares though? You've got me. I'll protect you,' she said. 'I missed you too, C-dog, I was just saving face when I said I didn't.' She reached out her right hand and squeezed my tits, one by one. 'Promise me you won't let it get that bad again.'

'I promise,' I said, and hoped that I meant it.

'Bros before hos,' she said, ruffling my hair.

'Bros before hos,' I said, as she stood up and made her way to the door.

'Donna,' I said, just as she was leaving.

'Claudette,' she said, turning and walking slowly backwards.

'What do you think happened to Sarah?' I asked.

She thought for a moment and shrugged.

'I think,' she said, and sighed, 'I think Sarah went wherever girls like Sarah go. Wherever it is. I doubt it's a good place.'

5

Smoke and Mirrors

My room must have been on fire during the night.

When I first opened my eyes it was filled with smoke.

I didn't smell burning so I blinked once then rolled over and went back to sleep.

When I woke back up my arm was outstretched and numb. My alarm clock lay in two halves on the bedroom door.

The smoke was all but gone.

'Paula said she might pop round for a cup of tea later on,' Dad said as we were getting ready to make our way into school; a meeting had been arranged to discuss the possibility of my return.

I would be faced with a panel of disapproving teachers.

I would act remorseful for smashing the window.

I'd apologise for the mirror.

I'd acknowledge it was probably wrong to have sworn so much at Mrs Bradley as she grasped at my bloodied arms, trying to hold me to the floor while people took video clips on their phones and the receptionist called Dad, the police, the hospital – just about any authority that they could think of.

I sighed, feeling almost as nauseous at the thought of Paula popping round as I did about heading back to school. Paula and Dad had been in some form of a relationship for as long as I could remember. I used to call her my Aunty Paula until she became my nemesis. By the time I hit secondary school I could just about bring myself to grunt at her. By the time the depression hit I would physically recoil from her attempts at bonding.

'Fine,' I told Dad, putting on my jumper, ready to go.

'She's been worried about you, Claudette. You got her letters.'

'I know,' I said, and tightened the laces on my trainers.

'And the perfume she sent,' he added.

'I wasn't allowed it, in case I fashioned a weapon.'

'Oh,' Dad said. 'Still, it's the thought that counts I suppose.'

Paula was not a bad person and I knew it. Paula had what people describe as 'a good heart'. In her spare time she ran exercise classes at the old people's home and volunteered at the food bank. Dad loved her and she loved him. They made one another happy. I wanted Dad to be with someone – I really did (though nobody would believe me). I guess I just thought he could do better. In that sense my problem was with him, not her. I wanted him to want more from life. Paula was low-hanging fruit. She wore fleeces with Alsatians on them that she bought at the indoor market. She hand-made most of the presents she gave. She clipped a pedometer to the elastic of her jogging bottoms every morning without fail. She walked ten thousand steps a day and still ended up back in the same place that she started.

Just watching her exhausted me.

'Try, Claudette,' Dad said. 'For me.'

'For you, my dear, anything,' I said, aping one of Dad's preferred phrases.

'Good girl,' he said, sounding not entirely convinced.

There were police cars in the school parking lot by the time we arrived.

'Bleak, isn't it?' I said as we made our way towards the back entrance. Two policemen were walking dogs across the playing fields and looked over towards us. I stifled a yawn and leant into Dad, still not entirely awake.

Some nights I just wouldn't go to sleep at all. I'd lie with my eyes wide, watching the minutes drip past. Other times sleep would be all around me, like fog. No matter how much you gulped down, that thirst could not be quenched. This was one of those times. I wanted to sleep for ever. It was my true love and my only fate. I felt only hatred for those that stood in our way.

'Nonsense,' Dad said. 'It's a shining beacon of education. It glows brightly even on the darkest of days. You should be as proud of it as it no doubt is of you.'

'This way, my learned friend,' I said, leading him in through the rear entrance.

My school smells of industrial detergent, mostly – synthetic citrus top-notes suffocating the stench of cheap deodorant and nervous sweat. But school is also a feeling. Being in school, especially out of hours, feels like a memory even when you're still a pupil. It's a nostalgia for something that hasn't yet happened. Some feelings we can't describe. Some feelings we can't explain. In these cases we attach them to the nearest sensation to hand. With school it's the smell.

It felt strange walking the halls with Dad.

There were the parts of school that I know he knew about:

the lunch hall, the head of year's office, the art room with the drying paint and the shoddy clay pots, the French room with the conjugated verbs and the cartoon baguettes on the walls, the playing fields and the dining hall.

Then there were the other parts. The illicit parts.

There was the bathroom, where Sharon Marshal had opened the toilet door with the faulty lock to find me digging into my legs with a pair of nail scissors.

There was the cloakroom where the Sixth Formers would sell cigarettes to the Year Tens. A pound a pop and a free match with every purchase.

The science block where Donna and I once spent a lunchtime sniffing solvent so strong that at one point I fell backwards and collapsed onto a plastic skeleton, snapping most of its ribs and all of my phone screen in the process.

The physics lab where Sarah would meet Mr Darvill and nobody would mention it.

The German class where they found me, asleep.

The other bathroom, with the mirror I broke.

Silently, Dad and I walked past a hundred different secrets that seemed to moan like ghosts.

Donna's bizarre devotion to the athletics team meant my lunchtimes would often be spare. So I'd wander the corridors until I found a space for myself, or a girl as lost as I was.

More often than not I found Sarah.

I laughed the first time I saw her, sitting alone in the copier room of the library (her usual lunchtime haunt, I learned), with Brian Farrell's Doctor Who lunchbox open.

'What the fuck is this?' she asked through a mouthful of borrowed crisps, holding up a capped syringe.

'I think it's Brian's insulin,' I said nervously.

'Will it give me a buzz?' she asked sceptically.

'I doubt it.'

'Or turn a profit?'

'I don't think there's much of a black market for that kind of thing. It'll probably kill him if he doesn't have it though,' I said, taking a seat on a copier.

Sarah shrugged and slipped the needle into her back pocket.

'He's in my maths class,' she said uncertainly. 'Or at least one of his crew is. If I'm still around last period I'll hand it over then. Say I found it in the yard or something.' She went at his biscuit bar with the hunger of a lion before clocking my awe at her appetite. 'What are you staring at? A girl's got to eat.'

'Most chew first,' I said, and Sarah laughed, scattering biscuit crumbs which we both ignored. 'You went at that like an anaconda. I didn't know you could unhinge your own jaw.'

Sarah thought for a moment before raising her eyebrows.

'Yeah you did,' she said and again we laughed, only this time sadder.

'I haven't seen you in a while,' I said, as she began hiding the remains of her borrowed feast behind a photocopier. In truth I'd even started leaving the house with the specific intention of finding Sarah at night.

'I'm keeping a low profile,' she said.

'Are you in trouble?' I'd asked quietly, as footsteps in the corridor slowed and then paused and then carried on their way.

'Almost always,' Sarah said, listening at the door to check the coast was clear for a swift and unobserved exit. 'You ever feel like you're in over your head?' she asked quietly.

'Almost always,' I said. The air in the room became thick with longing, as if Sarah wanted so desperately to say more.

'You know you can always talk to me. Tell me anything. I won't tell anyone else. I promise.' She turned and opened her mouth, before shaking her head. 'Is this why you've been in school so much recently?' I asked and she shrugged.

'Got to hang out somewhere, might as well be here. At least it's free,' she said as dismissively as she could manage.

'And why you've been going to homework club every night even though you've never completed a piece of coursework in your life?' She shrugged again. 'Sarah, come on. I can see Dan Vesper parked outside school every night at home time, I see Ross talking to him. If something is wrong, you can say. I can help,' I said. Her face froze momentarily at the mention of Dan's name.

'Nothing to tell.' Sarah was clearly done with sharing. 'Just keep your mouth shut about this place, or you'll know about it,' she said, as she made her way out and closed the door behind her.

'Mr Harper will see you now,' said Miss Spence, popping her head out of the head teacher's door.

The teachers sat three abreast behind a desk that didn't contain them entirely. Miss Spence, my head of year, Mr Harper, the head teacher and Mrs Archer, the guidance counsellor, all nodded politely as I sat down.

'Thank you for agreeing to see us out of hours,' Dad said, as he took his seat before the panel.

It was the weekend before the last week of term. Already posters and artwork had been removed from drawing boards in the hallways. The whole place was being stripped back to its skeleton in anticipation of a fresh new year.

'We had to come in for the investigation anyway,' Mr Harper

said, as he handed a sheet of paper to Miss Spence. 'Otherwise it would have been on Monday.'

'Oh,' Dad said. 'Still, thanks anyway.

'How are you, Claudette?' Mrs Archer asked, nodding encouragingly at me. 'You look well.'

I smiled and shrugged.

Mrs Archer had taken to me as one of her personal projects. When I had my first real crash, Dad got in touch with the school to let them know. I was as furious as someone who couldn't physically get out of bed could be, and once the fog subsided and I was back on my feet I felt mortified when every teacher asked me *how I was doing*, always with a sideways smile. Mrs Archer was convinced that she alone could cure me. She signed me up for music lessons and exercise classes – neither of which I attended; and brought in self-help books from home about Finding Your Inner Light – none of which I read.

She was kind and she had tried, which I appreciated.

'We're all very proud of the progress Claudette has made since she went into hospital,' Dad said, filling the silence from me. It's not that I didn't know how to explain how I felt; it's that I felt nobody really wanted to know. Not properly. There are only so many times you can say that you are fine before the word becomes rusted and redundant. 'She's back home with me now, we're doing well.'

'Yes, well we all need a rest every once in a while,' Mr Harper said, not quite meeting my eye. 'I had a niece that stopped eating. She had a rest and had to drop out of school altogether. Now she's a section manager at River Island and studying for a Geography degree on the OU, so . . . '

'You should give me her number. We could be friends,' I said with a sneer.

'Claudette,' Dad said with a stern smile and nodded at Mr Harper. 'What we really want to know is that after the summer holidays Claudette will be able to return to school and that she will be treated with the care and attention she needs.'

'I don't need care. Or attention,' I said. Miss Spence smiled awkwardly and nodded. 'I just want to know it's OK to come back. Can't we deal with the rest afterwards?'

'Well ...' Mr Harper offered, stretching his words. 'Normally, in cases of ... vandalism ... permanent exclusion would be the only solution.'

'It was an accident.'

'You broke a bathroom mirror and a full-length window, Claudette,' Miss Spence clarified.

'You spat at a dinner supervisor,' Mr Harper added.

'And the language ...' said Miss Spence.

'We've been over this on the phone,' Dad said, more bluntly this time. 'Claudette's behaviour that day was symptomatic of an illness over which she has no input nor control. Her grades are vastly above average in a school where average is considered an achievement, her approach to learning is exemplary and her attendance is ...' Dad tried, 'OK, I suppose.'

This was Dad at his most impressive, I had to admit.

'But there are other things to take into consideration,' Mr Harper said. 'The welfare of other pupils for one.'

'Claudette has never hurt anybody in her life.'

'And Claudette herself,' Miss Spence offered.

'*I disagree,*' Dad said curtly.

'What I mean is that children can be cruel. There will be a lot of questions. We've already had to shut down two websites with videos that were posted of Claudette's last day here.'

'What you don't understand about the situation is—' Mr

Harper began, only for Dad to cut him off with a raise of his hand.

'*Please*. I have lived with this – *situation*, as you put it – since Claudette was a girl. I've watched it come and I've watched it go and through it all I've seen a bright, intelligent, caring young woman grow, despite the occasionally huge odds stacked against her. I recognise that Claudette is occasionally unwell. I recognise too your predicament. What I am saying is that if you do not find a way to accommodate my daughter at your school solely because of a terrible illness from which she suffers and with which she copes as best she can, I will inform the education authority, the government, the press … anybody that will listen. So. What I suggest is that we spend a little while here, now, going over just how we're going to work this thing out.'

Dad took a deep, shaken breath.

He was on fire. The closest Dad usually got to real anger was when it started raining after he'd hung the washing out. I could tell that confrontation was a new experience for him. I liked it. I'm pretty certain he didn't, not judging by the vibrating table leg.

'Well,' Mr Harper said, taking control, while Miss Spence was looking straight down at the desk and Mrs Archer was beaming at Dad like she wanted to punch the air and cheer. 'I'm starting to see where Claudette gets her spirit from.'

'We're passionate people,' Dad said, with a hint of pride.

Mr Harper sighed and looked at Miss Spence, who seemed to shrug with her eyes.

'I suppose there may be a way around this.' He took out a file from his drawer and opened it on the desk in front of him. 'But I tell you now it won't be easy.'

*

'You didn't have to do that,' I said on the bus on the way home from school. 'I mean, I could have just moved schools.'

'Nonsense,' he said, pressing the bell as we neared our stop. Donna was waiting for me at the bus stop, eating a bag of chips. 'You've got your friends there. Or at least Donna. It's all you've ever known. And they know you, Claudette. I know it won't be fun going back, it never is. But it'll be worth it in the long run.'

'Time will tell,' I said as we got off the bus.

'Anyway, you've got the summer yet. Have you got any plans? Anything you'd like to do?'

'I suppose I have,' I said, thinking about Sarah and my goal as we stepped off the bus. 'I'm a woman on a mission. Watch me soar.'

Dad said hello to Donna with a hug. I looked at her and sneered and she sneered back.

'You look after one another,' Dad said as he faded into the distance.

I apologised for Dad's familiarity as we stepped down onto the beach. The tide was frothed white and dragging out like a pulled sheet. The police tent that had been erected cast a long, lazy shadow in the sand, and people began making their way home after a day of determined sunbathing.

'I love that man,' Donna said. 'So, what's the news?'

'I'm going back to school after summer,' I told her. 'They didn't want to let me, but Dad went full on 'eighties Arnie with Mr Harper when he started umming and aahing.'

'Good lad.'

We climbed up and took a seat on the lip of the old waste pipe while Donna described, in alarming detail, a series of sex dreams she'd been having about a ticket inspector who'd recently ejected her from the bus. 'I wish I liked sex the way you do,' I said. Our legs dangled down, catching brown flecks of the rusted metal as above us shadows from the promenade passed us by.

'You will,' Donna said, eating the last of her chips. 'You just haven't been given a reason to like it yet. It'll come. Maybe that's where it started going wrong. Sexual frustration.'

'It's a strong possibility.'

'Maybe you just need a boyfriend,' she tried.

'God no!'

'Or a good seeing-to.'

'*Well . . .*' I said, slightly more open to her Plan B.

'I could get drunk and try giving you a hand job?' she offered.

'No, thank you.'

'Prude.'

'Plus we'd make terrible lesbians.'

'How dare you!' she said in mock horror. 'I'd make an *amazing* lesbian. As long as there was no mouth stuff. Just me and the ten commandments.' She flexed her fingers at me like a cat.

'You're disgusting,' I said, as two brown Labradors sprinted ahead of us and gambolled into the sea.

'*Disgusting like a fox.* I'd treat it like a craft. Like crocheting. Remember that tote bag I made?' she asked.

'That was a good tote bag,' I conceded.

'You know it baby. *Imma show you a good time,*' she said, digging her hands into my sides, causing me to squirm so hard I nearly fell off the pipe.

I was steadying myself on the pipe with one hand, and trying to push Donna off me with the other, all the while attempting to catch my breath, when above us a shadow loomed and a man cleared his throat.

'Oh look,' Donna said, 'it's the filth.'

'Can you move along please girls,' Adam said.

Adam was Donna's older brother. He was a community officer and a scourge of underage drinkers the town over. No bottle of ill-gotten cider survived un-poured when he was on patrol. Adam was always sweet to me, which didn't stop Donna from treating him as her own personal punch bag.

'Hi Adam,' I said. 'You look nice in your uniform.'

'Claudette,' said Adam. He smiled at me briefly and then set his jaw to serious, a Man on a Mission once more.

'Why do we have to move? It's a public beach,' she said.

'Littering,' Adam said, pointing to the crumpled chip packet on Donna's knee.

'I haven't littered yet, dumb-dumb. It's still on my person. God, Adam, it's not the fucking *Minority Report*. You can't accuse someone of a crime they've yet to commit.'

'And which bin are you going to put it in exactly?' he asked, as I stood up.

'You are literally the worst person of all time. What exactly would you do if we refused to move?' she replied, as I dragged her to her feet and we tottered carefully along the pipe to the lower promenade.

'I can arrest you,' he said.

'No, you can't,' Donna said, holding onto my outstretched hand and making the final leap onto terra firma.

'I can perform a citizen's arrest,' he said, as we climbed to the top promenade and leant against the railings beside him.

'So can anyone, dummy. It's our fundamental right as a citizen.'

'It's no wonder you've only got the one friend,' he said as he made his way from us.

I shook my head at him and gave the best *don't mind her* smile I could muster.

'Your earpiece is flashing, Adam,' I said to the blinking light in his Bluetooth headset. 'Does that mean you're getting a call?'

'Is it the whole world ringing to say you look like a tit?' Donna said, brushing sand from the bottom of her jeans as Adam mumbled under his breath, tapping the gadget like he was trying to rid his ear of a water blockage.

'Anyway,' I said. 'This is all very nice, but I have to be getting home. Bye, Adam.'

'Bye, Claudette,' he said. 'Watch how you go.'

'Keep it real homegirl,' Donna said, as she knocked Adam's hat off his head and made her way towards her block of flats. 'Don't be a stranger.'

6

The French Connection

I don't remember much of my mum.

The parts that I do remember I don't especially miss: a few notes sung in a voice higher than Dad's. Two hands softer than his, lifting me up. A patch of time during which all memories seem shrouded in thick, heady, cigarette smoke that makes everything feel like a dream-sequence in a cheap soap opera.

That's not to say she didn't occasionally fascinate me.

'Do you remember your mum?' I asked Ross as I sat in the café. I'd arrived ten minutes early to meet Donna and, having passed the window and noticed a spare seat and a fresh plate of chips, he had invited himself to join me.

'Not really,' he said with a shrug. On the television an advert for fabric softener gave way to the news as Ross tried to eschew conversation in favour of carb loading. 'I see her around town sometimes.'

'And you don't say hello?' I asked, genuinely curious as to his setup.

'She never says hello to me,' he said flatly, stuffing chips into his mouth before changing tack. 'I don't even know her that much anyway so it doesn't matter.'

I wasn't convinced. In truth there's no way you can gloss over a missing parent, no matter what you tell yourself. Even if you were lucky, like I was, and had one remaining parent willing to try their hand at both roles, the void is too huge to ignore. I didn't even have a mum to miss in real terms – more like an idea of a mum who she sometimes merged in my memory with characters from shows I'd watched as a little girl. And yet something about it weighed heavy. It wasn't so much that I missed her presence. More that I mourned her absence. Like I'd been denied something I'd been promised, or irrevocably short-changed.

'I remember yours though,' Ross said with a forced smirk, squeezing a sauce sachet into his mouth.

'Yeah?' I asked, genuinely surprised.

'Yeah,' he said, his lips red and sweet. 'Big tits,' he said, as I rolled my eyes and kicked him under the table. 'Family tradition, eh?' he said again and I shook my head.

'Keep that smart mouth up and Donna will punch you in the throat,' I warned as Ross widened his eyes in mock horror. 'And anyway, I know it bothers you,' I said.

'And how do you know that then?' he asked and I shrugged.

'Because it bothers me,' I said. 'How can it not? You can't have half your roots ripped out and be expected to grow the same way as everyone else. We're the same, you and me.'

'Are we fuck,' he said with a smile and a shake of his head, taking my Coke and washing down his hurried feast, as Donna passed the window and made her way into the café.

'Bye, Ross,' she said, coming towards us and clicking her

fingers. Ross stood up without question and took the last fistful of chips before leaving.

'See you, Claudette,' he said, making his way from the café as Donna sat down and marked his exit with elaborate side-eye.

On the news a reporter stood on the promenade and held up a coat that I recognised all too well.

'It is believed that this is the coat Sarah Banks was wearing when she was last seen,' said the reporter, holding up a wool jacket for the camera. Midnight blue, fur collar, belted at the middle. *'As CCTV images of her last hours have emerged over the weekend . . . '*

'Didn't Leah have a coat like that?' Donna asked, picking at the shards of chips that had escaped Ross's ravages. 'A bit warm for this time of year, isn't it? Though I never saw her in anything even remotely suitable for the season, it has to be said,' she added, mock haughtily.

'Sarah was a creature of the night,' I said. 'Gets a bit nippy then.'

Donna nodded in agreement and picked up a menu.

They say that drowning is the most peaceful way to die. That if you can resist the temptation to clamber frantically for the surface, life will just leave your body like steam from a pan, until you are sleepy and then asleep and then gone.

Probably they're right, context permitting.

Clearly they did not mean during a Year Eleven water polo match in a comprehensive-school swimming pool.

But this is where it happened to me.

And that was the moment, all those weeks ago, that everything started to fall apart.

The moment I'd been trying not to think about.

The moment I think I understood that Sarah was in danger. And so was I.

Even before the lesson I was feeling weak and out of sorts. Donna had practically had to change me into my swimming costume and my legs had buckled on the steps getting into the water. While the lesson proceeded, I stood terrified against the side of the pool, feeling the world drag farther and farther from me.

Sasha Culk's leg moved slowly and smoothly through the water, hitting my thigh with a silent thud that both stung and ached. She and Demi McKenzie laughed as they splashed towards Donna, who was wrestling the ball from Charlotte in the middle of the pool. A gang of slick, flailing arms surrounded the ensuing struggle as Miss Clarence blew her whistle – the long, pained shriek bounced off the tiled walls in spears of sound that pierced but did not quite kill the battle of Red Caps versus Blue Caps.

The warmth of the water against my arms was the only pleasant thing in my life at that moment. It was all I ever wanted to feel again; I wanted to sleep, to let the entire sensation engulf my body and never wake up.

'Enough, girls,' Miss Clarence yelled. '*Donna, ENOUGH!* It's water polo not Mexican wrestling,' she said, as Donna grabbed Charlotte by the waist and bounced her in and out of the water with glee.

Miss Clarence was fresh out of university and took the girls for swimming and the boys for rugby every other week. She was pretty and slight but had an easier time than most newbie teachers at our school. The popular girls liked her because she had a designer handbag and played R&B music quietly during lessons. The boys liked her because she was female and under thirty and occupationally obliged to wear short-shorts and loose fitting T-shirts. She talked about nightclubs and bars in town that most of us knew about but few had ventured into, and one morning was dropped off at the gates by a man in a soft-topped car. The general consensus was Miss Clarence was the type of woman we'd all like to either grow up to be, or grow up to shag. Often both.

Across the pool, the bodies made miniature tsunamis that ebbed against the tiles. The sound of shouting and the shrill whistle clawed at my dull thoughts like a child kicking the back of a bus seat.

I slipped down.

Further and further.

Inch by inch I became surrounded and safe by the water.

It rose up my chest and my throat.

It swallowed my mouth and my nose.

Then, with a rewarding pop, it sealed around the crown of my head.

I exhaled and felt myself sink farther and farther down.

Submerged, and with my eyes closed, I felt my lungs begin to roar but I chose to ignore them. The bodies – all life – were like a retreating army, and the caw of the whistle was camouflaged by the deep until it became a tropical bird calling out for a mate.

I felt a hot urge to escape and clenched my fists tight at my sides, determined not to give in to my demand to push upwards for air. I opened my eyes to see the cool, blue world around me and felt a fleeting moment of pure tranquillity before a vice-like fist clamped at my arm and pulled me to the surface.

I gasped.

'You're a bloody liability, Claudette,' Miss Clarence hissed as she dragged my arms over the side of the pool.

I blinked the sharp chlorine from my eyes and shuddered at the chill of the air. I looked up. Confused faces stared back at me.

'If you're not going to join in then there's no point in you being here. Go on. Get changed. Detention on Wednesday,' she said.

I hauled myself onto dry land and walked to the changing room. Behind me, Miss Clarence's whistle cut through the sound of sniggering.

My clothes were in a tangled lump where Donna and I had left them. My bag was upturned and face down on the floor, my underwear soaking up the filthy chill of the wet floor. The prospect of getting changed filled me with dread. Instead, I wrapped my towel around my body and lay down on the low slats of the changing bench, dragging a coat across me for warmth as I closed my eyes and drifted off.

I mustn't have been asleep for very long. By the time I woke up the lesson was still in progress, though I was not alone in the changing rooms. I lay still and watched as, across the way, Sarah made her way slowly through bags and coat pockets, pilfering the meagre riches of the girls that she hated the most.

Sarah swore as I sat up slowly in my wet towel and my damp coat, and leaned against the changing room wall.

'Thought I was alone,' she said.

'So did I.'

Sarah gave a smile and a shrug and carried on her task.

'You not cold?' she asked as she re-zipped a coat pocket. 'I'm freezing. Everyone's going on about how summer's coming and I can't get warm. Especially at night. Properly Baltic.'

'I'm fine,' I said, sitting up, mesmerised and impressed all at once.

68

'Leiah Corelli's brought in her deposit for the Belgium trip. I heard her talking about it in assembly this morning,' I said, suddenly keen to help Sarah out and to stick the boot into the more deserving of our year group. 'Her dad's on the taxis so it'll be in cash, too, not a cheque,' I said, pointing to a pink tote bag hung around Leiah's new French Connection coat – a coat that would later be shown on the news like a *memento mori*.

Her eyes widened as she found the envelope containing the cash and pocketed the lot into the right hand side of her bra.

'You want to split it?' she asked reluctantly and I shook my head.

'Good,' she said. 'I was only saying it to be polite. I'd have done you in if you'd have said yes.'

'Chelsea Bishop's taken up smoking too since Maxine Donnelly told her she looked fat. I saw her at the shop by the bus stop. There should be a twenty deck in her pencil case,' I said, rooting through a bag on the bench next to mine and throwing over a virtually untouched packet of Benson & Hedges. 'The Year Tens will buy those off you for sure,' I said as Sarah nodded.

'You don't know next week's lottery numbers do you?' Sarah asked and I did everything I could to smile. She was many things but a natural humourist was not one of them. That she'd made the effort for my sake seemed special, though I didn't have it in me to belly laugh the way I think she'd hoped I would. 'You see everything, don't you?' she asked, straightening herself up so that the stolen goods were not as evident upon her silhouette as they had been before.

'It's a talent,' I said.

'What you doing in here anyway? You gone mad again or something?' she asked with what almost sounded like concern in her voice.

'No more than usual. Miss Clarence had to help me out of the pool,' I said, towelling myself off slowly without standing up.

'She do that to your arm?' she asked where a hand-shaped bruise had begun to bloom. 'You could have her done for that. Make loads of money, too. Sue the school. Get the entire shithole shut down.'

'I probably deserved it,' I said, standing up as the bell rang and the sound of a dozen wet feet slapping the tile surface grew louder and louder.

'Cheers for helping,' Sarah said. 'We should team up, we'd make a killing.'

'Like Bonnie and Clyde,' I said, as a sea of girls raced towards the changing rooms.

'Or Thelma and Louise,' she said.

'Didn't end so well for either of them.'

'I wouldn't know,' Sarah said, as some girls made their way to the showers on tiptoes. 'I've never seen it, only read the back of the DVD. Isn't it about two mates who just drive away together?' she asked.

'Yeah, but they can't outrun what they're trying to escape, so they end up driving off a cliff.'

Sarah thought on that for a moment and shrugged.

'Sometimes it's a gamble worth taking. Cheers for ruining the ending for me anyway, *dickhead,*' she said with a playful smile as her crew made their way into the locker rooms and our acquaintance was put on pause for the sake of the school's carefully established ecosystem.

'Were you talking to Sarah Banks?' Donna whispered as she dried herself off. I shrugged and began pulling my school trousers over my still-damp legs. Next to us Sasha and Demi were laughing together the way girls like that do – sharp, focused laughter that never really connotes joy. Rather it was their warning signals – they wanted you to know that they were the loudest people in the room, and that you were not in on the joke.

'Um, *excuse me!*' Demi said, slapping the back of Tracey Dimple's head as she attempted to spray herself dry with Impulse. 'She has asthma,' Demi said, pointing at Sasha.

'Yeah you little creep,' Sasha said, twanging the elastic of Tracey's swimming cap so it slapped painfully against her skull. 'Have a little consideration. Maybe if you washed more than once a week you wouldn't need to spray so much shit on your body to stop you from stinking.'

The two girls laughed as Tracey collected her wares in a soggy bundle and moved to the far edge of the bench.

Once they were happy that they'd won that particular battle, Demi raised her eyebrows at Sasha and nodded towards me.

'What you looking at, crazy?' Sasha said, turning on her heels and staring down at me, half dressed and zoned out.

'Shit tits and cellulite,' Donna shot back. '*Fuck off,*' she spat, throwing my wet costume and towel into my bag. 'Claudette, get ready, *now*,' Donna warned as the girls eyed one another up.

'Was she talking to you? *Lezza*,' Demi asked as Sasha grabbed my arm. I went to pull away but it was no use. I was too weak to even begin to try fighting her.

'Shame about the bruise,' she said, loud enough for the entire room to hear, 'makes all those cuts look stupid. Purple and red don't really go babes,' she said with mock mindfulness.

'Touch her again,' Donna said, removing her hand from my

arm, 'and I'll show just how well purple and red complement one another.' The girls laughed, pleased to have gotten a rise though not willing to risk the very real chance of a hiding from Donna.

'Maybe one day you'll do everyone a favour and hit a vein,' Demi said.

'You're so *deep*,' Sasha said to me with a roll of her eyes just as Sarah bumped past her, knocking her with some clout against the coat-hooks.

'You want to be more careful,' Sarah said quietly, staring straight into Sasha's eyes as she and her crew left the changing rooms.

That lunchtime, I was due to leave for a doctor's appointment. Dad had written me a note. I was to leave when the lunch bell rang and was due back sometime before food technology.

I had zero intention whatsoever of returning, so when the bell rang and the rest of the class rushed for the canteen, leaving their stuff at the desks, I quietly packed up for the day.

On my way out, I heard Leiah Corelli tearfully screaming down the phone.

'Well it's not here! Yeah, well, how am I meant to know where it is! NO DAD THAT'S NOT FAIR I HATE YOU!'

The entire scene was nauseating.

Without thinking about it, I stopped, turned round, and went back to the classroom. I found Leiah's coat easily, still on the back of her chair where she left it. Very calmly I bundled it into a tight ball, wrapped it in my wet towel and jammed it into the depths of my gym bag.

Then, I walked down the corridor, past Leiah, still wiping tears from her eyes, right out of the school and towards the bus stop.

*

When I got home from school that night Dad had already left for work. I spent the evening in the bath, washing away the stench of chlorine, and going over the day's events. The episode at the pool had left me shaken.

I got out of the bath and got dressed, knowing what I had to do.

Downstairs, I stuffed Leiah's coat underneath my own and headed out again, bound for the beach with the specific intention of finding Sarah.

I sat on the sand waiting for what felt like for ever, but just as I was about to give up hope that she would appear, I saw her in the distance. She was coming from the lighthouse, towards the beach. I watched her as she gradually came close.

Wordlessly she nodded hello and sat down beside me.

'Sasha is a proper arsehole,' she said, lighting a cigarette.

'I know,' I said.

'You shouldn't listen to her.'

'It's hard not to. She's loud.'

'She's not hard to silence, her. Just give her a good whack. She'll soon get the message.'

I smiled.

'That Donna's all right, though. You should stick with her.'

We sat staring at the ebbing tide.

'I got you something to keep you warm,' I said eventually, standing up and retrieving Leiah's stolen coat from beneath my own. I chucked it at Sarah, who laughed as she recognised the garment. 'It's not like she's going to need it to keep warm in Belgium now is it?' I said and she sniggered again, putting the coat on and zipping it up.

'Cheers,' she said. 'That's really decent of you'

'I just maybe wouldn't wear it at school if I were you.'

'I'm not an idiot. Do you want some money for it?' she asked as I made my way back over the beach.

'No,' I said. 'Just knowing she's without it is enough for me.'

Sarah sniggered again and yelled down the beach at me.

'You really are a proper bastard aren't you?' she said as I turned and shrugged. *I love it.*

PART TWO

Most People Just Visit

7

Most People Just Visit

I met Jacob properly on the day of my birthday. In fact, that day I met him twice.

'Where's the birthday girl?' my Aunty Stella asked as she made her way through into the living room after breakfast. She was Dad's youngest sister though older than him by a decade, and like all of Dad's family she was afflicted by an unaccountably sunny outlook that I could not fathom. I always felt most comfortable with glib asides and lazy sneers.

I truly was a Veronica in a land full of Heathers.

'Well, haven't you been spoiled?' she said, placing my presents on the table in the front room and attempting to wrap her arms around me. As usual I tried to sidestep this but still found myself on the wrong end of a hug. 'You're looking well. Nice to see you back on your feet. No point in being miserable, eh?'

People did this occasionally, I found, around mental illness. They'd come at you with this forced joviality. It's as though they imagined the excess happiness would rub off somehow; that maybe you'd become well again as if by osmosis or some shit.

'I'm so glad you're on the mend. You've got the world to be happy for, birthday girl. You're young . . .' she said, taking a handkerchief from her pocket and dusting a corner of the mantelpiece, ' . . . and I was just saying to your Aunty Joyce the other day you'd be the prettiest little thing if you made the effort.'

I managed a noble eleven minutes before making my excuses and leaving half an hour early to wander the promenade before my annual birthday lunch with Donna, and to tend to an errand, whose prospect had made my stomach churn all night.

I had decided that if I wanted to know what had happened to Sarah then I'd have to walk in her footsteps, follow her ghost down some of the paths she'd kept to herself. Only for a short distance, perhaps, but far enough to try and see where it was she'd been trying to get to.

It was clear to me now that Sarah had been frightened. She never told me as much, not in so many words, but I could sense it; I could see that she was running from something she couldn't escape. Hiding in plain sight from whatever dangers she feared the most.

I could never put a finger what exactly was wrong with her.

Something about Dan Vesper had sent a chill through me. I knew this fear and foreboding was precisely what I had seen in Sarah.

Dan was the key to unlocking the truth about what had happened. Somehow he was responsible and somehow he had to pay. No matter what anybody said, I knew he was the one who had caused her to disappear. If I could get to him then I could get to her.

*

Emma Nolan stopped and did a double take as I made my way towards the club's entrance. She was leaving as I was entering and seemed displeased with both situations.

Mostly at school she was known of, rather than known. Sometimes she spoke to Sarah, but mostly kept to her own dead-eyed clique. They were a group that laughed often but never smiled; their enjoyment came from the misfortune of others. Cruelty was their currency and any childhood charm – which was sparse to begin with – had long since been overlaid by thick foundation and laminated eyebrows permanently pencilled into arched disapproval.

'Hi,' I said flatly as she stood between the closing wooden doors, blocking my path.

'You're going the wrong way,' she said, tucking an envelope into her satchel, staring down at me from the subtle pedestal of the step. 'It's invite only.' She pushed her way past me.

'I guess I'm one of the lucky ones, then,' I said, opening the door.

'Don't say I didn't warn you,' Emma threw over her shoulder. I watched her as she climbed into the back seat of a waiting car with blacked out windows and the type of exhaust jigged to make the sound of an explosion at even the gentlest press of the pedal.

I had texted Dan once, tentatively, when my curiosity had got the better of me. And then again in a panic, when his reply was more prompt and demanding than I'd have anticipated: *Glad to see you're a friend. Meet me at lunchtime. You know where to find me.*

My message back sounded jumbled, even with the benefit of spellcheck, but implied that my tight schedule may not permit our meeting at short notice. *See you tomorrow*, came his text in return.

A nightclub during the day was as sad a sight as I could imagine.

The scuffs and dents usually hidden by darkness and the glamorous swirl of strobe lights are writ large and obvious. The room was quiet, save the tinny sound of a song playing low on an iPhone somewhere. The floor was filthy and the walls were peeling. Even the smell of bleach masking the fading scent of bodies – the dim, jarring notes of sweat and scent – seemed sinister.

It looked like a crime scene. A tragedy.

One or two bodies milled about but it was otherwise empty. The sharp sound of a torrent of glass smashing into shards echoed in the distance. Bottles behind the bar were checked and sniffed for signs of skimming, and a man sat crouched by a hissing barrel as he struggled with a length of unruly piping, like a snake charmer urging his serpent into submission.

Dan stood behind the DJ booth counting some form of currency. When he spotted me hovering nervously beside the bar he dismissed the two cohorts that lounged either side of him and jumped down to the dance floor with a firm thud.

'Pleased you could make it,' he said, leading me by the waist towards the bar.

I smiled as best I could and followed his lead as the music faded to silent.

'Get us a drink,' Dan said to the barman's back, who turned grudgingly but obediently and then made towards the optics.

When I tried to object Dan raised his hand gently to my mouth, pressing my lips shut with his cold thumb.

'A toast,' he said, turning my head gently one way and the other, before slowly lowering his hand to his side. 'To our new enterprise.'

'I really don't know,' I said, as two shots of vodka were placed in front of us and Dan raised his glass to mine, clinking before knocking it back.

'Let's not ruin the special moment. I'm pleased you're going to be working for me,' Dan said, nodding towards my vodka. I downed it in one, and felt it bloom inside of me like some toxic rose.

I had to play along; no going back now. Nausea occupied nine tenths of my insides.

'It would just be some flyering, yeah?' I said eventually, when I could force my voice to work.

Dan smiled and leaned his elbow on the bar, knocking a half empty beer bottle onto the floor below.

The barman's eyes met his and Dan nodded once towards the mess.

'Go get the broom,' he instructed as the barman began pooling the glass with his foot. The barman nodded and made his way towards the back of the club and out of an emergency exit door.

Once we were alone Dan looked at me like I was a puzzle he was trying to work out.

'You don't talk much do you?' he asked, smiling as I shrugged.

He reached behind the bar and retrieved a stack of flyers bound with elastic. 'I want you to hand these out, to start with,' he said, slipping the flyers into a brown envelope and folding it once over on itself.

I accepted the package and slipped it inside of my bag.

'I'd assumed flyering was the beginning and the end,' I said suspiciously. 'Just a chance to make a bit of money.'

He grinned. 'A girl needs ambition.'

'A girl needs free time,' I said, attempting a joke as I stood up rod straight, desperately intoning it was time for me to leave.

'Nothing's for free,' Dan said, reaching into his back pocket and pulling out two crisp notes which he slid into the top pocket of my shirt.

'Cheers,' I said, trying not to show any kind of pleasure whatsoever.

'I'd like to have a proper drink with you sometime,' he said smoothly, as I readied myself to leave. 'Why not come to the club night next week? It's going to be a big one.'

'You celebrating something?' I asked and Dan smiled as he shook his head.

'I think I'm going away for a while,' he said as my blood ran cold. 'Might as well make the last night count. There'll be cheap drinks. And an afterparty, too, if I like you enough.'

'Where?' I asked, unable to stop myself. 'Why?' I asked, before checking myself and blushing at my outburst. Dan leaving town was a possibility I had never anticipated, even before his presence had mattered. He seemed to be as much a part of the area as the sharp breeze and the lingering sadness that pervaded even the warmest days. The thought made me as furious as it did panicked. My mission now had a deadline. I would have to get to the bottom of what happened to Sarah before Dan had the chance to slip away into the shadows.

'Just fancy a change of scenery,' he said, coolly but cautiously, as if he could see through the first layer of skin that most people took to be the surface. 'Nothing more sinister. So you're coming then?' he asked as I nodded on instinct. 'You'll be at my last hurrah?'

'I'll be there,' I said. 'I promise.'

'Good,' Dan said. 'And we can have that drink.'

'It's on me.' I took the money out of my top pocket and transferred it to the one on the back of my jeans.

'Go carefully,' he said as I made my way out of the club. 'Oh ... and Claudette,' he added, stopping me dead in my tracks just feet from the exit. 'Many happy returns.'

Safely outside I stopped to swallow what felt like vomit in my mouth.

'Oh what's this?' Donna asked, teasing her fingers over the envelope which prodded out from my bag as we waited in line at the café. 'A present from an admirer?'

She herself hadn't bought me a birthday present but had written an IOU for a hand-job in my card, so at least I knew that she cared.

I shook my head and closed the bag.

'It's nothing.'

'What's in the box!' Donna yelled, grabbing hold of me, doing her best impression of Brad Pitt in *Se7en*. 'WHAT'S IN THE BOOOOOOOX!' she yelled again as old ladies tutted and brushed past us.

'Just some prescriptions and stuff,' I mumbled as we reached the counter. She eyed me sceptically but let it go.

'Hi Deb, can we have ... '

'I'm on my break,' Deb snapped, heading back into the kitchen. 'Jacob, get up here now!'

A boy made his way to out front to take our order. He was older than us though not by much. You could tell by the way his arms were covered in tattoos. Long sleeves of characters and emblems grew up towards his elbows like ivy.

'Oh *hello*,' Donna said, in her smoky old-lady-letch voice. '*What do they call you?*'

'Jacob,' he answered. 'What can I get for you?'

Where I live a person's voice is like their postcode. You can pin someone down to within a three-street radius by the way they pronounce the word 'theatre'. Not Jacob. His voice was clean and infinite. He sounded like everywhere and nowhere all at once.

'Hmmm,' Donna said, clearly eyeing up her next move. 'What can you tell us about today's special?'

'We'll have two sundaes,' I said, in an attempt to stop her in her tracks. 'And two Cokes.'

'Coming right up,' he said, scribbling our orders down on an oil-spattered notepad.

'You've a hue not borne of these shores,' Donna said as he was writing. 'A foreign sort, are you?' she asked.

'I've been travelling, if that's what you mean?'

'Cultured,' Donna said. 'Where?'

'Australia, then Thailand, then China. Then Europe.'

'And now the splendour of the North-East coast?' I said.

'It's a stop-gap,' he said, looking up at me.

'What were the rest? Failed attempts at taking root?' Donna asked as she took a lolly from the top on the counter and placed twenty pence on the till.

'Something like that,' he mumbled, and made his way to process our orders.

'Just nipping to the bathroom,' I said as Donna made her way to the table.

By the time I got back, Donna had true to form made her way through half of her sundae and most of the cream on mine too.

'Here, get this down you before I beat you to it,' said Donna, pushing my ice-cream glass towards me. 'You're going to need a sugar rush for the arcade session later.'

I sighed and took a token spoonful of ice cream as Jacob cleared tables behind us.

'Happy birthday,' he said quietly, as he walked past our table.

'How did you know it was my birthday?' I asked, my mouth sticky with ice cream and sprinkles.

'*I'm psychic,*' he said, pointing to the birthday card Donna had placed beside our menu.

Later that day Donna was sleeping off a sugar coma and Dad had banished me from the house for an hour – ostensibly to make some important phone calls, but I knew the routine. He would be inflating balloons and hoisting banners around the dining table in preparation for my birthday feast. Every year I pretended I had no idea. Me walking in and pretending to be floored by surprise was part of the ritual, and who was I to deprive him of his fun? So, with little else to do, I was walking alone along the beach. That's when I saw Jacob for the second time.

Jacob was poised in downward-facing dog on a rock by the shoreline. He stayed in position for a minute or two before his body began to tremble slightly, and slowly he untangled himself before sitting on the rock and, curling his legs beneath him, back towards me, facing out to sea. After a while he gently leaned back and inhaled, face up to the skies.

'Are you doing yoga?' I said behind him.

'It's very centring,' he said as he exhaled so that his words sounded like a whisper on a breeze.

'You'll sharp be back out of line when you get your head kicked in,' I said, making my way towards him

'Excuse me?' he said, raising his head up to the sky.

'I don't mind. It's good. I tried it once but my body doesn't bend that way.'

'Everyone's body bends that way, it's just a matter of practice.'

'Whatever. I'm just saying. It's not a yoga-in-public type of town. That's all. Someone at school once found a picture of Chris Farrow doing sword dancing and he had three teeth knocked out.'

'You must be so proud of your hometown,' he said.

'Aren't you the boy from the café?' I said after a moment, pretending I'd just found his place in the rich Filofax of my social interactions.

He unfurled his long legs and allowed his feet to dip into the water of the rock pool that was forming with the ebb of the tide.

'I'm so much more than that,' he said dryly. 'Aren't you the girl with the loudmouth friend and the attitude?'

'That's just about the size of it,' I said, sitting down next to him and removing my shoes, rolling the cuffs of my jeans before dipping my feet in the water next to his. 'I'm Claudette,' I said, and anticipated the inevitable tension that followed.

'Oh,' Jacob said in a tone of voice I was fast getting used to. It lay somewhere between realisation, pity and primal fear. 'So you're the . . . ' he said and then stopped himself, the way a good liberal always should. Because there is no way to end sentences that start like that and get away with it entirely scot-free.

'Yep. That's the one,' I said, stretching my legs further into the water, letting it swallow me inch by inch by inch until I was on the edge of the rock, my hands digging into rough stone to keep myself from slipping under. 'Just to be clear I'm the crazy one, not the one that's missing.'

'I gathered that,' he said, wiping his mouth with his hand and trying not to blush. There was a moment's pause before he looked pained and sheepish and muttered, '*Sorry.*'

I smiled and shrugged.

'What for?'

'How are you . . . feeling?'

'What does it matter?' I said.

'I'm just trying to say the right thing,' he said half apologetically and half defensively.

'Smart-ass is my default setting, I'm afraid,' I said, and smiled. 'I guess it's hard to explain. I feel like I have to describe myself to everybody that knows me at the moment. Everyone I've ever met . . . All I mean is that you don't know me, or you didn't before. Can't I just be however you find me, in this moment? However I am to you now? This is me. Lets take it from here.'

'I like that. You sound like an inspirational meme. The type of thing people write over a picture of Marilyn Monroe whether she said it or not.'

I laughed and leant back so that I was resting on my elbows, staring straight ahead. The rocks beneath us were invisible. Beyond my body was the grey infinity of the ocean.

'You're funny. *Ish*.'

'Thanks. *Ish*,' Jacob said, leaning backwards and mimicking my pose.

'Where are you from anyway?'

'Everywhere,' he said. '. . . Nowhere.'

'That's deep.'

He twisted his face as the rough rocks scraped at his back and sat up again.

'My dad was in the army. We moved around a lot. Every year, just about. I never stayed in one place long enough to be *from* anywhere, really. I was always the new kid. Just about on the verge of inventing myself when we'd be dragged to another base and I'd have to start again.'

'I hear that,' I said, sitting back up.

He told me about how he travelled from place to place, never staying anywhere for longer than a month.

'The next stop just always seems so exciting. I'm always convinced the next one will be the place for me,' he said.

He showed me his arms. Each tattoo had been drawn in a different city, and each meant something different to him. From his wrist to his elbow he traced a map of the world and the parts he'd managed to see before taking flight once more.

'What if you never find what you're looking for?' I said. 'What if you pass over the place that's meant for you because you were too eager to leave or too impatient to give it a proper chance?'

He shrugged. 'Then I'll die trying,' he said. 'With a ton of interesting memories.'

'How come you ended up here?' I asked as a seal's head pierced the water in the distance before disappearing beneath. 'It's not a natural progression from Thailand.'

'Ran out of money. My aunty and uncle own the café, said they'd give me twenty quid a day and let me sleep in the stock room if I helped out with the summer rush.'

'How long are you here for?' I asked.

'As long as it takes.'

'Where will you go next?'

'Wherever I can,' he said.

'You talk like a seventies rock star,' I said as a breeze blew a shiver across my spine.

'*Poetic and insightful?*' he asked hopefully.

'Stoned and pretentious,' I corrected him.

Jacob thought for a moment and then shrugged.

'When you're right you're right,' he said.

We sat in silence for a stretch of time that felt longer than it was. Jacob shifted on his seat and looked in his bag for something that wasn't there. I dragged my legs out of the water and let the sun dry the saltwater in tiny crystals between the folds of fabric.

'What happened, really?' he asked. 'You know what it's like around here. People talk. A story gets to your ear so stretched out you can't even recognise its origin. Was it as bad as people said?'

'I don't know,' I said. 'It didn't feel like I was there at the time. Not totally. Not the me I recognise.'

'Like a blackout?'

'Sort of, but brighter – like, fiercer? It was like someone opened the cages at the zoo. Suddenly this wildness that had been more or less contained got out. But I don't mean to make it sound glamorous and exotic. It wasn't. It was boring and frightening and it hurt. That's all there is to it.'

'Was it that bad?' he asked and I nodded.

'Then after the light comes the dark. The part before, the wildness, that bit's different. In that moment, you've stumbled upon the meaning of life and you're invincible. When the depression hits – that's the hardest bit.'

'I know what you mean,' he said.

'You do?'

'Of course. Everyone gets depressed from time to time,' he said and I shook my head.

'Yeah, but I *am*. *It is*. Like pigment or faith or hair colour or something. It really is always there.'

'You live in a place most people just visit,' he offered.

'That was cheesy as hell,' I said. 'But pretty much on the money.'

We walked back up towards the promenade together as Jacob

buttoned his white shirt in preparation for his evening shift at the café.

'It was nice meeting the girl behind the legend,' he said as we reached the point at which we would have to part ways.

'You too,' I said. 'And believe me, I don't say that often. We could hang out again if you like. I could do with as many friends as I can get at the moment. Besides, you could use a girl like me. I know these streets. Know where it is and isn't safe to do yoga. I could be your bodyguard.'

'And I can be your long lost pal?' he said and I smiled.

'Sure thing, Betty,' I said as I made my way from him.

'Stay safe, Al,' he yelled back after me.

8

Blessed

They say it's a shame that you never get to enjoy your own funeral, and I couldn't help but feel it was the same with Sarah and her absence. The longer she was gone the more she got what she had always needed when she was here – to be acknowledged, to be missed, to be thought of as more than just a problem to be dealt with.

She was like a child's toy, unwanted until somebody else had her.

I was in my room, watching the local news. All these weeks on and Sarah was still the main story, but I'd noticed the narrative around her change in the days and weeks after she went missing. She'd gone from being the Big Bad Wolf to being Little Red Riding Hood. Sarah Banks; the fairy tale with a twist. And now we were left to consider in her absence what no one had taken the time to consider while she was still here: that maybe she didn't choose to veer off the beaten track. Maybe she was led. And maybe the reason she'd never found her way home was that, for her, there never had been a home to go back to.

Dad knocked on my door as I was switching from the news

report to a lifestyle make-over show where they were discussing the merits of a pastel capsule collection.

'Planning a change of look?' he asked. 'What are you up to on the laptop?' I made a concentrated effort not to roll my eyes at him. Dad was of the belief that the internet was essentially a holding pen for thieves and sex pests all waiting to take what they could. When I'd informed him that I was just as likely to be raped and murdered by a stranger I met on the street as in a chat room he hadn't been as placated as I'd assumed he would be. I got away with the laptop on the grounds of schoolwork, but I could tell he still wasn't happy about it.

'Revision,' I said, as he bent down and kissed my head, lingering to catch sight of my screen.

'I'm off to work, then. It's just a few hours overtime,' he said unsurely. 'And if you need me . . .'

'The number's on the fridge,' I said. 'Got it. Go.'

As soon as he was out of the door, I reopened the Facebook page. It was time for my weekly spruce-up.

In Hollywood all the famous actors have body doubles. They literally pay another person to act out their most intimate and epic scenes. The scenes we remember them for are often the very scenes in which they didn't ever appear.

Most of us can't afford shit like this. We just have the internet, where we pick and preen at our replicants.

Spellcheck.

Edit.

Filter.

Photoshop.

Then, once we're happy with the electronic footprint that everybody else can see, we sit back and feel lousy about how our real lives are never as fun and exciting than the artisanal ones we share online.

I logged on and scrolled down the page to glean the most pertinent pieces of news and information from my friends and classmates.

That week, unsurprisingly, every second post was a link to a news report about Sarah or a clip of the town on YouTube.

A girl in the year below me had uploaded a photograph taken from above; her face was in a pout and two-thirds out of shot, but her tits were enormous and perfectly central. 62 Likes.

'Six years today Granddad, Never Forget X x x x x x x' posted a girl I had met at an underage disco. Her sadness and bravery garnered 21 Likes, a 'U OK HUN?' and a heart made out of a pointy bracket and the number 3.

Donna had papped her brother visiting a porn site and tagged her mum, aunty, uncle and every one of her cousins in the photograph. 42 Likes, three LOLs, an expletive from her brother and a 'Take this down and call me now' from her mum.

Charlotte had added a 'Which Biscuit Are You?' quiz (she was an iced gem). Dylan Tovey's new football boots rendered him #blessed, and Stacey Brisket wondered 'Why Is It Always Me?' (12 Likes, one 'Inbox Me, bbz.')

Along the right-hand side of the page were various adverts. One for a local psychotherapy centre, from the time I had searched the words 'suicide methods'; another for an S&M singles dating site, presumably from one of the evenings when my pornography consumption ran to the exotic; and an Amazon link for a book I once tried to Google a cheat-essay on for school, when I was too depressed to write it myself. I hovered momentarily over the dating site before ignoring all three potential futures – health, love and knowledge.

I clicked through to my profile page. I was in dire need of a makeover.

First, I changed my photo to a shot of me and some 'friends' (social butterfly). In the picture I look like I've been caught beautifully off-guard when in fact I had been painfully aware my photo was being taken at the time.

Next, I crafted my status update: a link to a semi-obscure song that everybody knows (accessible) featuring at least one line that alludes to homecoming (enigmatic) by an old band (cultured) but in a rare live recording on YouTube (edgy). I added a veiled reference to my triumphant return from the crazy house (informative) and hit 'Post'.

I wrote a comment on Donna's wall (sociable) making sure to include an in joke (beguiling).

I Liked three posts by almost-strangers (generous).

Then I shared a page that had been set up to try and raise awareness of Sarah's last sightings and appearance (selfless and caring).

Finally, I topped it all off by following an art gallery in town that I will never visit (wanker) and gifting three stars to a book that I would never finish (learned yet discerning).

At last I allowed myself to admire my handiwork, my own virtual body double. At least there's one dimension where I'm complete and whole and functioning. For another week anyway.

Later that day I knocked gently on Mr Fitzpatrick's front door. He lived in a downstairs flat, like us, but his curtains were almost always closed. Somehow it made even his front yard look gloomy and overcast.

I knocked once more, and was about to turn and leave when

the door opened slowly and the old man's pale face peered at me from the dingy hallway.

'I brought you some cake,' I said, presenting him with a napkin that was beginning to soak through with sugars from a home-made cream sponge. 'Dad made it. He's pretty good. It was my birthday yesterday, we had plenty left over so it's not like we're going without or anything.'

Mr Fitzpatrick looked at me uncertainly, and then glanced towards the end of the street.

'What's this in aid of?' he asked suspiciously, opening the door another inch.

I shrugged and handed the gift towards him.

'I don't know,' I said. 'I suppose you were nice to me the first day I got out of hospital, when nobody else was.'

'Manners should be expected, not rewarded,' he said.

'Look. Do you want the cake or not?'

'Are you alone?' he asked.

I nodded yes and the door opened another inch or so as he stepped to one side.

'You'd better come in then I suppose.'

His house was warm and damp, with a sharp, ripe smell, like a fruit basket left out in the sun.

His living room was cluttered, but with an odd sense of order about the place. Scrapbooks and photo albums on every shelf and surface – stacked high on top of his boxy old television set, lined up along the length of the upright piano, left higgledy-piggledy along the mantelpiece. On the low, wooden coffee table one album was open at the picture of a boy – around my age, maybe older – and a newspaper cutting that had been glued to the page and folded back on itself, so that only the bottom half of a toothpaste advert was showing.

'You can sit down if you must,' he said, indicating to one of two single armchairs in the front room.

'No thank you,' I said. 'I'm not staying. I just thought I'd say hello.'

I placed the cake down on the coffee table and tried to get a better look at the open album.

'It's kind of you, to have brought the cake,' the old man said, clearing his throat as if he was trying to interrupt my train of thought, or intercept whatever question I was about to ask. 'Unnecessary, but kind. I shall enjoy it with a cup of tea later on when I listen to the evening news.'

'Are these all albums you've made?' I asked. 'Or are some of them ones you've been given by family and stuff?'

Some of the albums were dated; others even had titles.

'Torquay, 1962' one said in swirling, old-fashioned handwriting. The type nobody bothers with any more.

'Graduation' said another.

'They're all mine. Just a little hobby,' he said, sitting down heavily in his chair. 'My way of remembering the good bits.'

I perched on the arm of the chair opposite his.

'Of your family?' I asked and he nodded. 'Is that your son?'

'At my age memories are all you've got,' he said, reaching forward and closing the open album.

'I doubt my dad could fill an entire album with my good memories the way I'm going. Let alone a whole room of them.'

'Well, he can always devote a page to the time you delivered cake,' Mr Fitzpatrick said, and I smiled at what may well have been his first ever attempt at a joke.

'Baby steps I suppose. Anyway memories don't have to be all you've got. My grandma didn't have any friends after Granddad died. Then Dad got her a computer and signed her up to Silver

96

Surfer classes at the library. Now she lives in Tenerife with her new husband and works two days a week in a shop that sells magnets.'

Mr Fitzpatrick smiled and shook his head. 'So there's hope for us all.'

'Well, I wouldn't go that far. Grandma was a real catch. But there's no harm in trying. Anyway, why do you never talk to anybody?' I asked, pacing over to the piano and playing one of the two chords that I knew.

'I talked to you,' he said, standing too, and placing his fingers next to mine, playing a mirroring chord that hung heavy in the room like smoke.

'It took you sixteen years to say anything even remotely nice.'

'You'd never given me reason to be nice. Besides, people don't talk to me.'

'You scare them,' I said.

'They scare themselves,' he corrected me. 'People have an idea. An impression. Of who you are. What you are. It can be very hard to change that, even if you are inclined to try. Which I am not. You of all people should know that.'

'*Preach*,' I said, thinking of Jacob.

'You're religious?' Mr Fitzpatrick asked, clearly surprised.

'God no,' I said. 'It's just something people say, you know, when you agree with something. *Preach*. It's supposed to be funny. But now that I'm explaining it I'm not entirely sure why.'

'Hmm,' he said. 'As pleasant as this has been, what exactly are you here for?' he asked, sitting back down in his chair.

I sat too, and dug my elbows into my knees.

'I don't know,' I said. 'I honestly don't. I got out of hospital less than a week ago and it's like I'm spending my entire time trying to find the person I'm supposed to be now, this fixed, functioning, *whole* person.'

'I see.'

'My friends are treating me like I'm some volatile stranger and my dad's acting like nothing happened and everything's fine, and meanwhile everybody's looking for Sarah Banks and everything's the same but different and . . . ' I stopped to catch my breath.

'That poor girl,' murmured Mr Fitzpatrick, a shadow casting over his face.

'You OK?' I said.

'Yes, yes . . . ' He shook his head a little. 'Go on.'

'The only parts of me that I remember clearly are the bad parts. I guess I'm just trying to remind myself that there's some good in me, somewhere, sometimes.'

'Where exactly do I fit in with all of this, Claudette?'

I shrugged.

'Well, I've got this book I'm supposed to fill in to help me get better. And I'm meant to set myself these goals and targets and stuff, things I can achieve in the short term and long term and all the type of stuff most people just do without even having to think about it. The problem is I do think about it and I never have anything to put. So, I don't know . . . Maybe I could visit you? That could be one of my things.'

'I don't need charity,' he said, looking a bit affronted.

'Yeah well that's good, because I've got no money and even if I did have I wouldn't give you any,' I said and he smiled. 'I just mean, you know, as a friend. We can talk. You can tell me about your albums, if you want to. I just . . . need to be able to do something that isn't inside my own head.'

Mr Fitzpatrick stood up slowly and opened the door to the living room.

'Time to go now,' he said, as I made my way to the door.

Assuming his lack of enthusiasm was a polite decline of my offer, I let him walk me to the door, when all of a sudden he cleared his throat and removed his glasses, polishing his lenses with an embossed handkerchief he fished out from under his cardigan sleeve.

'Wednesdays and Fridays,' he said, as we made our way to the front door.

'Excuse me?'

'Wednesdays and Fridays I'm sometimes dragging my feet a bit. Not much to do those days. Especially the afternoons. If you were to drop by I'm sure I'd be able to spare ten minutes or so.'

'I'll check my schedule,' I said, as I strolled out into his front yard. 'And thank you,' I said, shutting the gate behind me, 'for being nice to me.'

Mr Fitzpatrick smiled and shook his head.

'*Preach*,' he said, as he shut the front door.

9

Elemental

Nobody thought that Mr Darvill had taken Sarah, but everyone knew that he'd had her. One way or another, Mr Darvill was guilty.

They announced the news on television. The report showed Darvill's bug-eyed photograph from his school entry pass. The reporter talked about inappropriate relations and an imminent statement from the school. Then it cut to images of Darvill's wife, her jacket hood pulled low over her head, trying to make it through her own front gate through a swarm of photographers all snapping their lenses in her face.

I was dozing on the sofa; Dad was running a wet wipe across the skirting boards.

'Awful stuff,' Dad said, scrunching up the cloth and resting it on the edge of the mantelpiece as he stared at the television. 'Haven't I met him?'

'Maybe parents' evening,' I said distantly, haunted by his image. 'I'm late for therapy,' I said, standing up and collecting my things.

As soon as I was outside I sensed it – the palpable shift in atmosphere that happens when something significant occurs in a place. Others felt it too, and all around me a steady trickle of curious dawdlers headed in the general direction of whatever it was. My bus was due in five minutes but before I knew it I was following them, back down our street towards Stepney Parade.

A small crowd had formed outside the retirement flats, along with the usual array of cameras and police vans. They now seemed as much a part of the town as the promenade or the crap cafés and high teen-pregnancy rate. It's strange how quickly you get used to something. I almost couldn't remember a time when we weren't being investigated somehow – observed and analysed; documented and judged. It was like the crazy thoughts that had plagued my mind in the run up to my manic break were suddenly becoming a reality. There really were cameras everywhere. Our entire presence was being observed by sly, unseen authorities. Somewhere there were bad people. Somewhere notes were being made. Somewhere fingers were being pointed. Somewhere fates were being sealed and decisions were being made over which we had no control.

It was almost a comfort to see the communal madness that gripped the town now that we were all pinned under the microscope of the media and the police presence. Some revelled in the attention, vying to offer a soundbite or stake some claim to Sarah, readily spreading gossip and hearsay, stoking the flames. Others weren't so brash. They scurried and hid in the shadows, forever glancing over their shoulders. Just as vain as the camera-hogs, they felt that their own boring secrets were floating closer to the surface and were keen to avoid the reveal of the spotlight.

I spotted Adam in the crowd and headed towards him. He wasn't in his community officer uniform, but still looked on with the authority of a man who could take charge, should the occasion require it.

'What's happening in there?' I asked him, as the police wove their tape into a boxy web outside of the building.

'That teacher . . . it's his mam's old flat,' he said. 'Apparently he's been visiting more since she died than he ever did when she was alive. At least that's what Gemma from the butcher's told me,' he said, biting into his bacon and egg sandwich.

'Mr Darvill?' I asked.

'Yep,' he said, as the tape was knotted at the post and the police returned to the van where they donned white jumpsuits.

A drop of yolk fell from the bread and landed in the middle of his T-shirt.

'Bugger,' he said, wiping his front with a napkin.

'I used to see him driving around here all the time even though I know he lives miles away. I used to imagine he was trying to assassinate me,' I said, moving forward in the crowd.

'Maybe it wasn't you he was after,' Adam said, reaching his arm out and trying to pull me back towards the edge of the crowd. 'Leave it, Claudette,' he said, as I turned to meet his gaze. 'They'll let us know if they find anything important. You shouldn't be here.'

When I found out about Mr Darvill and Sarah I put a brick through the laundrette window, because I didn't know what else to do.

I saw them together in the science room one lunchtime. It was about a month before everything came to a head but I could already feel the deep tremors of a rupture building inside of me. I was focused but confused. The specifics still eluded me. All I knew for certain at the time was that an apocalypse was coming

102

and I was building towards something – a mission, a duty, a destiny – for which I had to make myself strong.

I had gone into the science cupboard looking for a textbook but had stumbled upon a poster of the periodic table and that was that. In my mind it was a sign: whatever my mission was would require intricate study of this colour coded map of letters and numbers. I missed two lessons in a row. The bell didn't interrupt me, nor did the buzzing of my phone when Dad was trying to call to ask where the hell I was. Someone from school had phoned his work to inform him of my sudden absence. It was the scraping of a chair that eventually broke my trance, and I soon realised Darvill was in the room adjoining the cupboard, marking coursework.

I was still wondering how I was going to get out of there, when I heard Sarah's voice and heard Darvill answer her. I couldn't hear what they said but I could hear the tone. Sarah sounded bored, but Darvill's tone was not one that teachers usually use with their students. He sounded amused and then angry. I looked through a crack in the door. The view wasn't clear, but I could see him standing over her, one hand on her arm. His face was too close to hers, I thought, and he was whispering sharp words in her ear. She looked him dead in the eye and leaned her neck to one side. And then, with a cautionary glance at the door, he pressed his lips to her exposed neck and put his arms around her shoulders. They stayed like that for a moment and then they left, Sarah first, then him.

I couldn't move.

I was utterly afraid.

I didn't know what to do about any of it.

When I felt too heavy with secrets to contain it any longer, I forced myself to stand up.

I started walking and I kept going, walking and walking to try and make myself feel light again.

At some point after that, my memory goes blank.

By the time I came round it was dark and I was sitting on the bonnet of a police car. Adam was standing nearby. He was in uniform and scribbling something in his notepad, while a policewoman sat next to me and rubbed my shoulders to keep me warm. After a moment I clocked the pharmacy shopfront and the broken glass.

'What've you been playing at, love?' she asked as I felt myself slip back into the world from wherever it was that my mind went when I blacked out. 'What's that she's saying?' the woman asked Adam as I whispered the periodic table under my breath.

Silicon, phosphorous, sulphur, chlorine . . .

'What you saying pet?' the woman asked as I clung desperately to the clean structure of the chart that had gotten me into the mess in the first place.

Potassium, calcium, scandium, titanium . . .

'What's she going on about?' another policeman said from inside the car.

'I dunno,' said the policewoman, giving my leg a shake. 'I think she's foreign or something.'

Tin, antimony, tellurium, iodine . . .

'Claudette,' Adam said, making his way over. 'Claudette, can you hear me?'

Iodine . . . iodine . . . iodine . . . iodine . . .

'Told you she was foreign,' the policewoman said as Adam repeated my name over and over again.

'That'll explain it then,' said the policeman inside the car, fiddling with the radio and casting out a net of static over the stillness of the night.

'She's not foreign, she knocks about with our Donna.'

'That's just as bad if not worse,' said the policewoman flatly as Adam turned back to me.

'Claudette . . . can you hear me,' he said, lowering his face so that his eyes met mine.

Iodine . . . iodine . . . iodine . . . iodine . . .

'It's xenon,' he said after a while, holding my face in his hands. 'Xenon, Claudette,' he said.

I looked into his eyes and stepped back into myself. It was as if the needle had hit the groove and momentarily I was lucid.

'*Swot,*' I whispered quietly as Adam smiled at the flash of familiarity that crossed my face.

'Come here,' he said, holding me tightly to his chest as I began to sob.

Once they realised that there would be no great discoveries made that day at the flats on Stepney Parade, the crowd had begun to disperse.

'That's that then,' Adam said as we made our way towards the sea front. I was by this point twenty minutes late for the bus, which meant I was half an hour late for therapy. Which meant that there was really no point in going. 'What are you up to today?' he asked.

'Therapy,' I said.

'Oh,' Adam said, awkwardly.

'Don't worry,' I said, sensing his unease. 'Everybody feels awkward. Don't. It's fine.'

'It's not though, is it?' he said as he ushered me across the road.

'It's getting there. At least you were kind to me, when things got bad,' I said.

'You weren't well,' he said. 'It was obvious.'

'Not to everyone. They just thought I was being a dickhead,' I added. 'Smashing stuff up and banging on about all sorts of nonsense.'

Adam shrugged and looked around him.

'I had to talk to someone you know, after Dad died.'

'I know,' I said.

'Donna just blasted through,' he said, taking a seat on the bench overlooking the sea. 'She's a pain in the arse but she's tough. She got on with it. Cried the right amount. Laughed the right amount. Remembered him just enough. I don't know. I just . . . drowned in it all.'

'I know,' I said, sitting down.

'I was the man of the house and I hadn't even lost my virginity yet,' he said with an embarrassed laugh that brought another flush of pink to his cheeks. 'I have now though, just so you know.'

'Congratulations,' I said, ruffling his hair.

'One of the reasons it's so hard to get into the police force,' he said flattening the tangled mass I'd created on his head. 'Nobody wants a kook with a gun ruling the streets.'

'I didn't know that. Isn't that discrimination or something?'

'Not if they do it carefully,' he said. 'Anyway, I'm just saying. I don't know what it's like for you. I know things got bad. Things . . . *get bad* at times. But I understand, as much as anyone can. And I think you're brave, I really do.'

'I think you'll make a fine policeman one day, Adam. Just so long as Donna doesn't completely destroy your soul in the process,' I said and he laughed.

'Yeah. Well, time will tell,' he said, and we were quiet for a moment. 'Anyway, can I give you a lift? To the doctor's. I've got a one-on-one at the gym in twenty minutes, but I could drop you off close by?'

When I declined on the grounds of needing that salty blast of air to clear my mind he nodded and said he understood.

'If you do ever need anything though, Claudette, don't be scared to ask. People do care, even if it doesn't always feel that way.'

'I know,' I said, as I made my way towards the amusements.

'And don't worry yourself about all the other stuff. There are people whose job it is to sort the world out. You just concentrate on yourself.'

I bought an ice cream for lunch and ate it in the amusement arcade.

I did not want to see anybody, and more importantly I did not want to be seen.

I was so late for my therapy appointment by this stage that no amount of hurrying could rectify it. Better to start box-fresh and raring to go at my second appointment than spend the remaining moments of my first red-faced and apologetic. Besides, Dad would only worry and Donna would only judge me. I figured they'd done enough of that over the last few months. An afternoon off from my bullshit was my gift to them.

Dreamland Amusements was the largest of the arcades that was still open and it looked like a set for a seventies gangster film. The games pinged out prizes that had been preserved behind their glass screens since I was a kid. The neon lights flickered and spun so that once you were inside time ceased to exist. Back in the day it had always seemed the most glamorous and exotic of places. A land of sparkle and luck; of chance and hope. Now the only real link it seemed to have to its given name was a look of constant exhaustion, like it had battled through a fitful evening of nightmares and cold sweats and still had to get up and put in a full day's work.

I sat alone in Dreamland for almost an hour. I was more than content watching the cartoon fruit spin and stop in odd concoctions. The lights were too bright and the carpet too sticky, but the odd sensation of a room so removed from the outside world – a place where day and night were one and the same, where the same songs played in the same order over and over again – was comforting in a strange, removed sort of way. It was like the world was on hold while I sat on the cracked, leather stool, eking out my loose change for as long as humanly possible.

I was about to get up and leave when I realised somebody was sitting at the booth opposite me.

There was a wailing of notes and then a cascade of coins.

'Jackpot,' I heard a voice say, and recognised it to be Ross. I was gathering my things when I saw two men entering. One I didn't know. The other was Dan Vesper, carrying a small bag. They made their way over.

'Must be my lucky day, Ross, son,' I heard Dan say as a hand scooped the shrapnel from the tray of the winning game. His voice was jittery and jagged though not through nerves. He had the energy of an angry beast thrashing against a cage door.

I pressed against my machine so as to not be seen.

Ross groaned but did not object as he watched Dan pocket his money. There was a cold silence that followed and I leaned closer, trying to hear their conversation over the sterile dirge of the music.

'You owe me,' Dan said.

'I'm good for it,' Ross said, as another coin was slipped into the slot.

'I know. And now it's payback time,' he said.

'What am I supposed to do with this?' Ross asked.

'Work your magic,' Dan said.

'What?'

'Make it disappear,' Dan said as Ross's machine sounded out and another shower of coins clanked in the tray. 'You want a roof over your head then you earn your keep. I'll be in touch,' he said. I watched him walk back out of the arcade minus the bag he had entered with, his henchman trailing after him.

There was a lengthy pause, certainly enough time to give Dan an ample head start, before Ross made his way out of Dreamland into the harsh light of day. He was carrying Dan's bag with him.

I let him gain some distance before I got up and began to follow in his wake, hanging back just far enough to be out of sight, but not too far that I couldn't keep track.

I followed him across the road, through alleyways and side streets. With each turn he seemed to grow smaller on my horizon, until eventually I was almost running to keep up with him. I followed him across the green and along the estuary bank to the rock pools beneath the pier where we used to take fishing nets to catch minnows. The soles of my shoes slid on the damp stones, but I steadied myself with my hands on the rough, wet rocks.

At first there was no sign of Ross. The tide had been pulled far out and the sun dried the rocks in blotchy patches.

And then, there he was.

'What are you doing?' he asked, crouched in the pebbles between two overhanging boulders. I had been just about ready to give up my mission and, as much as I was pleased to have secured my prey, hearing his voice made my skin turn cold.

'What's in the bag?' I asked as Ross stood up.

'What bag?'

'The bag you had.'

'There was no bag.'

'What was in it?'

'I don't know what you mean?'

'Yes, you do.'

Ross sighed. 'Spying? Really, Claudette?' He tried to push past me but I stood firm in my tracks.

'I won't let you go,' I said and he smirked and shook his head.

'Look. The bag's gone. You can't really stop me now, can you?' He took a half-smoked cigarette from his pocket and pressed it to his lips. He struggled with a lighter that clicked three empty sparks before he gave up and threw both the lighter and the stub of a cigarette into the distance.

'*So cool, Ross,*' I said. 'Why are you getting rid of things for Dan Vesper?'

'Because when he asks you to do something you do it.'

'Was it anything to do with Sarah?' I asked and Ross's face turned white.

'Don't get involved,' he said. 'Please Claudette.'

His voice was becoming more panicked and suddenly I felt myself pity him the way you pity a dog that has wrecked the front room because it had nothing better to do.

'Did Dan know Sarah?'

'Look, he didn't take her, if that's what you think. But you know how it is. If people found out they knew one another it wouldn't look good.'

'How well did they know one another?' I asked and Ross shrugged. 'How well do you know him?'

Again he shrugged and looked to the ground.

'I just started doing some flyering for his club night, that's all,' said Ross.

'You seemed thick as thieves,' I said.

'You wouldn't understand.'

'Wouldn't understand what?'

'What it's like having nowhere to go,' he said, as he made his way past me. 'At least Dan gives you what you need. Gives you money, a place to stay. You think your life's so hard, Claudette, but you don't know shit.'

'I know Dan doesn't give anything without taking twice as much back,' I said, following him across the rocks, up onto the pier and back along the shore.

'Why do you care so much?' he asked, as I met his pace and we walked awkwardly side by side.

'Because I want to know what happened to Sarah. Don't you?' Ross stopped in his tracks.

'Maybe she doesn't want to be found,' Ross said knowingly as a bus came into view in the distance while he fished a torn ticket from his back pocket.

'What was in the bag, Ross?' I tried one last time, gently.

'Honestly? I don't know.'

'Then tell the police.'

The bus hissed to a stop before lowering its deck for the prams and wheelchairs.

'There's nothing to tell.'

'Ross,' I whispered, as an old lady fiddled in her coin purse for the right change. 'Who took her?'

'Sarah?' he said, going to step on to the bus. He turned and looked at me then, with an odd smile, a smile that was proud and kind and sad all at once. 'She's wherever she's supposed to be. And you should leave her there, for her sake and yours.'

And with that the doors sighed closed as the bus pulled away.

10

The Darkroom

The next day I walked past the Mariners six times in an attempt to spot or be spotted by Dan Vesper. His replies to my texts first shortened, then became spaced out and eventually stopped altogether. It felt like he was pulling away. Either he was on to me, or he no longer had use for me. Either way I couldn't allow it.

After half an hour he was still nowhere to be seen so I gave up and walked along the beach feeling useless, having made no progress. With days as empty as mine and expectations so universally low, a failed task had the ability to cloud proceedings like a drop of ink polluting an ocean.

I went to text Donna but the words just wouldn't come. I didn't know what exactly I wanted from her. I certainly wasn't in the mood to see her. I just felt the need to remind her that I existed.

In the end I decided to go and bother Jacob at the café instead.

'He's not here,' said Deb, acting all harangued and put out despite a distinct lack of customers. 'Never is here when I need him, he's a cheek to ask for paying if you ask me.'

'OK. I hope the rush dies down for you soon,' I said, gesturing to the empty tables. Deb mumbled something about me being a cheeky little so-and-so before sighing and clanking a metal canister of milk against the bench.

'Said something about the pier. Can't say I was listening properly. Took his camera with him. You don't go getting him into bother now,' she warned me as I closed the door behind me.

Jacob had taken up temporary residence underneath the pier, arching out over the darkest patch of sea like a half-built cathedral, its dark wooden slats ridged with barnacles and spangled black from saltwater. He was sitting in the damp sand, the water edging menacingly closer and closer to him, as he craned his neck back in odd angles, taking photographs.

'Updating the 'gram?' I asked, making my way over.

He didn't look up, didn't stop what he was doing, but he must have known it was me as he smiled. 'Just trying to capture the moment.'

'All the college kids come down here with their little tripods – finding the beauty in darkness or some shit. It's well *hack*.'

'There really are no original ideas left,' he said as I lay my bag down on the sand.

'Well, this is nice,' I said, staring up at the base of the pier. Mouldy rope hung down from the boards in loops, like some dishevelled mummy.

'I like it,' he said. 'It's like the staring at the bones of the town. It's peaceful.'

'It's depressing as fuck down here,' I said eventually. 'It always feels cold, even in summer.'

'It's depressing as fuck up there,' he said. 'I tried taking a photo from the pier and some kid called me a nonce and threw a beer can at me.'

'Them's my people,' I said with a shrug.

'You want to go somewhere?' he said then.

I shrugged. 'I want to go anywhere but here. I hate it so much.'

'We can go back to my place?' he said with a wan smile. 'I can show you my darkroom?'

'Sold,' I said.

We snuck in up the back stairs of the café so that Aunty Deb didn't suddenly feel Jacob's services were required up front, and navigated our way past open boxes of napkins and spilled sugar sachets that lined the rickety staircase.

'Wow, it's even more depressing behind the scenes,' I said, steadying my foot on a loose floorboard. I paused to pick flaking paint from a patch on the wall. Jacob took my hand and hauled me past a pile of stacked menus.

'Such is life,' he said, as he fiddled with a shoddy lock and opened the door to his space.

'Just to reiterate,' I said, as I made my way inside and was confronted with the sparseness of the old stock room he called home. 'I'm not here to shag you. I really am just keen to see your photographs.'

Jacob was quiet for a moment and then laughed once with an exhale.

'Good,' he said, and locked the door behind us, leaving the key jutting at an angle. 'I thought you might be after me for my money.'

Minimalist is what they would've called it in the lifestyle supplement of a Sunday paper. A rail of clothes, a desk, a futon against the back wall and several strung-up clothes lines pegged at intervals with freshly developed photographs.

I took in his photographs one by one, displayed and grouped in semi-themes. There were pictures of the beach in daylight and by night. There were shots of individuals, some of whom he'd even managed to pose. Mostly they were close-ups and obscured angles of sights most of us walked past a dozen times a week without stopping to pay heed. There was the rotting wood of the far pier, taken so closely that the gaps in the wood looked like canyons from the sky. A stack of rope and a neon sign with three letters bust out. A burnt-out ice-cream van and a weather-beaten Missing poster. Two magpies chatted on a memorial bench as the tide drew out before them.

Click.

'Stop it,' I said, as Jacob began making wider circles around me, dipping in and out of the hanging photographs, snapping my picture as he went.

'Why?' he asked as his lens sealed again, like a lizard's eye.

'Because this precise moment in my life isn't one I want to suspend forevermore,' I said, reaching a fresh line of photographs. Jacob cooled his enthusiasm and relaxed his camera around his neck. 'I'd sooner minimise all evidence.'

'That's a shame,' he said.

I looked closer at the photographs taken in the aftermath of Sarah's disappearance. Mostly they were of police procedurals – the evidence hunt, the fresh tents on empty beaches – but in all of them there was a crowd; a gathered chorus narrating the sorry state of affairs.

'I like these ones,' I said. 'The crowds. They're good. You should see if the newspapers want them,' I said and he laughed and moved closer to me. I could feel his body at my shoulder.

'Maybe,' he said.

I leaned right in to the photographs, as something caught my eye. In each photograph, always in a different place, seldom in a different pose, was a little girl slightly removed from the action.

'Who's that?' I asked, as Jacob made his way towards the cupboard at the back of the room.

'Dunno,' he shrugged.

She was mostly out of frame, incidental really, but once I'd noticed her she was all I could see. In each picture there stood a girl, her face blurred but her stance unmistakable, observing the entire event of Sarah's disappearance like a ghost.

'It's the school holidays, could be any number of kids.'

I stared closer, trying to will her into focus.

'No,' I said. 'No, it's the same girl. In every shot. In every crowd she's there. What kind of a kid spends their time doing that? What kind of kid spends their time alone, just watching?'

Jacob held up a key and pointed towards a locked door. 'You want to see the darkroom?' he asked, ignoring my question.

'Why not,' I replied.

I reached out my hand in the pitch black, and touched Jacob's now-familiar shape as the door closed behind us and all light disappeared. Total darkness is a rare and frightening thing. It wasn't just the absence of light that made me uneasy. It was the absence of myself. In those moments between the door sealing shut and the warm glow of the red light being turned on, it was like I myself had disappeared, not the room around me.

'You all right?' he asked, as my breathing slowly returned to normal.

The red light gave a warm dreamy quality to the room around us, made all the more strange by the wires in the walls humming their gentle tunes.

'Yes,' I nodded. 'I just didn't think it would be that dark.'

'Needs must,' he said, clipping and teasing film into shallow pools of water. 'This is where the magic happens.'

I watched as outlines began to haunt the glossy blank paper, emerging slowly like a mirage in a desert.

'Have you always done this?' I asked, fascinated by the process as a figure began to emerge on a park bench on the green overlooking the promenade.

'Yeah,' he said. 'I dunno why, really. It's just ... people are never still enough to really get a real look, you know? In an unguarded photograph, it's like you can see the real person. They can't turn away, can't hide. They're as real as they'll ever be.'

As the figure in the pictures became clearer, my skin grew cold. The outline was familiar, though it was only once the chemicals and the waters began to calcify its features that I recognised the stranger as a gradually sharpening image of myself.

'Did you know Sarah Banks?' I asked, as my mind began to cloud.

'No,' he said, distantly. 'No, I never knew her exactly. But I met her not long after I moved here. I actually photographed her one night ... ' he went on, and then stopped as his watch began to bleep and he peeled a photograph from its pool with plastic tongs before hanging it to dry.

The red light began to suffocate me as my insides turned to ice. Slowly I edged backwards, feeling for the wall with my heel, my hand behind me while Jacob continued, oblivious.

'Sarah?' I said, quietly, as I felt my way blindly across the back wall of the small room, watching myself slowly appear in an alleyway on my first day out of hospital.

'I saw her on the beach one night and asked if she'd let me take her photograph,' he said, like it was no big deal.

'And what did she say?' I asked, watching in alarm as my own image started to form in the developing tray, my face unaware it was being captured tight by the camera lens.

'She charged me twenty pounds,' he said with a laugh, as I felt my way towards the door handle just as Jacob turned to see me.

'No!' he yelled, and shot forward, slamming the door behind us.

'Jacob, I have to go,' I said, pressing myself to the door. 'I don't feel good. It's this place, it's the dark. Let me out, please.' I tried, fumbling for the handle.

'It will ruin everything,' he objected, pressing himself against me and sealing the door in the process. '*Oh shit,*' he said.

His hand was still firmly against the door as he turned and we both saw the photograph of me emerging beneath the shallow pool, staring out towards the waves. The image he had taken was not just unguarded, it was oblivious; the lens capturing me at my most vulnerable, unaware I was being observed.

'Claudette, it's just a photo, I didn't even think. I'd forgotten I'd even . . . '

I worked to prise his fingers from the door handle, feeling my breath quicken.

'I thought you looked interesting,' he tried. 'Sad, but interesting . . . '

'Jacob, let me *go*!' I said, driving my heel down his shin.

He doubled over, releasing his grip from the door as light flooded the room. I scrabbled at the lock of the bedroom door before hurling myself down the backstairs half-blind, sending menus and supplies flying as I leapt down three steps at a time before dashing onto the promenade and vomiting onto the sand below.

I walked shakily but determinedly through town, taking sharp corners as if to outrun my own thoughts. Having only skimmed the edges of Sarah's world, I already felt like it was drowning me. I could not begin to think how stuck she must have felt there in the middle of it all.

And so I walked.

I walked until my legs felt like they were burning. Then I walked further still until I became numb to any sensation other than that of pure movement; the sense of being thrust towards something, away from something else. I became so hypnotised by motion that before I knew it dusk had settled and I'd run out of dry land. I was standing on the edge of the old fishing quay. The day had disappeared without me. This happened a lot, I found.

Light is fleeting.

Light moves fast.

It's darkness that lingers.

The fishermen hoisted giant, stinking ropes onto the clapped-out boats and pulled tarpaulin sheets over their tools. The boats all had names like mistresses and bodies like wives – *Crystal*, *Blue Rose*, *Dynasty Belle*, *Diamond Di* – all curled in fancy fonts that had faded beneath the rust and the dents.

'Got a nice bit of cod you can have if you like, love?' said one of the fishermen as he made his way up a metal ladder onto the quay.

I was awake and conscious but my soul still hadn't recovered, so that when I opened my mouth to reply no sound came out. Instead I just shook my head and turned back and began retracing my steps.

It was dark by the time I made it onto my street.

'Now then, Claudette,' Ross said. He and two of his friends from the year below circled me with their bikes as I made my way towards my house.

'Why are you here?' I asked.

'We're going to teach Darvill a lesson,' said the taller of his friends, shaking a can of spray paint that he blasted into the air.

'It's an upstairs flat, how are you going to manage that?' I asked.

'We'll just do the downstairs flat and draw an arrow pointing up, *duh*,' said the second boy in a voice that hadn't quite broken yet.

'Come with us,' said Ross.

'I'm fine for revenge vandalism, but thanks so much for the invite, boys, it really boosted my self-esteem.'

'Your loss,' he said, wheelie-ing off into the distance before I yelled for him to stop.

'Ross,' I said. 'What do you know about that new boy, Jacob?'

'The posh one?' he asked and I nodded.

'Not much. Think he might be gay or something. That's about it. Why?'

'He had pictures of me,' I said, and Ross and his friends shared a knowing look.

'Oh yeah?' he asked, one eyebrow raised.

'Don't be a dick. Pictures he'd taken of me, out and about, without me knowing.'

'He's probably just a creep.'

'He had pictures of Sarah, too,' I said, and regretted it immediately as Ross's face clouded.

'How?' he asked, edging his bike towards me as I shrugged. 'Where?' he demanded.

'On the beach,' I said, feeling a sudden narcoleptic fug drench my body, no longer keen for Ross's limited input on the subject.

'No,' he said, growing frustrated. 'Where were the *photos*?'

'In his room, the old stockroom, above the café,' I said and Ross nodded, turning his bike from me.

'I wouldn't worry about him,' he said, 'he's nobody.' He pulled off into the distance. 'Oh and by the way,' he yelled back to me, 'someone saw you hanging around the Mariners today.'

'Who?' I asked as loudly as I could without drawing the attention of our neighbours.

'That'd be telling,' Ross said, showing no such concern. 'There are eyes everywhere around here, Claudette. Nothing stays secret for long.'

Once I had got inside and said a cursory hello to Dad, I crawled into bed fully clothed and felt a tear run down my face. Just as sleep began to slowly take me, my phone buzzed against my thigh and I retrieved it with a leaden arm.

The text was from Ross.

Please don't go near Dan again. I'm scared for you.

I went to hit reply but hit delete instead, before I slipped into twelve hours of sweet, blessed, oblivion.

11

A Poem on the Underground Wall

Mr Fitzpatrick accepted my company grudgingly at first. We'd sit in almost silence. I'd ask him questions and he'd shirk the answers. He'd try to get me to describe myself and my condition in words that I wasn't sure I had, and I'd change the subject, keen to be more to him than just the girl who went mad.

Our only smooth conversational rallies came when we chatted about innocuous subjects. The state of the town, on a whole. The graffiti on the harbour walls. The weather. The press intrusion. Television. The summer that we had been promised but which so far hadn't materialised.

Before long though, I think he came to not only expect but also to enjoy my visits, as much as anyone ever did. Small details were telling. Perhaps they were a coincidence. Perhaps they wouldn't have meant anything to anybody else. But to me they showed affection and an appreciation of my time and company, and I grew to like him for it.

Saturday was his established day for cleaning, he had told me proudly one day, but after my first couple of visits the house suddenly became immaculate. On the days I'd pop in, the place would smell like a meadow, heady with room-spray and polish. The cushions would be plumped, the surfaces swept. His myriad photographs and albums would be piled and filed as neatly as could be for such an abundant collection in such a modest front room.

There would be treats, too. Unopened packets of luxury biscuits sometimes, which we'd gorge on together and that he would insist I took home on the rare occasion there were leftovers. A fresh cream-cake here and there from the bakers behind the bank. Once an entire meal: lasagne made from scratch, with salad and garlic bread – and a small glass of wine to boot.

'You know how to treat a lady,' I said as he cleared the plates.

'I extend to you the courtesy I'd show any guest,' he said sternly, with all of his usual warmth and humour.

For a long time his past was deemed a no-go area.

'Mine was a small and inconsequential life, Claudette,' he'd say with a smile, when I'd go the long way round a conversation to try and wean some minor detail from him. 'I'm not worth discussing.'

'Everybody's worth discussing,' I'd argue. 'Everybody has a story inside of them.'

'Some stories are best left untold,' he said.

That's not to say he applied the same indifference when it came to me. More and more he'd urge me to reveal more. He didn't just want to know about the hospital, or about the more colourful details of my illness, which were what most people seemed fascinated by. He wanted to know about where I was in it all. He talked to me and about me in a way nobody ever did. He separated me from the madness – as if it were a separate entity, a spare limb. He was keen to find out how I coped with it all. In essence, he wanted to understand just how much 'me' existed within 'it'.

Perhaps most importantly, it felt like he really listened.

'And were you aware at the time?' he'd ask me after I'd finished telling him one detail or another. 'I mean, did you recognise your father? Did you know he still cared?'

His interest always came back to that. Dad and I. What he did, how he did it, whether I appreciated his efforts even at my worst.

'At your worst, how aware were you of your behaviour?' he said delicately, encouragingly, though firmly enough that I knew he wouldn't be fobbed off. I groaned.

'When things get bad I feel like – I don't know, I feel like I'm searching for myself in a crowd,' I tried and he nodded.

'That must be terrifying.'

'It is,' I said.

'And is there any respite? Does anything help? Or is it a case of hoping the storm will pass?'

'Some things do help I suppose,' I said.

'Friends?'

I shrugged.

'Family?'

Again I shrugged.

'Dad, I suppose,' I said, taking another biscuit. 'He's the one thing I can see in the dark. It's like my mind remembered to tag him with some neon collar so I can always spot him even when the rest of the world is like ... *phwooooah*.' I illustrated this by rocking my head from side to side so that the room blurred and my hair coiled to my face.

Mr Fitzpatrick laughed, whether at the performance or the sentiment I'm not sure, but whatever answer I had given him seemed to soothe him.

'When I used to do gymnastics we were told to focus on one point in the room whenever we did spins or pirouettes. This way we wouldn't trip and fall once the dizziness set in. I could spin on the spot for minutes at a time, just by learning how to focus on the tiniest sliver of a wall, how to move my head so fast it was as if my eyes never broke that focus. That's Dad, to me. When things get bad he's my focal point. Anyway, quid pro quo Mr F. Now you have to tell me something about yourself.'

He smiled took a biscuit.

He ignored my question. 'The missing girl. Sarah. Were you aware of her troubles?'

'Everyone was,' I said, cross that he had managed to unearth the one subject I found more fascinating than him. 'The worst part was she was smart enough to know exactly how bad things were for her. It pisses me off the way people talk about her, as if she was gone long before she went missing. She wasn't. She was right here. We all knew her and we all saw her, every day and every night, and we turned away. Everybody saw but nobody looked and certainly nobody spoke out. And if we'd given her a fraction of the thought then as we are now then maybe she'd be home, and safe.'

I sat and seethed at the injustice of Sarah's life.

'Most people would rather clean up a huge mess than tidy up as they go along,' said Mr Fitzpatrick eventually. 'I don't think for a moment they even realise how messy things are until they can't find something specific. It's a crying shame, really. We have to become emergencies before we are tended to properly.'

I didn't know that Sarah would go missing, but I could tell that bad things were coming.

It was no secret that she took what she could from those she felt wouldn't miss it. And, on more than one occasion, those she felt deserved to be without. The incident in the changing room was hardly a revelation in that sense. That she did it never made me think less of her. To some Sarah was bad all the way through. Not me. To me she was strong, not hard. She was neither a master thief nor an opportunistic entrepreneur of the underworld. She didn't take to get more; she took to get by.

Her survival instincts were impressive, but then again so were her morals, as skewed as they were. Sarah only seemed to take from the very worst our school had to offer. And so she would skip past Melanie Coolidge's bag (bullied for her overbite, big brother recently jailed) and the scant offerings of Sharon Fielding's third-generation parka (both parents dead, grandparents hanging in there by a thread), and dipped straight for the knock-off designer number of Tanya Binks (blonde, suspended three times for bullying) and Ashleigh Davis (mum ran the local Cash Converters, dad ran the local BNP group). Money, phones, cigarettes – anything that could get her as far away from where she had gotten seemed to be her main objective.

So when she started taking from me, I wasn't filled with a sense of rage and injustice. I was pissed, for sure, as much as anybody on a limited budget would be to discover they'd been relieved of a crisp note with nothing to show for it. But more than anything I was concerned. To me, this new behaviour meant that Sarah was no longer just trying to get by, the way she had been before. Now, she was trying to get away from something, trying to escape. Now, she was desperate.

On one of our final nights together, as Sarah grew more withdrawn and I began to bleed irrevocably beyond all clearly defined lines, we walked back from the beach in the dark.

'I thought you'd be happier, given your lot in life,' she said, after a while.

'Why's that?' We plodded through the loose sand towards the concrete underpass which separated the dog-walking stretch of the beach from the car park.

'You've got everything. You've got a dad. You've got that old lass who knocks about down the social centre.'

'*Paula*?' I corrected her and she shrugged.

'You've got friends.'

'Not as many as you,' I objected and Sarah scoffed.

'I don't have friends. I've got a group of lads that want to fuck me and a group of girls that are too scared to disagree with anything I ever say.'

'You do rule with an iron fist.'

'*Bitches get stuff done*,' she shot back, and we both laughed. 'Maybe that's why you're mad . . .' she went on, thinking out loud. '. . . Like, I haven't got time to think whether or not I'm happy or sad. I'm never in one place long enough to feel anything, really. Always doing something. Always going somewhere. With you it's like you've got all this stuff, this family and this house—'

'It's a flat,' I tried and she gave me a look of disgust. Sarah never seemed to contemplate others all that much, so on the one hand I felt almost touched that she had clearly spent so long considering my predicament. On the other hand, I quite wanted to kick her teeth back into her skull for the conclusions she was making.

'There's no fire under your arse, is what I'm saying. You've got all this time so you sit around feeling bad because you can.'

'What a luxury,' I said, half hurt and half angry.

'I'm not saying it to be tight,' she said sharply, and suddenly I felt the same pang of fear which her devoted fan base at school must have lived with on a daily basis. 'It's not a bad thing. I wish I could be like that. I wish I had time to decide how I felt. I wish I could let myself feel without . . . ' Her breath trailed off into the night air as we made our way through the concrete underpass.

'It is a bad thing,' I said quietly as Sarah turned her phone light on to illuminate her pathway, clutching it in the same fist as she held a stubby bottle of half-drunk vodka.

'I know,' she said. 'I was just trying to make you feel a bit better. It looks well shit being you sometimes,' she said, bumping her weight against me.

The walls of the underpass were daubed with misspelled and misguided teenage hymns – love, lust and hate all scribbled in thick marker and cheap spray paint. Sarah lit the walls with the sharp light of her phone. We walked slowly, contemplating these outbursts and pleas. In a different life we'd have been two happy schoolgirls on a trip to an art gallery.

Suk Ur Dick NE Time NE Place, said one message in black ink on top of which a phone number had been written, scribbled out and rewritten in a different thickness of pen.

Jack and Lydia 4EVA, another message read.

I once was here, here I was, was I here, yes I was . . . , some poet had daubed in sharp bubble lettering, clearly proud of their flair with words.

There were spray-painted names and tags in fonts so elaborate they may as well have been in a different language, as well as crude outlines of body parts and the odd gun thrown in for good measure.

'Here we go,' she said as we reached the end of the tunnel.

'*I've arrived*,' she said sarcastically, and held the light up to reveal one patch of wall in particular.

Sarah Banks Is A Junky Hore With ADES.

We both stood and giggled for a moment.

'There's none about me,' I moaned.

'Give it time,' she said, stepping closer to the wall. We were so close to the leaching amber lighting of the car park entrance that she was able to turn off her phone. Beneath the colourful description of Sarah's character and wellbeing was a darker message, sprayed in pink.

Sarah Banks Is A Dead Girl.

Sarah stood in front of the message and giggled to herself, unscrewing the lid of her vodka bottle and taking a mouthful which she spat half of into her right palm.

'There you go,' she said, pressing the wet outline of her palm beneath the message. 'Not many girls my age can say they've got their own star on the walk of fame.'

'Do you want to thank the Academy?' I asked. 'Your family? Your God?'

Sarah resealed the lid on her bottle and thought for a moment.

'Nah,' she said. 'Anywhere I go I go alone.'

I asked Sarah to hold my bag while I relieved myself behind the locked toilets in the car park.

'Don't be long, it's freezing and I want to be getting home,' she said, taking my tote bag as I minced behind the concrete shed.

The sound of me pissing was louder than I'd have liked but absolutely unavoidable. A brazen jet cut through the silence of the night like a sandblaster as I watched my piss worm its way downhill towards the sand.

When I got back Sarah was swallowing the last drop of her vodka. She threw the empty bottle behind her. It shattered invisibly.

'Here,' she said, suddenly in a hurry. 'I've got to get going.'

'Me too,' I said, as she began making her way across the grass verges at double speed.

'Sarah,' I called after her, in that night-time whisper that's as loud as a scream. She slowed down grudgingly before stopping completely. 'You have got one friend you know.'

'Yeah?' she asked, without turning to face me.

'Yeah,' I said. 'Me.'

She winced as I said it, before carrying on her walk.

'Believe me you're better off out of it,' she yelled as she vanished into the night. 'I'm not worth the effort.'

It would be days and days before I saw her again.

The next day I arrived at school late, having slept in.

Sarah hadn't turned up at all.

'You look like shit,' Donna said in the lunch queue, as we waited with our congealing trays of chips and beans.

'I'm fine,' I said, as Donna helped herself to a chocolate tray bake and a bag of salt and vinegar. 'I just don't really sleep.'

'All you ever do is sleep. You're like Lazarus without the resurrection, which I would know about because I finished my RE coursework. Did you?' she asked, but my mouth wouldn't work to answer her. 'Maybe you should ask your dad for a day off school? Get some rest? You literally look like you've died,' she said, sounding almost concerned.

The room felt like it was filling with water and even putting one foot in front of the other was proving a trying task. Yet through the thickening of my mood I found myself craning my neck around the dining room, trying to see if Sarah had at least shown up to school for her free meal.

'When you're ready, big lass,' said the dinner lady at the till.

'Oh,' I said, trying to cling to an appropriate response. 'I'm sorry,' I said, rifling through my bag for my purse.

'Loony toons,' said a Year Nine boy, throwing a chip my way and hitting me near my ear. It bounced off onto the cash register.

The dinner lady tutted, as Donna became impatient and put her tray of food down, taking my bag from my limp hands.

'I'd love to know where you go sometimes,' she said, locating my empty purse and opening it up.

'Me too,' I said quietly, as Donna rolled her eyes at my melodrama.

'Clearly not to the fucking bank,' she said as the dinner lady scowled.

'I could have you suspended for that,' she said coldly to Donna as the line behind us grew more and more impatient.

'Sorry,' I said, assuming from past experience that the ire was directed at me.

'Claudette, there's literally not a penny in here,' she said, tipping the purse upside down to prove the point.

'Today!' yelled Scott Brennan from the back of the line and Donna gave him a high-salute middle finger for his input.

'There's a twenty in the notes bit. Dad gave it to me this weekend for lunches.'

'Think again,' she said closing the purse and slipping it back into the bag. 'This one's on me.' She handed fifty pence to the dinner lady with a curt smile and managed to hold both our meals in one hand whilst guiding me by the arm with the other. 'Well. I hope you realise it means you have to put out later.'

12

The Dead Girl

'Before you kick off, I'm just doing my duty,' Donna said, as I swung my body into the bus shelter and slumped onto a plastic seat. At the other end of the bench sat a man with one leg cocked up like a dog's ear, as he sipped from a can of no-brand beer.

'I cannot believe you're doing this,' I said, staring angrily into the distance. 'It's bullshit.'

Word had reached Dad that I'd bailed on my last therapy session. As punishment he'd arranged for Donna to act as chaperone. (He was unable to frogmarch me to the couch himself whilst he was still on day-shifts.) Donna coming with me didn't bother me in itself, but for some reason the fact it was arranged behind my back made me seethe.

'Whatever,' Donna said, putting her earphones in and switching on her iPod. 'Give me a shout once you're speaking to me again.'

'I hope you're fully charged,' I said, and turned my head to the wall.

I could tell that somebody was staring at me but I didn't want to look up. I tried to focus my anger at the ground, where globs of chewing gum formed odd maps in the concrete, but eventually the urge to look was irresistible. The man was leering at me with wide, expectant eyes.

'Cheer up love,' he said with a wink. 'Might never happen.'

All of a sudden I had a target for my fury.

'How the fuck do you know what has and hasn't happened to me?' I barked at him as he recoiled into the opaque glass wall of the shelter, clearly taken aback.

'Yeah,' Donna said, taking out one of her earbuds. 'And you're drinking extra strength lager in a bus stop at half ten on a weekday morning. We're fine for life-hacks, *dickhead*.' The man shook his head and drained his can.

'Bitch,' he spat as he made his way past us.

'Everyone's the worst,' Donna said, sitting down next to me.

'Right now you're still very much in that category as far I'm concerned.'

'*I love you,*' she said, in a dumb sing-song voice. She wasn't fooled by my temporary bad mood.

'Give me that,' I said, taking the bud that hung down her shoulder and plugging it into my ear. 'You are dead to me.'

'The colder you are the hotter I get, *baby*,' she said, bumping her weight against me gently. I bumped her back, harder, so that she flopped to one side, laughing as the headphone yanked from my ear.

'Careful,' I said, pulling her back up and returning the song to my ear. 'If you *must* come, then you may as well make it worth my while with a soundtrack.'

'So I'm good for something?'

'One thing. If it wasn't for the iPod I would have killed you in rage,' I said, as she turned the volume up and pretended to scratch at invisible turntables.

The bus into town took a long route over a short distance. We dipped past the new-builds behind the old tennis greens and I leant my head to the window in an attempt to connote sadness and despondency. But the road was uneven and the glass vibrated with such powerful intensity that my brain felt like it was in a blender. I could feel my eyes moving in odd, panicked directions, like an old doll being dropped down some stairs. I sat up and cracked my neck, trying to ignore Donna as she glared at a toddler a couple of rows down, trying to make him cry.

'Give it up,' I said, as Donna turned slowly to me.

'Are we friends again?' she said, scrunching her bus ticket and tucking it into the neck of my top.

'No.'

'Good,' she said.

'What do you know about Dan?' I asked abruptly.

'Which Dan?'

'Vesper. Daniel Vesper. Wasn't he in Adam's year at school?'

'Why do you care all of a sudden?'

I shrugged and remained mute, forcing Donna to fill in the silence as she was prone to do.

'I don't know. I know what everybody else knows about him. That he's best avoided.'

'I want to know where Sarah is, and I think he has some-thing to do with her,' I said quietly, taking the headphone from Donna's right ear so that she was forced to listen to me. She clicked her iPod to off and turned to me, looking concerned.

'Everybody wants to know what happened to Sarah. Hence the police investigation and the never-ending camera crews.'

'But what if they're not looking in the right places?' I asked 'What if she was doing things that people didn't know about?'

Donna shook her head and looked at me with a sense of imminent disappointment.

'OK,' she said, in the type of voice teachers use when they think you're being unreasonable. The type of voice that warrants a swift fist to the jugular. 'So let's just take one step back here. You think Sarah was into secret stuff, yeah?'

'Yes.'

'Everybody knows that, Claudette,' Donna said.

'Yeah, but nobody knows exactly what. What if we could find out? What if we could save her?'

'Then we'd be national heroes or something. But let's be realistic, chances are that if *you*, a sixteen-year-old girl—'

'*Seventeen*,' I corrected her.

'—*seventeen*-year-old girl,' Donna said, rolling her eyes, 'who spoke probably no more than a dozen words to Sarah in the entire time she knew her, has an inkling about Sarah's misdeeds then chances are the trained detectives are one step ahead.'

I went to correct her but thought better of it. Sarah always seemed like she wanted to be kept a secret and so I'd adhered to her wishes. Since we'd become friends I had told Donna about almost every aspect of my life. She was the first person I ever confided in about my depression, and she knew that I'd lost my virginity before I'd even stepped off the bus home that afternoon. Yet Sarah was the one part that I had kept to myself. I liked to think that on those nights together Sarah had allowed herself to be more vulnerable with me than she'd ever been with anybody else. Not that I did anything particularly significant. But I was there. I'd listened. And I'd asked for nothing in return. To tell Donna, or anybody else, would have been to put a chink in Sarah's armour – and I understood, right from the start, that Sarah's armour was necessary to her safety.

'But the police have to go by the book,' I said. 'They need search warrants. They have to do things properly. Slowly. Someone could get away.'

'And you're, what?' Donna asked, as the bus pulled in to stop and opened its doors, making a plume of sweet vape smoke curl out from the driver's cubbyhole. 'You're going to go rogue? Just focus on yourself for God's sake. Let the world work itself out. When they have the answers they'll tell us.'

'It's harder for me,' I tried. 'I feel like I have to know, I can't explain it and I can't let it go. It's like I get an itch that I need to scratch.'

'Yeah and look what happens when you scratch an itch that isn't really there?' Donna said angrily, taking my arm and rolling my sleeve, exposing that the scars latticing all the way up to my elbows.

'Jesus, Donna,' I said, pulling my sleeve back down. 'That's not cool.'

'*No it's not*,' she said, sliding to the other end of the back seat. She looked furious for a moment. 'Look, I'm not shaming you. I'm saying it because people care. No matter what you think. No matter how many dumb jokes we make about hating one another or whatever. People care and people love you and it hurts us to see you hurt yourself. Part of that is accepting that sometimes you don't know it all. That sometimes a third party really is the best perspective on your bullshit. And another part is accepting that as much as the world affects you, you also affect *it*. Everything you do impacts on everybody you know. So dumb shit like this is never anything other than exhausting and avoidable. You're setting yourself up for a fall on purpose. Just stop.'

I slid my fingers up inside of my sleeves and traced the cemented furrows and ridges that tattooed my lower arms, feeling the all-too familiar pang that came with the sensation, somewhere between regret and nostalgia.

The scars, interestingly enough, were perhaps the catalyst that led to me receiving the one and only tangible gift Sarah ever gave me.

It happened a few days after the swimming lesson, when Sasha had voiced her opinions on my scars in the changing rooms and I'd handed Sarah a stolen coat on the midnight beach. I was walking along the hallway at school one afternoon when Sarah had passed me coming the other way.

'Watch where you're going, tit bags,' she said with a sneer, pushing me against a wall. I felt her slip her hand down into my satchel and deposit something inside, before strutting off to evade another lesson.

I waited until I was alone in the toilets before investigating what it was she'd left for me.

Towards the bottom of my bag, beneath the leaking pens and the crinkled pill packets, was a scrap of square-lined maths book paper, annotated in pencil and wrapped around a small, hard object.

Cheers 4 the coat, said the note. *Here is something in return. Sasha is a twat. Maybe now she'll be a bit more careful with her hot air haha* ☺

The note was scrunched around Sasha's emergency inhaler.

I pressed the mini canister down, felt the cold spray against my fingers and smiled to myself.

'There you go,' I said to myself, dropping it into the toilet water, careful not to flush. 'You want it, you fish for it.' I scrunched the note into a ball and placed it in the torn lining of my schoolbag.

My fingers worked along the ridges and welts in the soft of my elbow. Donna's words stung. I hated how much truth they contained; and I hated how hard it was for me to allow that truth to stand. For all I felt I couldn't help it, I had to push back.

'Sorry I'm such a burden,' I said and Donna heaved yet another sigh in my direction.

'Oh my God you're such a *victim*,' Donna said. 'Seriously. That shit won't fly with me. Nobody's criticising you for being unwell. When things get bad nobody ever thinks less of you for it. But this sort of thing? *No*. You do it time and time again. You latch on to some dumb idea like a rabid dog until nothing else exists. You make your whole life about one thing that deep down you know you can never control and when it doesn't work out perfectly you just drown. It's selfish and it's stupid and it happens slowly enough for you to realise and stop it. So give it up, Claudette. There are people out there hunting for Sarah. You are never going to find her. And even if you did, it wouldn't fix you.' She pressed the bell and stood up.

'So nothing about Dan then?' I asked, stepping past her towards the bus exit.

'Sometimes I wish we really were lesbians so I could break up with you,' Donna said, leaning against me as we got off and walked towards the office block where my therapist did her umming and aaaahing.

'You wish we were lesbians because I'm so goddamn fine.'

'This is true,' Donna said, wrapping her arm around my waist.

'Don't hate me,' I said, leaning my head awkwardly against her shoulders as we walked towards the main entrance.

'Don't give me reason to then,' Donna said, holding the door and beckoning me through with an elaborate hand gesture. '*Dumb-dumb.*'

Paula was stroking my hair as I lay on the couch that afternoon. Paula's big thing was playing with people's hair. She said that it was mutually therapeutic. Usually I'd have run a mile from such a harrowing interaction, but I was in a post-therapy slump and couldn't be bothered to create my usual stink. It was just me and the sofa. That was all I could manage. I was powerless to resist Paula's paws.

I groaned and turned round to face her, hoping that this would indicate I was very much done being used as a human doll. Far from being put off, Paula kept twirling a strand of my hair and pulled me towards her. My nose pressed against the belly of one of her wolf-patterned fleeces.

There was to be no escape. I groaned again and tried to sit up but my body felt like lead.

I was exhausted. I found almost everything tiring, but therapy took it to a whole new level. Talking about myself nonstop for an hour was draining in ways I could never quite articulate to anybody. Donna said she found talking about herself invigorating. And Paula said she'd quite like to pay someone to listen to her moan for an hour twice a week. What they really meant was that I was an ungrateful child for not relishing this blessed opportunity I'd been gifted.

'Dead leg,' Paula said, lifting my head and placing it on a raised cushion as she slid to the far side of the couch, rubbing her thigh back to life. 'I'm just pleased you're home and well.

I take it now you're up and about you'll be joining me for the Wednesday afternoon Jazzercise class on the beach?'

'I'd rather die,' I mumbled, rolling over and facing the room.

'That's my girl,' Paula said. 'Nice to have the old you back. Even if your energies are all saved for plotting my destruction.'

I sat up and took a sip of water, along with one of my tablets. It caught on my tongue before sliding down to my throat in salty, scratchy slow motion and I felt my eyes rim with tears.

'Come on,' Paula said, catching my mood as I drew the cuff of my hoodie across my cheek. 'Let's say we nip out for an hour. Quick walk and a drink at the pub. My treat.'

'I don't want to,' I said, sulking back into the couch.

'Give it a go, sweetheart.' Dad sat down next to me and put his arm around my shoulder. 'We can come straight back if you think it's best. May as well make the most of the offer. You know I was only ever after her money in the first place.' He grinned as Paula gave a tut and a *what is he like* roll of her eyes.

'I promise nobody will say anything while I'm there,' Paula said, giving my hand a squeeze and standing to zip up her fleece. 'I've done three karate lessons so one wrong look and they'll be for it.' She chopped the air with requisite sound effects.

'Fine,' I said, sitting up and wiping my eyes. 'But I'm not talking and I don't want you to talk to me either.'

'I hope that's a promise,' Paula quipped, handing me my shoes from behind the door. 'We don't want you cramping our style.'

There was a pink limousine parked outside of the pub when we arrived.

Inside it was too full for teatime on a weekday evening and the whole room smelled of spilled beer. There was a low, constant hum of chatter that was interrupted only by the buzzing of mobile phones vibrating on the wooden table-tops.

A misshapen line of regulars sat across the length of the bar, with their backs to the room and their pants tugging low on their bodies. Lined up, their arses formed a pasty row of sad, fleshy bunting that it hurt to look at.

In the far corner, a group of slurring women wearing heels and dresses shrieked as the bride-to-be – wearing a sash and a veil – opened her hen-night presents. Slightly removed from the group, a pair of girls in golden veils and sashes that read **Maid of Honour One** and **Maid of Honour Two** were huddled around a mobile phone, as tears dragged mascara down their faces.

The bride seemed nonplussed and continued poking sex toys up towards the wide-screen television so that the Housewives' Favourite teatime presenter was taken from every angle known to man and then some.

Dad spotted a free table, while Paula went to get the drinks. The sound of static rang from upstairs as the boys from tonight's band tuned their amps for rehearsal, and across the other side of the bar a boy flicked peanuts into his sleeping brother's mouth while his dad circled hopefuls in the *Racing Post*.

'A pint, a Pinot and a Coke for the little lady,' said Paula, placing the drinks down on the table and throwing a bag of salt and vinegar in my direction.

Dad took three deep gulps of lager before releasing a rewarding 'aaaaaah' sound as he placed his glass down onto the soggy beer mat. He and Paula made relaxed small talk as I flicked through screens on my phone, more keen to appear occupied than anything else.

The group of hens began humming along to the theme tune of the show that was ending and before long the drunker barflies began joining in too.

'God help town tonight,' Dad said, with a wink at Paula, who shook her head and took a prim, sensible sip of her Pinot.

The music ground to a halt and was replaced by a moment's murmur before a loud cheer sounded out from the front of the room. The town was on TV again. The lady presenting the news that night wore a dark-purple suit that made her look like the aubergine emoji that was never really an aubergine. Behind her an old picture of the beach taken on May Day looked golden and enticing.

From behind the bar Maxine increased the volume as the cameras cut to a panning shot of the beach in real time. It was overcast and shadowy and across the bottom of the page the words **Breaking News** were stamped in bold letters, the way they always were on election day or when a royal baby was due.

'Shut up,' yelled someone from the back of the room, as even the increased volume of the television was drowned out by the excited murmurs of the afternoon drinkers.

'There's Dean!' said one woman with glee as the crowd gradually subdued. People began standing up, one by one, as the cameras cut to a male reporter standing outside of the school where trails of police vans were driving through the gates with their lights flashing.

His words still couldn't be heard exactly and more and more people were growing impatient. Dad stood up to try and get a better look. I stood between him and Paula, leaning against his shoulder as I tried to see over the thick forest of bodies towards the screen.

It was then that the text at the bottom of the screen began moving. Suddenly the pub plunged into near silence. *Body found in search for missing schoolgirl Sarah Banks. Police launch murder investigation.* The camera cut back to the newsreader in the studio.

Nobody knew how to react. Dad's hand curled around my waist and he pulled me tightly to him. He put his nose to the top of my head and breathed in deeply, as if to remind himself that at least I was still here.

Even Paula rubbed her hand gently across my back as she wiped a tear that had run down the side of her face.

Everybody glanced awkwardly at one another. Nobody wanted to be the first one to speak. Nobody wanted to establish the tone of behaviour in the face of a tragedy.

It was the sound of the bell for last orders – usually rung at quarter to eleven on the dot each night – that cut through the sharp silence of the room.

Maxine stood behind the bar as she always did. The sound of the bell dimmed to pulse as the attention of the room turned to face her.

'Go home to your families,' she said quietly, but in a voice that commanded respect; a voice that had stopped more fights and ejected more miscreants than most of us could comprehend. 'We're closing early tonight. There'll be a collection behind the bar for flowers tomorrow.'

The back doors were opened, and we began to trickle out into the evening light.

PART THREE

To The Lighthouse

13

Somewhere They Can't Find Me

I spent the best part of a week in bed after learning of Sarah's death.

A small part of me had been jealous of Sarah when she was gone.

Depression made me want everything and nothing all at once, so that no matter what happened I would never be content. I'd crave company and solitude; light and dark; cold and warmth; love and hate.

Everything and nothing, always and for ever.

I wanted more than anything to disappear.

I wanted to disappear and for everybody to see.

I wanted to be the conductor of my own search party; the chill in the room at my own memorial.

Sarah had managed this. She was an absence and a presence. She had disappeared and she had pulled the attention of the world to the space she left behind.

But now she was gone, for ever.

She'd never get to enjoy her status as the most wanted girl in the country. The one we missed. The one we craved.

The cruelty of the situation weighed me down until I could see nothing else. And so I did exactly what I was so prone to doing.

I hid.

Dad tried for days afterwards to get me out of bed. He'd cook food he knew I liked, and leave my bedroom door open, aware that the promise of a feast would usually rouse at least some form of curiosity in me.

He'd sit on the end of my bed and tell me about his day, something I usually found so unbearable for so many reasons that it would have me up, dressed and out of the house in no time.

He let visitors in and out, to observe my souring lump of a body like an open casket viewing in a mausoleum.

Nothing helped.

Nothing changed.

Sometimes you just have to ride it out. Whatever shut you down will start you back up again, if you're patient enough and lucky enough.

It took five days before something like light began to cut through the fog, and I rose from the dead like Lady Lazarus.

'Good evening sleepy head,' Paula said, as I made my way into the front room, where the soap operas were beginning on television.

The only thing fully penetrating the haze of confusion was the stench that was emitting from every one of my crevices, as if my body were the smelling salts to the fug of my mind. Dad was standing in front of the TV trying to plug in the new DVD player as I sat down on the sofa next to Paula.

'Piss off,' I mumbled.

'*Claudette*,' Dad said, before Paula raised her hand to him and shook her head.

'I'm sorry,' I said, holding my hair flat to my ears as I began to sob. 'I'm just so sorry.'

'I know, my girl,' Paula said, gently drawing me towards her and wrapping her arms around me as I leaked tears and snot into the cream wool of her jumper. 'We all are.' She rubbed my back gently. 'We all are . . .'

'Maybe we can just get some flowers,' Jacob said as we sat in a pub sharing a bowl of chips.

During my lull I had ignored all of his attempts at contact. Missed opportunities from Dan and Donna stacked up on my phone's memory, too, though these held less interest. The phone had buzzed between my legs as I lay motionless, tangled up in the shroud of sheets that held me safe. Envelopes arrived which I opened and scanned – a letter, at first: Jacob apologising for upsetting me. Then came the photographs. There were images of myself. Of the town. Of the crowds and the police.

And there were images of Sarah, captured unknowingly at first, on her way from the lighthouse. And then closer, this time aware of her observer, her eyes staring down the camera defiantly, though you could tell she was uneasy at the arrangement. Curious at the strange boy with the gentle request who expected nothing more of her.

I point and I shoot, he wrote, in his second and last missive. *There's nothing in it, or at least nothing sinister. Here is everything I have done since I got here. No more, no less. Please don't hate me. I'm here if you ever want to talk. Your friend, J.*

He told me to name the time and the place and finally I relented and texted him back.

'I'm so sorry I frightened you,' he said sheepishly, stroking my arm.

I shrugged and shook my head.

'I scared myself,' I said as dismissively as I could manage. 'You'll get used to it.'

There was an awkwardness to our initial exchange that didn't even thaw with our mutual apologies. Jacob looked uneasy and eventually I snapped.

'What is it?' I barked, as he shifted his eyes from side to side.

'Did you send them?' he asked nervously as I shook my head.

'Send what?'

The day after I had fled, he told me, he had been paid a visit whilst working at the café. Dan Vesper had timed his morning coffee-run with Jacob's break, and at Dan's insistence the pair had sat together in a shady corner of the café, getting to know one another.

'He wanted to know about you,' Jacob told me, clearly still shaken by the ordeal. 'And about you and me. And about you and Sarah.'

'What did you tell him?' I asked and Jacob shrugged.

'The truth. That I knew nothing.'

'Good,' I nodded, as Jacob sighed. 'Then,' he said, 'after my shift I went upstairs and—' he reached into his bag and retrieved his camera, whose lens had been cracked clean down the middle, '—the entire place had been ransacked. The dark-room had been cleared out, everything was a mess.'

'Oh, God,' I said, taking the camera and examining the smashed lens. 'I'm so sorry. Did they find anything?'

'Nothing to find,' he shrugged. 'You had all the photos by that point. I don't like any of this.'

After a while, I told him that I knew Sarah more than most. Given what he'd just told me, I felt he deserved to know.

'We used to talk. Sometimes. Not at school. I saw her on the beach one night,' I told him as he leaned in closer, hungry for details. 'And, well, we became friends.'

'So Dan has a right to be wary?' he asked, and I felt the blood rush to my face like fire. 'I mean, I assume he is. He doesn't seem like the type who'd come and welcome someone to his community just to be neighbourly?'

'Dan has no rights. Dan has no rights whatsoever,' I snapped, before taking hold of myself and apologising.

Jacob raised a dismissive hand and changed the subject as promptly as he could.

'What were you doing on the beach at night?' he asked.

'Trying to drown myself,' I said matter-of-factly. 'But I'm a really strong swimmer and also quite buoyant, so it would seem.'

'Jesus,' he whispered as I rolled my eyes.

'Crazy does crazy,' I said with a shrug. 'I only tried it once, when I was really bad. After that I'd just go for a walk when I couldn't sleep. Sometimes to be alone. Sometimes because I thought she might be there and I liked having a secret friend. Anyway, we would chat sometimes. She told me she had secret hiding places.'

'Like where?' he asked, as the waitress came and collected our empty bowls and ketchup bottles

The first night I saw Sarah at the beach was the night I'd jumped off the pier.

I was walking back towards the shore through the cold, low tide. I knew I wasn't dead. But I didn't feel alive, either.

Then I saw in the distance a pale figure. It moved slowly across the causeway from the lighthouse towards the beach.

I thought it was a ghost.

I stopped still and watched. The water was just above waist high and my legs were trembling beneath the surface, but on top my hands were stretched out flat and still, gently moving to the rhythm of the ocean.

All of a sudden it dawned on me: it was Sarah.

All of a sudden I had an anchor to the world.

She reached land and trod on the soft sand towards the dunes, where car headlights cut through the sharp grasses. She disappeared into the dunes. The car lights dimmed. And I made my way to the beach.

I don't know how long I sat there staring out at the water before she found me. Maybe a minute. Maybe an hour. But at some point I heard the sound of a car engine starting and wheels fading on gravel, and soon afterwards Sarah was standing right behind me.

'You're soaking,' she said, sitting down. I turned to look at her and then turned back to the ocean. 'You been trying to top yourself?' I shrugged and ignored her. 'Stinks of shit out here. All this seaweed. Rotten . . . ' she went on, lighting a cigarette and taking three long drags. She handed it to me and I shook my head, still not meeting her gaze.

'Why do you do that?' I asked as she extinguished her cigarette in the sand.

'What?'

'Do what you do? Go with those fat old men in the dunes. Let them touch you. Let them have you.'

Sarah laughed the way only tough people can. Her laugh was not a mark of joy. It was armour.

'They don't have me,' she said. 'I have them. You wouldn't understand.'

'Try me,' I said, turning to look at her. The back of her hair was ruffled and beaded with sand that caught on the moonlight

152

like diamond fragments. Her right wrist was adorned with a bruise, where a bracelet might have gone, had her conquests been the wooing type.

'Sometimes you just need to remind yourself that you're alive.'

'By shagging fat perverts in a car park?'

'By disappearing. Going somewhere else, even if it's just somewhere else inside your own body. Somewhere else inside your own head. It helps.'

'Couldn't you just do volunteer work or something?' I asked, as my bones began to jitter and my teeth started clacking. Sarah scoffed and shook her head.

'I don't do anything for free.' She stood up. 'I won't tell anybody,' she added, steadying herself on the sand and slipping her lighter into her back pocket.

'Tell them what?'

'That I saw you. What you were trying to do.'

'I don't care,' I said and pulled my knees close to my chest to try and bring some stillness to my juddering frame.

'You should,' she said. 'Whatever. I don't give a toss. Just don't tell anybody you saw me either, OK?'

'Everybody knows what you do.'

'Yeah, but they don't know where I do it.'

'It's the location that bothers you?' I said and she breathed out with an angry, short laugh.

'You've got no idea, have you?'

'About what?' I asked.

'Having nowhere in the world that is just yours,' she said. 'This—' she gestured to the shoreline, '—is the closest I've got, for now. And I don't want it ruined. I need my own space. Somewhere they can't find me. Somewhere only I can go.'

'Where who can't find you?' I asked and she scowled.

'Look, you're nuts, yeah?' she said 'You've got problems. You've got, like, *demons* or whatever?'

I nodded.

'Well so have I. Only mine are on the outside. If I'm smart enough and fast enough I can outrun mine, and you of all people should understand that. If you could get away from whatever it was you're frightened of then you would, wouldn't you? *Wouldn't you?*' she asked, angrily, and I nodded. 'Just don't fuck this up for me. I'm not like you. I get the one chance and the one chance only. I need this. Please.'

We were quiet for a moment and when it became apparent that a response was expected I shrugged and turned to look up at her.

'Fine,' I said. 'You know I wouldn't have said anything anyway, but fine.'

'A girl can't be too careful,' she said as she nodded and turned to leave. 'There's eyes everywhere in this town.'

'Why haven't you told the police?' Jacob asked as we made our way towards the pier. In my pocket my phone buzzed and I ignored it.

'She asked me not to.'

'*Claudette,*' he said. 'I think the barriers have widened a bit now. Don't you think?'

I was saved from answering by my phone vibrating again, and I pulled it out.

Hey queen, what's happening? read the first message from Donna.

I'm bored. Come and entertain me, read the second.

Jacob was peering over my shoulder. 'Who's that?' he said.

'Donna.' I put my phone away.

'The girl you were with in the café?' he said. 'The funny one?'

A sharp breeze made my hairs stand on end.

'Didn't think you'd noticed,' I said, feeling threatened for some reason, but uncertain whether I had a right to be.

'If you know things about Sarah then you should let people know,' Jacob said, changing the subject back.

'It was only really the last couple of months that she'd chat to me. Besides, all I ever really knew was that she wanted to leave town, to get away from it all. To get somewhere else.'

'But where would she go?' he asked and I shrugged.

A family with two children wearing stormtrooper masks raced towards us and I stepped to the edge of the pier to allow them to pass. I stared down at the water below. My phone buzzed again in my hand and I glanced at the screen showing half a message before shoving it into my pocket.

The tide lapped at the concrete, leaving long strands of black seaweed as it retreated back out. 'Will you come to the light-house with me tomorrow afternoon?' I turned to lean back on the wall of the pier.

'Why?'

'To investigate.'

'This is getting dark,' he said, turning and leaving to go back to land.

I caught up with him, matching his quickened pace as we walked against the wind.

'No one will follow us. I know the sea around here. If we go just as the tide is coming in, we'll be sealed off. We'll have plenty of time to look around without anybody bothering us.'

'What if we get stuck there?' he said.

'For a seasoned traveller you are really unadventurous,' I said. 'Come on. It'll be interesting. We might find something.'

'And then what?'

I shrugged.

'Fine,' he said. 'Whatever. But I'm going to see a local landmark, that's all as far as I'm concerned. What you get up to is your business.'

'Fine by me,' I said. 'Meet me at the far bus stop for half three. We'll have enough time then.'

'I think I could spend a lifetime with you and never get to know you any better, Claudette,' he said, after a long pause.

'And that's just how I like it,' I said as I turned to leave.

'I really did think for a moment that I'd find her, you know,' I said, with a small laugh as Dad poured me a cup of tea and wiped the spout, so that nothing spilled on the freshly washed couch.

Paula was taking her Pensioners T'ai Chi class for their annual night out – a Chinese set meal and happy hour at the chain pub behind the supermarket – and having ignored six missed calls from Dan, and had as many texts ignored by an increasingly absent Ross, he and I were alone for the evening.

'That you'd just happen upon her.'

'Yeah,' I said, dunking two biscuits at once and sliding them sideways into my mouth, which stretched around them then demolished the soggy mess in one go. 'I know it sounds mad,' I said through biscuity mush, 'but I thought. I don't know. I just thought ... she had to be somewhere. I thought I had as good a chance as anyone.'

'I think everyone knew, deep down, that this wasn't going to end well.'

'I think I want that on a tattoo,' I said, 'on my forehead.'

'You've had a rough week. Maybe we should talk about something else.'

'Who will arrange her funeral?' I asked. 'The school? The police?'

'That's a no on the breezy chat then?' Dad asked and shook his head. 'The children's home, I suppose. Social services. Her parents.'

'They shouldn't be allowed to go.'

'You don't know their circumstances.' he said. 'Maybe what they did they did for the best.'

'Why can't you just hate like everyone else, Dad?'

'Stricken with joy at the richness and beauty of the world,' Dad said, drinking the last of his tea. 'Why is this affecting you so much?' he asked, with concern in his voice, as he poured himself a second cup.

It was hard to put into words how Sarah had affected me. I tried.

'You know when I was a kid?' I asked. 'When I wouldn't sleep?'

Dad shuddered. 'All too well.'

'I used to think if I never went to sleep then I'd never die.'

Dad smiled and nodded. 'You told me that once when we were sat on the sofa at four in the morning in tears.'

'I know, and you lulled me to sleep with the soothing promise that whatever I did I'd die anyway.'

'Not a vintage year for parenting.'

'Yeah well. I think one more night and you'd have killed me anyway. The thing is, I really believed it at the time. Like if I didn't stop then I'd never stop, or something. I knew there was no logic there, not really. But I just felt it, felt like

157

I could get around it. And with Sarah, I don't know, it was like that. I thought if I found her, if she was safe, then … maybe I'd get better.' I made an uncertain face. 'It's ridiculous, I know.'

'Not really. We all pin our hopes on impossible things,' Dad said. 'Put chance to the test, then blame the rules we've set ourselves.'

'Yeah but it's different at five than seventeen,' I said. 'I really did think it would work. I still sort of do. Like, what if I know who killed her, what if I find them?'

'You think you'll find yourself?' said Dad. 'Is that it? That it will make everything clear?'

'Maybe. I don't know.'

'You're going about things the wrong way, Claudette.'

'But—'

Dad raised a hand, a rare forbidding look on his face.

'This is not negotiable,' he said sternly. 'Enough.'

We were quiet again as outside birdsong carried in the soot of dusk.

'A boy at my school died when I was about your age,' Dad said, getting up and handing me the packet of biscuits again by way of apology for his sudden and uncharacteristic severity, 'and nobody quite knew how to react. We were sheltered,' he said.

'I don't think anyone is ever ready for that kind of thing to happen, especially not children.'

'He wasn't taken or killed or anything quite as horrible as your friend,' Dad said. 'He fell off his motorbike. Had no helmet. All too familiar. Anyway, we couldn't make sense of it, but people kept talking about him. Everyone had a story, no two ever quite the same. So before long someone had an idea to

158

make a memorial booklet for the leaving year. Commemorating his life.'

'That's sweet.'

'You can't save Sarah. But you can help in shaping how she's remembered. Why not try to tell people about the good parts?' he asked. 'Show that she was more than just . . . just what everybody thought she was.'

'I'm not sure there were any,' I said after a while, 'at least nothing she enjoyed.'

'She was a sixteen-year-old girl. She must have had the same hopes and dreams as everybody else your age, no matter how muddied her waters became. Find them, let people hear the good bits.' Dad went to collect the tea tray.

'*Look closer, Claudette, focus on the task at hand instead of the unmanageable whole. Sometimes there is no context.*' Dr Chastin's words played through my mind.

Right now, the whole world seemed to be doing just the opposite. No one could not accept that a person, more than likely a person they knew, had simply taken Sarah, hurt her and destroyed her because their urges were greater than their notion of consequence. No one could not accept that if they'd looked more closely when she was alive then maybe they'd have seen just how much danger she was getting herself into.

The more I thought about her, the angrier I became. In Sarah I saw parts of myself – a girl trying to escape something she might never be able to outrun. Perhaps she had gone about it the wrong way, running from her demons by throwing herself at monsters. But the fact remained: we had all failed her. Myself as much as anybody.

Even if I hadn't looked away from the awful things she did, what exactly had I done about it?

I hadn't been able to help her in life, but in death I would do my best.

I would give her the peace she had never found for herself.

It would be my mission; my gift to the friend I had lost.

14

To The Lighthouse

The lookout stank of rotting fish and old saltwater.

'This is not what I had in mind,' Jacob said with a sigh.

He had met me as promised, albeit ten minutes late and lacking the enthusiasm I'd hoped he'd bring to the operation. Because of his lax approach to timekeeping, we'd been forced to wade to the lighthouse across a low, approaching tide, stopping occasionally so that he could take pictures with his freshly replaced lens. I'd had the good sense to wear ample footwear. Jacob, ever the indie darling, wore his barely fastened Converse knock-offs, which he'd had to remove, tying the laces together and wearing them around his neck so as to avoid coming down with trench foot.

It had not put him in the best of moods.

'Teamwork makes the dream work,' I said, once we'd made it over. I pushed a lid off a tin drum which turned out to be empty, save for a cloying odour that gripped my throat tight and refused to let go for some time. 'You could try and be more help.'

'I told you, this is sightseeing for me,' he said, taking a

close-up photograph of the brickwork in the old stone shack that sat at the foot of the lighthouse. 'Your business is your business. Anyway I still think you're wrong. If there had been anything here to find, they'd have found it by now.'

'Oh ye of little faith,' I said, stepping over a pile of petrified old rope that had been abandoned many years ago, coiled up into a point like a sleeping cobra. 'Whatever she was hiding, it's here.'

I knew Sarah used this island as her safe space. She didn't have a room of her own, but this lighthouse was the next best thing; and like any teenager, she needed a place to tell her secrets to.

Sometimes I'd sit alone on the beach.

Sometimes Mr Fitzpatrick would be in the distance, out talking to the ocean, oblivious to my presence.

Sometimes there would be people having sex in the sand dunes. Or in the back of family station wagons in the unlit car park.

Sometimes the night air would be broken by the sound of music swelling and dimming as the doors to the nightclub were thrust open, muffling to a hush as they closed again.

Sarah would always walk alone to the lighthouse. If ever she was carrying something with her when she left, she never was when she returned.

I walked carefully around the base of the lighthouse now, kicking larger rocks with the side of my foot, desperate to unearth any clues that may have been hidden. Jacob had left me alone and was at the edge of the causeway, now sealed off with a low ocean that would be impossible to cross for hours, taking photographs of the land from behind a pile of artfully arranged rocks.

The mission was proving to be futile. There were shopping bags and condom wrappers. Occasional syringes and Coke cans dotting the rocks like rubies. Sections of rope and seaweed clung to surfaces, and the air felt damp and off.

The sea made a different sound towards the back of the lighthouse. It was a hollow sound; a tight echo like a space being filled and emptied over and over again. I followed the noise, stepping down towards the lowest edge of the island where the water kissed the land like the seal of a love letter, and followed the broken paving to the back of the lighthouse.

The grate covering the tunnel was rusty and almost sealed shut. A girl like Sarah could have snuck through the gaps with relative ease but, as I discovered, for anyone with a fair set of tits and a noteworthy arse it was a chore to squeeze through the bars that shed dirty brown smears onto anything they touched. You had to crouch down to make it into the tunnel, but once you were inside there was room to stand.

The floor dipped in the middle, collecting a pool of filthy water that channelled steadily beneath the lighthouse and out of sight. On the walls were old hooks long since stripped of purpose, and a long, stone bench the colour of dirty pennies. In the middle of the bench there was a box, so rusted it was almost undistinguishable from the stones around it, and secured by a metal clasp with no padlock.

I snapped a fingernail the first time I tried to open it. The gritty catch had sealed itself shut and the lid was heavy and sharp at the edges. My second attempt was just as futile and I was about to call for Jacob when the lid came open with a loud clang which echoed around the tunnel and made my skin tingle.

Strapped to the box's lid were two fading orange lifejackets, side by side, with once white strings that had come loose and hung like Halloween decorations.

I reached in and felt along the bottom.

It was beneath a long tarpaulin sheet that I found Sarah's stash.

There were three sandwich bags full of money – tightly packed wads with elastic bands at their waist. Two carrier bags full of clothes, most of them about Sarah's size, some of them children's, all of them still with the labels attached, a few smeared with ink from an exploded security device. Piles and piles of undelivered flyers from Dan's club night created a safe layer for the stash against the damp base of the lockup.

I lifted the items out one by one and sat them on top of the box. Each item of clothing had been carefully wrapped and placed inside of a carrier bag. Paper, folded up like a treasure map, was revealed to be a child's drawing of two girls, one older, one younger; in its creases was a small, red friendship bracelet, with tiny shells beaded through it.

'What's that?' Jacob asked and I jumped, grabbing the bag I was holding tightly.

'It's Sarah's stuff. I found it.'

'Careful,' he said, pointing to the carrier that had flopped to the edge of the tin box.

'Shit,' I said, doing my best to save the entire thing from falling into the water before stopping in my tracks. 'Is that what I think it is?' I asked as dozens of small white plastic bags – like no-brand sugar – fell into the water.

'That's a shit-tonne of drugs, is what it is,' Jacob said. 'We need to get out of here.'

'Wait,' I said, as the packets began to disperse on the water's surface and were slowly sucked into the stream, wherever it went. 'The police need to know this is here.' I bent down to grab as many of the packets as I could, only to be met by Jacob's hand grabbing my upper arm and yanking me to my feet.

'Don't touch them,' he said angrily as I shook from his grasp.

'It's not like I'm about to hoof the lot, for God's sake. I just want to put them back where they were.'

'You don't want to be involved in this. You don't want any trace of yourself here. Look . . . ' he said, moving in front of me and squatting down towards the water. 'Hold on to me.'

I grabbed his hand and he lowered his leg into the water, kicking the bags up and back onto the bench. 'There, that's enough for them to get the gist,' he said, standing back up. 'The rest is up to them to fish out.'

'But I need to put everything back where I found it,' I said, suddenly concerned with the exact placement of each item beneath the tarpaulin. I placed the money to the far left hand side, with the bags of clothes next to them.

'Come on,' he said, nervously jerking his knees up and down.

'I just need one thing before I go,' I said, carefully raising the lip of the old first-aid box and ferreting through the bag.

'Claudette, this is getting far too dark.'

'Just one minute,' I said, finding the refolded picture with the friendship bracelet inside. I slipped it into my bag and as I did, I felt the envelope full of flyers from Dan Vesper. I smiled to myself as I carefully removed them from my bag and placed them tidily beside Sarah's undelivered stash, before teasing the tarpaulin back over the haul and closing the box.

'Now we're done.'

*

We sat on a rock, watching the seabed emerge slowly as the tide moved back out.

'Nearly time,' I said. 'It shouldn't be long before it's low enough to cross.'

'Thank God,' Jacob said. 'What are we going to do?'

'Tell the police.'

'I don't want to be involved.'

'I'll call it in from a phone box. Do it anonymously. Nobody will know it's us.'

'Jesus, Claudette.'

I fastened the bracelet around my wrist. I had asked Jacob to help but he'd refused to touch it. 'It's not like we're the villains of the piece.'

'So what are we? Heroes?' he asked sarcastically and I shrugged.

I knew I shouldn't feel so energised. I knew the gravity of what we'd just done, and knew that I should react with severe caution. But in the midst of it all, all I felt for certain was that I had been right. I had known Sarah – not well, perhaps . . . but enough to have helped.

'Whatever we are, we've found more than anyone else has so far. And I think I know what we need to do next. Are you busy on Friday night?' I asked as Jacob's face clouded.

In Mr Fitzpatrick's front room. We ate some biscuits that I had brought with me, and looked through some photographs. It was becoming a routine for us both by that point.

'She was a beauty,' I said about the dark-haired woman who seemed to appear in photo after photo, and he told me about his first ever trip to the cinema with his soon-to-be fiancé. The woman he would go on to marry.

166

Turning a page, I found a brilliant hand-drawn copy of a painting I recognised from an art book at school.

'Did you trace that?' I asked, and he'd relayed his time at university.

Then, retrieving a photo of a young man that had slipped onto the floor beneath his chair, I held it up. 'What was your son's name?'

He went quiet and just offered me more tea.

'You're keen on the boy from the café, I assume?' he said now, as he sipped from his small cup of water.

'Jacob?' I asked. 'God no. I just need a friend at the moment.'

'So no romance?' he asked, with a soft smile.

'Certainly not.'

'Good. Tattoos are a sign of bad things to come. He seems like trouble.'

'He's harmless enough. Strange, but harmless. I like him. Have you been to the new fish and chip shop yet?' I asked him, keen to shift the conversation away from a subject even I wasn't too certain of.

One of the advantages of growing up with a dad who never shuts the hell up is that I've just about learnt to ape the process of small talk. That's not to say it comes easily to me. The truth is that every bone in my body wants to break free in conversation and bombard people with a list of personal questions until I'm happy that I've accurately coloured the outline of them I have in my mind:

How much money do you earn?

Have you ever been arrested?

When did you lose your virginity?

Have you ever said you loved someone and not meant it?

If you could have your time over would you really have kids again, given the chance? Honestly now . . .

Important stuff. The things that make the story come to life.

With Mr Fitzpatrick I never meant for it to happen. I never wanted to pry or be hurtful. It was just that it had been nagging at my mind for as long as I'd known him, and with the photo still in my hand, I heard myself blurt it out.

'Your wife and son. What happened to them? Did they leave or are they . . . ?' I felt the room grow heavy and let the unspoken word linger between us.

'Excuse me?' he asked as he lowered his cup from his lips and returned it to the table with a gently shaking hand.

'All these photos. You must have loved them. Still love them. But you never talk about it. I don't understand.'

'Not everybody feels the need to broadcast their every thought and feeling, Claudette,' he said. 'It's the curse of your generation, assuming your every private moment has the right to be heard; that the world is interested in how you think and feel. We can't all make a song and dance out of every cloud like you do.' He sunk resentfully back into his chair.

'That's not fair,' I said, sitting up from the sofa. 'I'm sorry, Mr F. I wasn't asking to make you angry. I'm asking you because I am interested in you. And because I care.'

'Care?' he said. 'Are you sure I'm a not just a distraction for you? Like art therapy or gentle exercise. I'm something you're doing to make yourself feel better.'

'Bullshit,' I said. 'I mean yeah, maybe part of that's true. But so what? You get to chat to someone, which you moan about but I know you enjoy. Nobody loses here.'

'How dare you come into my home and talk to me like that.'

'Sorry. Look, it came out wrong. Like an accusation. It wasn't meant that way. Really it wasn't.'

He was quiet for a while and shook his head before he sat forward and removed his glasses, wiping the lenses with a cloth napkin on the arm of his chair.

'Well, you have a unique tone, Claudette. It does not always endear you. But I too am sorry. I snapped and that was wrong. But you have to understand, for some of us pain is something we feel we must keep secret. Something private.'

'I envy your restraint,' I said and he laughed.

'I'm not to be envied. I'm just an old man who can't let go of the past. It's the stone around my leg. When you've lost the way like I have, life is something that happens around you.'

'I want to understand. You do know that, don't you? I think deep down you want to talk about it, too,' I said quietly and he nodded.

And then Mr Fitzpatrick spoke. And spoke. He kept talking for longer than he'd ever talked to me before. And I listened without interrupting for as long as I could ever remember doing with anyone. Even Sarah.

He told me about the dance halls, where he met his wife. About their wedding and their honeymoon. He told me about how she had passed away in childbirth and left him with a son, Robin, whom he'd loved, and who grew up to be brilliant and successful. But who had had watched fade and disappear before his very eyes.

'Sometimes he'd leave and walk for miles, for days and days. It was like he was trying to . . . I don't know . . . '

'Escape himself?' I tried, and Mr Fitzpatrick nodded.

'I suppose so.'

Mr Fitzpatrick said he'd get calls from hospitals, saying that Robin had been found dehydrated and exhausted, collapsed by some roadside in a distant town, or unconscious in some forest having been discovered by a dog-walker early one morning. He'd bring him home and nurse him back to health. Tend to his wounds, listen to his ramblings. Try to explain to him that he was loved, that he was safe. Watch with joy as he rebuilt himself and began taking footsteps back into the real world once more, and then watch with horror as he came apart again.

'And then one day he was gone, said Mr Fitzpatrick. 'He woke up one morning and went out for a walk. They found his shoes on the beach but not him. No note. No body. After seven years they stopped looking. But I never do. I walk to the beach every day, talk to him, ask him to come home. Of course I know he won't, can't. Wherever Robin is he's there for ever. But the thought of living without him, it's just . . . '

'I'm so, so sorry,' I said quietly.

'Robin was . . . different,' Mr Fitzpatrick said. 'He was a brilliant young man, but a troubled one. His mind never quite settled, and neither did he. There were spells, in hospital. Like you had. But of course it was a different time. Robin couldn't talk about his demons. About the darkness he felt coming for him. At least he didn't feel like he could,' he said in a whisper. 'You're lucky, Claudette. You live in a world that can hear your story without recoiling in horror. An illness is just that; part of a whole, not the cause and effect of everything you do, of everything you are.'

'It's hard,' I said eventually, still shaken by his disclosure. 'People ask you how you feel and you're "fine" for so long. Then one day you just think, to hell with it, and tell them, and then they look at you like you're an alien. People say they want to understand but they don't. They just want to seem like they do. Nobody really wants to get their hands dirty.'

Mr Fitzpatrick shook his head.

'You need to give the world more credit from time to time. Don't ever let your pain be yours alone. Don't feed it or hide it. Let it become everybody else's responsibility, too. Make them carry it with you. Hell, make them carry it for you if you can. Because if you don't it will destroy you completely. The biggest mistake I ever made was going into myself. Sometimes you go so far you can't get back out. It's too late for me. It would break my heart to see the same thing happen to you,' he said shakily.

'It won't.'

'We're none of us born alone into this world. Solitude grows, like mould, through carelessness, laziness, missed opportunities to stop it before it becomes all-consuming. Grab hold of everybody close to you and hold on tightly,' he said, becoming more and more passionate. 'That's the only way you'll ever really stay afloat. That's the only way worth living your life.'

'I don't really believe in any sort of God or afterlife,' I said as I stood up and placed my cup back on the low table that separated us. 'But wherever he is, wherever he went, I think he went there knowing, deep down that you loved him. And I think he went at peace knowing that.'

'I hope so.' Mr Fitzpatrick pressed his handkerchief beneath his glossy right eye.

'Take care,' I told him, as I made my way to the door, bending down and kissing the top of his head. It was the first time I'd ever been within touching distance of him.

'And you my girl,' he said, tapping my hand that I had rested on his shoulder.

'I'll see myself out,' I said.

'Claudette,' he asked, as I was in the hallway, tying my laces on the bottom step of his stairs. 'That bracelet, where did you get it from?'

I looked to my wrist and twisted the shells into view.

'Um, I don't know. Town maybe. Why?' I asked.

'It just reminds me of somebody I knew,' he said quietly. 'She had one just like that.'

My blood ran cold and as he drifted off into his afternoon nap, I slipped quickly from his house and ran down the street.

15

Girl Talk

There was a story about Sarah's death on the news as I straightened my hair to go out that night. It was nothing groundbreaking. Yet still just seeing her made my mind shrink tighter and tighter until nothing else existed.

It was the slow realisation of burning that roused me from my trance.

I swore and pulled the straighteners away from my sizzling neck, oblivious to the fact that I was still gripping a large length of my own hair in their scalding jaws, so that my head jerked sideways with my panicked reflex.

I swore again and unplugged them, scraping my hair back and fashioning some form of messy bun in lieu of the silky tresses I had envisioned for myself. Then I dabbed at the burn with Savlon and got to spend five minutes focusing on the twinge of physical pain, as opposed to the churning pre-club anxiety that had been festering in my stomach all afternoon.

I had tried to put on make-up, which was rare, and soon I remembered why I seldom bothered. I was not the beguiling goddess I'd envisioned I'd be with a tenner's worth of Paula's lipstick and foundation plastered to my face. Rather I came out resembling a child's crayon likeness of myself; recognisable as human, but by no means real. Eventually I settled on my usual; my dressiest nose ring, a lick of black eyeliner and some lip gloss that tasted like cherries.

Next, I tried on five outfits before I concluded that I loathed myself and all fabric for ever.

By the fifth attempt I had sweated so much that it had hardly been worth bothering with a shower earlier. I sat on my bed and enjoyed a calming moment, in which I hated myself for giving a shit about all of the stuff I knew I shouldn't.

Hating the way I looked was never about what other people said or thought. I was not some slip of a girl and never would be. No concerned relative would ever pull me to one side and ask if I was *eating properly* (though there was often concern, mainly tooth related, to my penchant for opening sugar sachets and pouring them into my mouth one after the other).

When Patricia Hewitt called me a fat cow in science it didn't bother me, nor did it bother me when the group of boys she was with spent the rest of the lesson sniggering and making mooing noises. I never was fat. You just couldn't see the shape of my skeleton. Besides, Patricia Hewitt had been held back a year and her mum was a dinner lady, so comparatively I felt superior.

No. Any hatred I had of my body was down to me. A frustration that the reality and the fantasy were always so vastly different, that when I looked in the mirror the image in my head was not reflected back at me in the same shimmering, glowing light in which I was bathed in my imagination.

I sat contemplating how awful it was being a woman when a knock at the door interrupted my glorious misandry.

'Only me,' said Paula from behind the door. Her voice was accompanied by the sound of glass clanking on glass. 'Thought you might like a little drink before you headed out. Just us girls. Our little treat.'

I sighed and stood up, opening the door. 'Don't sit on my clothes,' I said, turning off the television and the volume on my phone up, so that the music rose to an almost uncomfortable level.

'You look nice,' she said and I sighed.

'God, Paula, I don't care how I look,' I said. 'I'm only going out with friends and even if I wasn't it still wouldn't matter,' I growled.

'Absolutely,' she said, pouring a glass of wine for herself that reached the brim, and one for me that was so small she may not have bothered at all. 'It's who you are on the inside that counts.'

'Thanks,' I said. *'For the wine,'* I added, keen to nip any suggestions that Paula was my feminist role model in the bud.

'You looking forward to tonight?' she asked, fluffing the pillows on my bed.

'Better than staying in,' I said and lied. There was nothing about going to a nightclub that evening which made me feel anything other than dread. But the fact of the matter was that Ross had disappeared almost entirely since Sarah was declared dead. And, worse still, if what Dan had told me was accurate then soon he could also be gone for good. Sarah could no longer be saved. This part was true. But those responsible for her death could be held accountable. If Dan was to be exposed it would be up to me to do push him into the light. I had to tighten my grip on him, and the only way to do that was to lay my cards on the table; to make him understand that I saw him for what he really was, and wouldn't rest until the rest of the world did too.

'Ah the confidence of youth,' she said. 'I remember a time when I relished leaving the house. Don't think that won't leave you. Nothing a lounge-suit, two bottles of wine and a boxset is worth sacrificing for.'

'God, it's like you've given up,' I said.

'The opposite!' she said, laughing. 'We've cracked the secret to life, us oldies. One day you'll realise. You're not going to drink are you?'

'Probably.'

'*Claudette*,' she said, in her concerned voice, as I picked hair-pins from my curled lips and slid them into the more persistent lumps in my crown. 'You know it's not good with your tablets. Plus girls your age need to keep their wits about them in places like that.'

I'll say one thing about Paula. She always tried to treat me just like she would any other teenage girl in the world. I was going out, and she was being a concerned mother figure. The same scene was playing out in houses the length and breadth of the land. Most people weren't kind enough to even attempt this.

'Odd sentiment for the woman pushing the cheap rosé,' I said, still unable to verbally acknowledge my gratitude.

'It's £6.99 a bottle, full price, thank you Claudette, and I thought it would be nice to have a girly chat.'

'You were mistaken,' I said, backing up to her. 'Will you zip me up.'

'There you go, bonnie lass,' she said, as she clipped the tag of the zip beneath the low backline of my top.

Paula held me gently by the arms and stepped closer to me, staring at us together in the mirror.

'Such a lovely young woman, Claudette. I hope you know that. We're all so proud of the way you turned out.'

'I'm a mess.'

'You're beautiful,' she said, gripping my arms tighter. 'Not that it matters. You could be a hunchback and covered in slime, and everybody would still love you. But you are. And you're tough and you're clever, which is the best part. I don't know anybody who knows their own mind the way you do.'

'Shame I can't control it,' I said and Paula shook her head.

'We've all got our crosses to bear,' she said. 'Some are just heavier than others. Besides, you always bounce back. Tough as old boots, that's our Claudette.'

There was silence as Paula sat back down on the bed.

'You and Jacob seem to be getting close,' she said eventually, and let her words hang in the air. 'It's not often you go anywhere with anyone save Donna.'

I groaned. Here it came.

'He's a friend,' I said. 'And that's what I need at the moment. That's all I need at the moment.'

'He's older, isn't he?'

'He's forty-two,' I said.

'*Funny.*'

'What is this about, Paula?' I asked. 'It's getting on. I still need to put my pants on and then sit for ten minutes at least to dry up. I'm sweating like a bitch on heat.'

'All I'm saying is that if you ever did want a boyfriend,' she said, and I groaned. ' . . . *Or a girlfriend*, we'd be understanding. We'd make . . . allowances.'

'What do you mean?' I asked, suddenly curious. 'Like, pay a dowry or something?'

Paula shook her head and rolled her eyes .

'I just mean if you ever wanted the house to yourself . . . ' she continued, stretching the word to breaking point.

'I want the house to myself all the time, Paula; twenty-four-seven, three-six-five. You both know this.'

'Ever the wit,' she said, standing up and livening up my empty glass. 'I just mean, we've all been young once. We've all . . . experimented. But not out on the beach, or in the lighthouse . . . ' she said, grimacing.

'Oh God!' I said, taking a gulp of my wine and grabbing the bottle from her, topping up my glass. I was more horrified that our jaunt to the lighthouse hadn't been as inconspicuous as we'd imagined it was, than by any notions of al fresco sex, but still felt mortified all the same. 'We weren't shagging on some wet rock, Paula. That's gross. It's filthy out there. Besides, it's just Jacob. It's not like that.'

'I'm not judging,' she said, holding her hands up defensively. 'I've been on the beach at night. I've heard the . . . grunting in the dunes. I know what people get up to. I'm just saying. You don't have to be one of them. I know you think we're old stick-in-the-muds. But everyone is here to make your life easier, Claudette. All you have to do is talk to us.'

I sipped my wine and sighed.

In truth, I did sometimes think about getting a boyfriend. I didn't particularly want one. But it would shut people up and get them off my back. For all I consistently smashed just about every exam I took, it was still the first thing almost every person who met me would ask. I knew I wasn't the whole package. When it came to hunting for a mate I was quite aware of my strengths and weaknesses.

Pros:

Pretty decent set of tits for my age.

Skin OK on most days.

Hair acceptable.

Have given over five blowjobs and yet to experience
negative feedback.

Objectively perfect taste in film and music.

Pretty amazing at masturbating. Therefore, assume have
either amazing hand or vagina. Possibly both. Either
way: transferrable skills.

Able.

Willing.

Cons:

Prone to bouts of psychiatric sectioning.

Tits aside, am shapeless, such as an oblong.

Of the four people I've had sex with, three were stopped
prematurely when I sighed and said I was bored.

Arms and legs are fucked up with scars. Not an entirely lost
cause, but a balancing act if ever there was one.

For all that I was no easy ride, the problem would come when
it came to finding someone I could tolerate, let alone spend any
length of time with. My list of hates was comprehensive to say
the least.

'Claudette ...' she tried again slowly, pretending to fold a
top from the floor which had clearly been intended for the wash.
'Why was Daniel Vesper sat outside of the flat for nearly two
hours the other day?'

I felt the wine rise back up into my throat.

'Who?' I tried, as Paula stood up and dropped her usual tone.

'Don't pretend you don't know who he is. He was sat in a car yesterday, smoking so much I thought the house over the road was on fire. Plumes of smoke coming out of the windows. How he didn't choke I'll never know. Claudette, if you're in any sort of trouble . . .'

I sighed and turned to her.

'Look,' I said, softening as much as I ever could with Paula. 'I know I don't give you the easiest ride. And I'm sorry. OK. There, I am. And I promise, if I ever want to talk about boys or sex or being a woman or . . . grunting,' I said, suppressing a shudder, 'I will. I don't take you for granted. I just like taking the piss sometimes. But there is nothing going on with me and Jacob. Not now not ever. And I don't know why Dan was sat on our street, but I daresay it was for reasons known only to him and probably best kept that way. I'm not in any trouble. I'm not in any danger. Just stop pulling my dick, Paula, OK?' I tried as certainly as I could.

She paused for a moment, her suspicion clearly still not entirely assuaged, and then thought better of it.

'That wasn't so hard, was it, Claudette?' she said, with a smile that seemed oddly unconvincing. 'You really are a good girl. I'll let you get on.' She picked up the glasses and left my room.

'Yeah, well I am drinking tonight,' I yelled through the door, still shaken by the thought of Dan Vesper watching over me, but keen not to let any vulnerability show.

'Very good,' Paula yelled back cheerily from the kitchen.

'And having unprotected sex with strangers,' I yelled.

'Fantastic,' she said, just as chirpily.

'And doing heroin,' I hollered.

'Aren't we all,' she said in a sing-song voice before I gave up.

Just as I was navigating my jeans over the difficult terrain of my thighs there was a knock at the front door.

'Don't go, it's for me,' I shouted.

'I'll get it,' Paula said, completely ignoring me.

I lunged to try and beat her to the door but my jeans gripped tight at my knees and I ended up sprawled on my bedroom floor.

Shit.

I made my finishing touches as quickly as possible and made my way into the front room where Jacob was sitting nervously on the couch as Paula offered him a chocolate from her birthday box which he declined.

'Hello,' he said looking unusually nervous.

'We have to go,' I said. 'Now.'

'But we haven't finished our chat yet,' Paula said brightly.

'Next time,' I said, leaving the house.

'Call me if you need me, Claudette,' Paula said, following us to the front door. 'And Jacob ... *To be continued*,' she said as she shut the door behind us.

I apologised for Paula as Jacob walked silently by my side.

'It's OK. Well, she's terrifying. But OK.'

'Paula?' I asked, bemused. Paula was many things but a source of fear was not one of them.

'What did she say?'

'Not much. She asked me how long I was staying, and whether I'd visited the student art gallery in town.'

'Oh, she's always pimping that thing. It sounds awful.'

'I don't know, I'd quite like to go,' he said. 'And you have to come with me for making me come out tonight.'

'Fine,' I said.

'Then she told me if anything happened to you she'd have

my legs broken in so many places they'd look like they'd been drawn on an Etch A Sketch,' he said, and the imagery stopped me dead in my tracks, right in the middle of the road. 'Then she offered me a cup of tea,' he finished nervously.

It wasn't much after ten by the time we arrived at the club.

'You're barred for a fortnight,' the bouncer with the neck tattoo said, as his colleague dumped one comatose boy onto the kerb and left him to his concrete slumber.

Across the road, a girl in a white dress displayed her reproductive organs to the world at large as she leant across the railings of the promenade, vomiting onto the sand below.

'What do you mean we can't get in!' her friend in smudged eyeliner shrieked at a terrified cabbie, who had locked the doors on them and was trying to start the engine. 'She's not drunk, it's food poisoning!' she objected as he sped off into the distance.

From the pub down the street, the one with the bucking bronco and the girls in cowboy hats, a group of prematurely aged men, with bellies sticking out from underneath popped buttons, walked arm in arm, incoherently and discordantly chanting a song in which only the occasional swear word and racial slur could be made out.

Mercifully they passed almost entirely without incident, save one of them commenting that if I hung around for two more drinks he'd probably give me a go.

Something about it being night-time made them intimidating to me in a way I would never have felt during daylight hours, when I'd have given as good as I got. Tonight, though, I bit my tongue. The night felt stretched and tight; like a violin string turned to snapping point. Everything felt a hairs-breadth away from snapping – the wrong look, at the wrong time, was the difference between relative calm and all-out violence.

'I hate you for dragging me into this,' Jacob said quietly, as we approached the muffled thud-thud-thud coming from behind the closed doors, where two bouncers stood side by side – each hairless and round like some dystopian Tweedledee and Tweedledum.

'Well, we're here now. The only way out is through,' I whispered, bracing myself.

'ID please,' said the bouncer on the left.

There was a long pause during which nobody responded.

'He means you,' I said to Jacob.

'You're kidding? I'm five years older than her,' he said. The bouncers looked at one another, then set their eyes squarely on Jacob.

'We going to have any trouble tonight, soft lad?' said the one on the right.

Jacob rolled his eyes (a brave move, considering that each one of the bouncers' four legs was thicker than his entire frame) before reaching into his pocket and pulling out his provisional license.

'What do you think to this,' Tweedledee asked his mate, pressing a small torch at the license before shining it in Jacob's face. 'Look legit to you?'

'You never can tell these days,' said Tweedledum, taking the passport and scanning Jacob with a look halfway between contempt and daring; urging him to run his mouth just once, so that he could justify some violent attempt at restraint. 'You got anything else on you?'

'I've got a birth certificate at home.'

'Just the attitude then?' asked Tweedledee as Tweedledum jabbed his hand towards Jacob's chest, thrusting the small, laminated square at him with such force I saw his body jolt.

'In you go,' said Tweedledee, reluctantly. 'But watch what you're doing.'

'We're keeping an eye on you,' Tweedledum warned, as we passed them and made our way into the deafening lobby and their laughter faded behind the closing doors.

I leaned in to Jacob as it was the only way he'd ever be able to hear me and I could feel his body was rigid.

'We need to drink,' I whispered to him

'Heavily,' he mouthed back as he grabbed me by the wrist and wove me through the crowds.

'What's the end goal here, Claudette?' he asked as we moved outside to the smoking terrace and sat on a bench.

I swallowed hard, trying to extinguish the chemical fruit burn of the apple-sour shots I'd downed at the bar, before swilling my mouth with a beer.

'I just want to see who's about,' I said. A woman's leg sprawled over our laps as she reclined into her boyfriend's embrace on the bench next to us. 'Ross will be here. He can be a dick, but he's harmless.'

'And then what?' he asked and I shrugged.

'Then we meet up with Dan, I suppose, and get to the bottom of what he had to do with Sarah.'

'Sounds watertight,' he said and drained his beer.

'Look, we're here. We may as well make the most of it. Do you want to dance?' I asked and Jacob shrugged.

'Anything to avoid third base,' Jacob said, gently lowering the girl's curling leg from our laps before helping me up.

'Which room?' he asked.

'Basement.'

'To the underground,' he said, as we picked our way through the bodies.

16

Gin Lane

'I'm going to piss myself,' Jacob said, midway through a slower song, interrupting my glorious, masturbatory trance as I swayed in the darkness to the rhythm of an unfamiliar song.

'Aren't you a little charmer,' I said, following him towards the toilets. 'I'll wait here for you.'

People came and went as I waited in the corridor for Jacob to return. Men huddled chatting in corners as groups of girls walked past like pissed Mona Lisas.

One girl tripped on the stairs as she stared intently into the eyes of a man, who smelled so strongly of Lynx that I could taste it in my mouth from the other side of the room. He fumbled over to help her up and in that moment their eyes met and she locked her mouth to his like an *Alien* Facehugger, before they crab-walked up the stairs in impressive unison.

I grimaced as a boy from the year below me walked up and leaned his head towards my shoulder.

'All right,' he said, his breath smelling of beer and cigarette ash. 'How you doing, you OK. How are you, you doing well, yeah?' he asked.

'Great thanks,' I said, turning away from him.

'Nice to see you out, like, better, you know, you look nice tonight, like, you can't tell there's anything wrong with you or anything,' he said.

'Thanks,' I said, feeling like the belle of the ball.

'I'm getting a car soon, if you're interested,' he said, leaning further still until I was little more than a full-length crutch for the weight of his body. His hand stroked across the flies of my jeans.

'You're a God amongst men,' I said, walking away and letting his limp body peel slowly to the floor, backed by the jeers and laughter of his friends who were standing beneath the stairwell.

Unfortunately for the sisterhood, I'm cursed with the bladder of a camel, so I never really got in on the mutual bonding that goes on in the women's toilet. But even though it stank of piss and the floor was smeared with stiletto scars in black liquid, it felt like a sanctuary compared to the outside world. Bow legs with red-lace shackles prodded out from beneath the stalls as in the corner two women, who worked in the same factory as my Dad, were passing a bottle of poppers beneath the nose of a younger girl in a bid to freshen her up.

I stood in front of the mirror and soaked my wrists beneath the cold tap, careful not to make contact with the filthy ceramic of the basin. I felt the water rush across my wrists and sweet relief travel up my arms until I convinced myself that my whole body was at an acceptable temperature.

'Oi, dickhead, either piss or get off the pot. I've half an eyelash hanging off that wants fixing,' a woman shrieked, as I opened my eyes and realised that I'd zoned out and there was a queue forming behind me.

'Sorry,' I mumbled, making my way to the back of the bathroom where the empty condom machine had rusted fast to the wall. In the open stall at the back of the room three girls were exchanging money for the type of small, white bags that had fallen from Sarah's stash.

I hovered for a while, pretending to text, until two of the women left the stall, fifty quid lighter and giddy with excitement.

'God,' said the third girl in surprise, as she bumped into me on her way out of the stall. It was Emma Nolan. 'I didn't think you'd be here.'

'Surprise,' I said limply.

'Yeah, well, you better not tell anyone you saw me,' Emma said, pushing her way towards the sinks. 'Not that they'd believe you anyway.' She took a lipstick out of her handbag and crowned the thin slit of her upper lip with a lush, pink bow.

I elbowed my way in beside to her at the mirror.

'Do you make much money doing that?'

'I hand out flyers,' she said coldly, staring hard at my reflection in the mirror. 'Like you.'

'Yeah, I'm sure,' I said.

'You looking for a change in career? I thought you did Sundays at the chemist anyway,' she said, snorting as she washed her hands.

'Temporary leave of absence.'

'Because you're a nutter.'

'I was overqualified for the job,' I said and Emma snarled.

'You always did think you were better than everyone, Claudette Flint. You're nothing special, you know.'

'I know,' I said. 'Whereas you seem to be really going places.'

'*Bitch*,' she mouthed with a bent head as she zipped up her bag. 'If you tell anyone I swear to God you won't know what's hit you.'

'Fair enough,' I said. 'But I want something from you first.'

'You're not having a freebie,' she said and folded her arms.

'You couldn't pay me to take that shit. Drugs are for mugs and all that,' I said and she hissed at me to shut up. 'You've seen the way I behave sober,' I added, and she rolled her eyes as if she'd made the dig herself. 'I want to know how close Dan and Sarah really were.'

Emma looked around the bathroom and when she was convinced the vicinity was a safe space she moved closer to me.

'They got on all right at first I suppose,' she said, cooling her wrists in the sink. 'Dan likes the broken ones best,' she said, raising her eyebrows at me. '*They work harder when they're desperate*,' she added cruelly. 'So he started her off handing out flyers. Like you. But once she was *promoted . . .*' she said, 'things started going wrong. Dan wasn't happy with her performance. Figures didn't add up. So I took her patch after he got rid of her.'

'Got rid of her?'

She laughed. 'Think he'd have been stupid enough to kill her? You're even crazier than you look,' she said. '*And act.*'

'Maybe. But who'd be the best person to ask, about Sarah?'

'Her and Ross were close, before she got brave. That's all I know,' Emma said, as she made it to the door. 'Look, she wasn't thick. You don't steal from someone like Dan and expect to get away with it. Sarah was stupid but she wasn't a complete idiot. The girl knew what she was doing. She dug her own grave.'

'*Nice*,' I said and Emma shrugged.

'Whatever. I meant what I said, Claudette. If you tell anybody you saw me that'll be you done. It's not worth it. Trust me. Turn a blind eye. Some questions just aren't worth asking.'

*

'Where were you?' Jacob asked angrily once he had found me outside.

'You took ages, I had to pee,' I lied. 'You know how it is in the ladies. Then I needed some air.'

'I got you this,' he said, handing me another beer and a glass of water. I accepted the beer.

'Can we go yet?' he asked. 'Everyone is leaving anyway.'

'Not yet,' I said as something caught my eye from over his shoulder.

Coming through the crowds, nodding nervously the way a sober person does when greeted by drunken people, I saw Ross's blond hair.

'There's someone I know. Come on,' I said, dragging Jacob towards Ross.

Ross was reclining on a back bench, beneath a broken halogen heater.

'Hi,' I said.

'Evening crazy,' he said flatly, lighting a cigarette. He looked like a husk; as if he'd been emptied and only half refilled since our last encounter. 'This the creep with the camera?' he tried though I could tell his heart wasn't in it.

'Ross, Jacob, Jacob, Ross,' I said, and they nodded at one another with the stern uncertainty of two men who would normally never cross paths.

'You having a good night?' I asked, suddenly amiable with the warm rush that comes when you shift gently to the place between sober and whatever comes next.

'It's shit tonight,' Ross said. 'Full of oldies. Why are you here? You never come here.'

'Just making the most of the town's arts and culture scene. What about you?'

'I was working.'

'And now?'

'And now I'm not,' he said.

'Want to hang out for a bit?' I watched Ross look around the terrace, making certain that there was absolutely no other alternative.

'Whatever. Any chance of a beer?' he asked Jacob, who started to protest until I shot him down with a look.

'Fine,' Jacob said, heading for the bar.

'Few shots would be nice, too,' Ross yelled behind him.

Once we were alone, Ross and I made uncertain faces at one another in lieu of actual conversation. It was Ross who eventually broke the silence.

'Is he your boyfriend then?' he asked and then blushed.

'Jacob? Nah,' I said. 'He's just passing through town. The type of temporary friend I need at the moment.'

'I bet that's not what he thinks.'

'What he thinks isn't really high on my list of priorities at the moment. Anyway he's heard the rumours. I think he knows I'm a No-Go Zone right now.'

Ross nodded and went quiet again.

'What are you really doing here, Claudette?' he asked, looking concerned. 'You know you shouldn't be hanging round places like this.'

'Looking for answers,' I said. 'I'm like a dog with a bone.'

'Why can't you just leave anything alone?'

'I saw Emma earlier,' I said, ignoring his plea. 'Hawking her wares.'

He blushed again. 'I'm not like her. Not like them. I do proper jobs. I clean the glasses.'

'I'm not judging,' I said.

'Well you should,' Ross said. 'She's vile.'

'Yeah, that's the impression she gives off. She knows Sarah, though,' I said, and scanned Ross's face as he winced at the mention of her name. 'Said she was in on the flyering business, too. Pretty extensive PR campaign Dan's got going on, eh?'

'Sarah didn't last long,' Ross said quietly and then, realising the poignancy of his words, looked to the ground. 'She wanted out fast and she didn't care how many fires she left for everyone to put out behind her.'

'What did she want *out* of?' I urged him. 'What was she running from?'

Jacob came back from the bar with beer bottles and shot glasses jewelling his knuckles.

'That's your lot,' he said to us, as he sat down.

Now that Jacob had re-entered the fold Ross's entire demeanour changed. Gone was any hint of remorse; gone was the vulnerability and the regret. He puffed up like an inflated balloon and grabbed his drinks.

'Cheers,' he said shortly, downing the first shot. 'I owe you one.'

'You owe me two,' Jacob corrected him and we sat in strained silence for a moment.

Ross and I chatted about our vaguely overlapping interests – mainly our disdain for classmates and teachers alike – and Jacob did the honourable thing by occasionally nodding as if he had any clue about what we were talking about. Every so often he'd catch my eye with a glance of longing. Not in a sexual way; not like I was the geek who had taken off her glasses and straightened her hair for the prom and suddenly we were in love. It was more a desperate urge to get the hell away from the nightclub.

Just as we were reaching our wordless agreement to call it a night, there was a change in atmosphere as Ross's face became a stony stare. *Dan*.

'Ross,' said Dan, slapping his shoulder before turning to me. 'And my rising star,' he said with a wink. 'And who do we have here?' he asked, coiling his head towards Jacob. 'Ah, yes. From the café.'

Dan was reasonably tall and relatively lean but he had the enormity of a person who never smiled. His hair was gelled and there was a deep, purple scar across his face – the type that only comes from glass – which curved the socket of his eye and face behind his single stud earring.

Ross looked ruffled and he stumbled for the easiest option out.

'They were just going,' Ross said.

'No. We weren't,' I corrected him.

'All right, big lad,' Dan said to Jacob without looking at him, before turning his attention to me. 'I haven't seen you here before at night, have I Claudette?' he asked.

'It's my first time,' I said.

Dan breathed in the night air beneath the sharp slits of his nostrils that made a sizzling noise which grated my bones.

'Fresh meat,' he said with a smirk. 'And look at all these people?' he said, turning to the dwindling crowd. 'All here because of you.' Weighing down my shoulder with one of his arms, he took a flyer from his pocket and let it fall to the wet ground.

'I'm just the messenger,' I said. 'It's you they're here for.'

Dan thought for a moment and then nodded.

'That they are,' he said. 'That they are.'

On one side of me, I felt Jacob bristle, but we both resisted reacting.

'Aren't you going to invite them to the party?' Dan asked Ross eventually. 'There's always room for two more.'

'We were just leaving,' Jacob said.

'I wasn't talking to you,' Dan said coldly, turning to Jacob, before bursting into a smile and slapping him on the back, jovially but with enough force to rock him backwards. 'Only joking, big lad. Just my sense of humour. You're welcome to join. We're going to make the night last as long as we can.'

'They were leaving. Claudette has to be getting back,' Ross said.

'We'll come,' I said.

Dan terrified me the way few people did. Everything from his physicality to his deep, reptilian stare made my body and mind unite, unusually, in their desperation to run and hide. But something about me would not let it show, something inside of me wanted to get as close to the danger as possible, to stare until I was immune.

Dan was a key that I needed to unlock whatever it was about Sarah's life that nobody else had uncovered yet, the missing piece that I felt certain would explain why whatever had happened to her, had happened. I needed to know, the whole town needed to know, and I was not going to let my own fear get in the way of that.

'Now that's what I like,' Dan said, wrapping his arm around me. 'Someone who says yes to life. Come on, it's not far,' he said, releasing me from his grip and walking ahead.

Ross followed closely behind him, while Jacob slowed his pace, indicating that he wanted me to do the same.

'You're not going,' he whispered when we were at a safe enough distance as to not be heard.

I swallowed my nerves, along with the common sense that wanted nothing more than to agree with him.

'Thanks for the input,' I said. 'But I'll do what I like.' I noticed Jacob's concern turn to genuine panic, so leant closer to him. 'Just stay with me. We'll be fine together,' I whispered. Then Dan opened the doors for us and we left the club as his guests.

There was half a bathtub in the front yard of Grey's House.

Grey's was one of the huge old places that had started as some rich person's house back when the town had been something special. After a while, when the town was a thriving holiday destination, it had morphed into a bed and breakfast. Its last incarnation was one of many bedsits that parents warned us against walking past at night. Now it was like a cross between a squat and a grunge club.

It was the sort of institution that had fixed bars on the windows and glass on the hallway carpet. A place where nobody ever locked the doors to their rooms because everyone was either too poor to steal from or too frightened of one another to even try it.

In an upstairs room somebody spun dance music on a set of decks that jarred and scratched every thirty seconds or so.

'Don't worry about him,' Dan said of the DJ, as we made our way towards the kitchen at the back of the house. 'Evan's always been a stuck record. I'll sort him out once we've all got a drink.'

Jacob and I kept as close to Ross as possible as we entered the large, sparse kitchen. There were pockets of people huddled in groups, sitting on benches or folding chairs, sharing bottles of vodka and cigarettes.

The room felt heavy and full of regret. Nobody really wanted to be there.

'This one's on us,' Dan said, as a bottle of cider was passed to my lips and held upwards. I instinctively sealed my mouth shut. My hands gripped tight to my sides and I concentrated on not choking, but Dan tipped the bottle higher and higher until I couldn't help but drink. 'There's a girl,' he whispered through a rictus grin. 'You were thirsty.'

'Thank you,' I said shakily, wiping my lips as the bottle was lowered and handed to some unseen hands behind us.

'No worries,' said Dan, who began pushing slowly up against me, gently but insistently moving me away from the others. No more safety in numbers. 'Just remember you owe me one.'

As soon as were separated, Jacob was accosted by two red-eyed men in tracksuits, who held his arm and began admiring his tattoos.

'You enjoying yourself?' Dan asked.

Whether it was the drinks or the hour, my head became light and distant. Not in the buzzy way that hurried drinks in a nightclub could induce; rather, it was a shift in my sense of perspective. I felt as if I were suspended between dream and waking and I could not quite be sure what was real and what was not.

I squinted to stay focused as the noise in the room grew more frantic and, all around us, bodies moved more frenetically, convulsing. Low-level chatting became urgent and pitched, reptile tongues licking the air. Beads of sweat formed across the crown of my hairline. I gripped a kitchen counter tight. I focused on the Emergency Exit sign. The familiar object in the unfamiliar environment comforted me. Even better, it implied a way out.

'It's been a blast,' I managed. 'Thanks again for the job. And thanks for having us tonight. I can't stay long. I told my dad

I'll be home. I was once an hour late for dinner and he called the police,' I joked, laying the groundwork for a swift departure and praying that the notion of the authorities would at least buy me some leeway.

Dan smiled and looked at me, turning his head from side to side.

'Are you sure you're OK? You look like you're having one of your turns. Let me take you upstairs so you can lie down.' He tightened his hand around my wrist.

'No,' I said, perhaps more forcefully than I'd imagined. Something told me that if I lay down that night I would not stand back up any time soon. 'I'm fine. Thank you.'

'You'll have to make sure you have a good time instead of a long time then,' he said, and stood back an inch, expectantly. I forced a laugh from my throat like a splinter and he nodded approvingly.

'Ross is great,' I said. 'I've known him since we were kids.'

'He's still a kid,' Dan said, glaring over to where Ross had been. 'Are you cold?' He spun back to me, his eyes bloodshot, and his face a horror of angry vessels and pallid skin. He looked like Dad that time he came down with swine flu – only instead of the limp uselessness of illness, Dan had a jumpy, eager energy like a spider trapped beneath a glass.

'No, I'm fine.'

'You don't look relaxed,' he said. 'Do you want something to relax?'

'No,' I said. 'maybe I am just cold after all.'

'You go to school then yeah?' he said, his eyes darting from side to side he was trying to cross a busy road. He sniffed deeply and jerked his head towards me, urging an answer.

'Um, yeah. I'm in Ross's year.'

'So you knew Sarah?' he asked, increasing his intensity. When I didn't answer immediately, he repeated his question.

'Sort of,' I said. 'But not very well.'

'She ever say anything?' he asked.

'Like what?' I asked.

'The thing is, Claudette. Here I am paying you for a job, happy to have a new friend, and you fall so completely off the radar that I can't ever get hold of you.'

'I'm sorry,' I said, as the room began to fade in and out of itself like a revolving door spun too fast.

'I'm just confused, that's all. You know what it's like to be confused, don't you, Claudette?' Dan placed one hand on my shoulder, and whispered, 'Where is it that you've been? I texted. I waited. Nothing. Where is it that you go?' He moved closer to me, and I felt a numb black wave wash over me before I forced my eyes wide open.

'I don't know,' I said, gripping the countertop like a life raft. 'I lost my phone . . .'

'Funny that. So has Ross,' he said, his hot breath against my neck; the only thing in the room I could be certain of.

'I'm sorry,' I tried, as he moved even closer. 'I think I know what you're looking for. Sarah had something of yours, didn't she?' I asked, supressing my fear and excitement as Dan's eyes flickered sharply and dangerously like oil tossed on fire.

Dan grabbed my arm tight and pulled me as close to him as he could without possessing me entirely.

'What do you know?' he whispered into my ear, hot and jagged as the party played on behind him, oblivious to his fury.

'She kept them with her secrets,' I whispered back, as coolly as I could muster. 'Sarah was lucky; she did have some real friends in this world. Friends that knew her for who she really was. Friends that new about the places that were special to her.'

My speech cut short as Dan dug his hands into my arm until I could feel my bone give to his pressure. He breathed in deeply, raising the hairs on the back of my neck as he inhaled my scent.

'You're playing games you won't win, Claudette. That girl took a lot of money,' he said sharply into my ear. 'A lot of what was mine.'

'And you took *everything* that was hers,' I hissed back, feeling repulsed as my lips brushed against his ear. 'She needed help and you used her. She needed a friend and you hurt her. Only it's not like your shitty pile of drugs, is it? Because she can't get back what she lost.'

'Where is it?' he demanded, before loosening his grip as three men entered the kitchen, each carrying a gym bag. He gripped my shoulders, one hand on each, as the men clocked him, nodded once and headed out into a back room.

'*Shit*,' he whispered in their direction before turning back to me. 'This I have to sort out. But don't you go anywhere.'

'I wouldn't get too excited,' I said coldly. Dan's attention pulled towards the demands of the men. 'Like you said, I get confused sometimes.'

'You what?'

'Well, whatever Sarah had of yours certainly isn't where she left it,' I said, taking a bottle of spirits from the counter. 'I mean, after I told the police I'm sure they'll have taken them somewhere else. If you want them you'll have to ask them. I'm sure they kept them safe,' I said as Dan's phone began to vibrate in his pocket.

'You have no idea what you've done, Claudette.'

'Here Dan,' I said, handing him the bottle. 'You don't look yourself. Have one on me,' I said as he laughed once.

'You don't go anywhere,' he instructed, taking the bottle with one hand and grabbing the sleeve of my vest into a tight fist with his other, as if trying to pin me to the spot. 'We're going to have a real chat when I get back,' he said as he left, nodding his head as if certain of the repercussions I was to face.

I had no intention of staying put.

I slipped through the kitchen as carefully as I could. A man laughed and held on to my arm as I passed him, but I shook him off and continued. My head was pounding and my legs felt like lead, but I managed to make my way upstairs one step at a time, holding on to the wall for dear life.

Upstairs I slowed down at every open door, frantically looking for Ross.

In some there were couples awake and wired, lying together on filthy unmade beds.

In others, men sat facing one another, leaning against walls with their heads bent back and their open mouths pointing up at the ceiling; their eyes glazed and cloudy, like fish on the turn.

It was in an attic bedroom that I eventually found him sitting alone on a single mattress on the bedroom floor.

'Ross, I don't feel well,' I said as he hurried over and led me gently to the mattress.

'What have you done?' he asked when I was settled. He handed me a can of flat pop to sip from.

I looked around the sad room. My head was starting to clear, slowly and not entirely, but enough so that I could recognise myself and my surroundings. I noticed his school bag, lying abandoned at the foot of the makeshift bed.

'Do you *live* here or something?' I asked.

Ross shrugged and looked up at me. His eyes were red but not the way Dan's had been. All of a sudden it hit me: he had been crying. I wanted to hug him.

'Why don't you just go?' he said, rubbing his tired face, bending his knees up to meet his chest.

'I thought you were living back home?'

Ross never had a real 'home', so to speak. He had beds in houses – sometimes family, sometimes not. Never the same place for more than a few months at a time.

'Not everyone's got it as easy as you, Claudette,' he shot back nastily.

'Yeah, my life's a real bed of roses,' I said quietly, wiping a thick slick of sweat from my face, and he apologised.

'I just stay here sometimes.'

'One of Dan's lost boys.'

'At least with him I'm someone's boy.' His eyes welled up. 'I thought she'd got away,' he said quietly, keen not to be heard by anybody outside, and keen to do his best to disguise the fact that he was crying.

'Sarah,' I said. 'I thought you said that she was where she belonged?' Ross's breathing became heavier, and his tears more pronounced.

'I thought she was. I thought she'd really done it, escaped, made it out. I was just . . . I didn't want anyone to know that I knew,' he said, shaking his head as he pressed his eyes with his palms, chastising them for his tears.

'Anyone to know what? What happened to her, Ross?' I asked, stretching out my hand and gently rubbing the back of his neck, cautiously, the way you would a stray cat in an alleyway.

'I don't know.' He shrugged. 'She was getting away. And I thought she'd done it. I thought she'd gone.'

'Gone where?' I asked.

'*Just gone!*' he yelled before simmering back down and curling back in on himself, apologetically. 'You don't know what it's like to have no one, Claudette. Nobody helped her. Not her parents. Not the children's home. Not Dan. I thought she'd finally gotten away, like she'd always wanted to—' Ross said, wiping his eyes as I smiled sadly, thinking back to the girl forever walking ahead into the distance. The more he opened up about her it seemed that whichever version of Sarah you were presented with, the one aspect of herself she could never disguise was her insatiable yearning for another place. 'I thought I was helping by not saying anything,' Ross whispered, his head bowed as his eyes skittered nervously across the doorway, wary of the walls that didn't so much talk but listen in that awful place. 'I thought by not saying anything, not saying anything to you, not saying anything to the police, I thought I was helping her,' he said, his voice barely audible above his staggered breath. 'But it turns out I wasn't helping her. I was helping Dan without realising it. Helping him get away with what he did to her,' he said as a tear cut down his cheek and merged with the floor.

'You're better than them, Ross,' I said quietly, gripping the back if his neck as he squinted through tears. 'Don't ever let them think you're not.'

'What you doing?' he said, with a sad laugh, wiping his eyes as he sniffed and coughed his way back to a state not far from composed. 'You don't say nice things to me.'

'Yeah, well. You're a dick. But compared to what I've seen tonight you're golden.'

'I hate him so much,' Ross said. 'I hate him, and I know he hates me.'

'We can take him down,' I said quietly. 'But we can't talk here. Meet me one day this week. You've got my number, so use it. My dad works nights at the moment, so you can come round then. I want to know what you know.'

'I'm not sure you mean that,' he said, widening his eyes to emphasise the depth and weight of his burden.

'I do,' I whispered as heavy footsteps crossed past the door followed by lighter ones, following.

'Fine,' he whispered. 'Fine. But you really should go now. I don't want anything bad to happen to you.'

17

Proof

Half the town were out the next night, though the mood was unusually sober.

The police were re-enacting Sarah's last movements. We'd all been told in advance.

Huge lamps with silver surrounds blasted night-time into day. Men rode cameras along tracks laid down in the sand as they traced her last known steps.

It was a fortnight ago but it wasn't.

She was alive but she wasn't.

I couldn't take my eyes off the performance.

The girl playing Sarah pressed a hand to her freshly blacked eye as she wiped away a tear. She stumbled through the sand; whether she was supposed to be acting drunk or she simply wasn't used to the soft ground beneath her feet was not made clear to us. Nothing was. The directors and camera men had asked the crowds repeatedly to return to their houses lest a stray sneeze or a small child ruin a good shot on a tight schedule.

Nobody listened.

We just watched as Sarah's ghost moved towards the wooden

plinths beneath the pier before somebody shouted 'CUT" and the lights dimmed to black.

Nobody knew what had happened to Sarah, was the upshot.

Off the record, Adam told us as much as he knew.

The cause of death had been drowning. And yet for all she'd slipped and gone under there were still fresh wounds that nobody could explain.

An anonymous phone call had been made about fresh evidence in the lighthouse – the specifics of which Adam could not divulge – in what was fast becoming just another unexplained tragedy. The investigation had been under scrutiny from the start, but now questions were being asked about how the discovery was missed in the first place. Fingers were being pointed.

Still nobody knew how to find whatever it was they were still missing to bring this case to a close.

'It's a zoo in the station at the moment,' Adam told us, as we made our way towards the crowds. 'Everybody's just seething. It doesn't help that the reporters have taken the story and run with it.'

'Why are they still here at all?' Donna asked, as over the road two men in bomber jackets took photographs of the crowd and the film crew converging on the beach.

'She was young, she was pretty. Everyone loves a mystery,' he shrugged. 'All the better if it photographs well.'

'That's bleak,' Donna said. 'It's the sort of thing I'd say.'

'If you caught who did it, would they make you a proper policeman?' I asked Adam before correcting myself. 'I mean, not just a community officer.'

Adam shrugged again as we reached the crowd.

'Don't know. I don't think they've thought that far ahead. Just trying to keep afloat under the pressure of it all at the moment,' he said, as two clipboarded officials rounded us together like well-trained sheepdog and demanded our silence.

'Where were you last night?' Donna whispered as quiet descended and Fake Sarah made her first of many trips to the sea that night. 'You're never around any more. I miss you.'

I was about to answer her, albeit vaguely, when over the heads of the crowds, in the doorway of the Mariners, I saw Mr Fitzpatrick. Only he wasn't alone. He was with a girl. A small girl – no older than ten – wearing a filthy tracksuit and a look of pure, unadulterated horror as she watched Sarah's body double walking across the beach.

I recognised her instantly: the girl from Jacob's photographs. Almost as blurred and borderless in real life as she was in his pictures, but her stance and size left me with no doubt.

A stage-light popped quietly, raining glass and sparks onto the sand below.

'Who's the girl?' I whispered to Donna, nodding towards the Mariners, where Mr Fitzpatrick was ferrying the reluctant girl away from the re-enactment.

Donna raised herself to tiptoes and scanned across the crowd of heads towards the horizon.

'Dunno,' she concluded. 'Probably his granddaughter or something.' She turned her attentions back to the cameras.

'No . . .' I said, watching him lead the girl down an alleyway. 'Mr Fitzpatrick doesn't have anyone,' I said. 'Only me.'

'*Jesus,*' Donna whispered. 'There's a good line to take anyone to the end.'

'Dickhead,' I hissed, as an old lady eating a sandwich from cling-film wrapping turned and glared at us.

'Shhhh.' Donna briefly pressed two fingers to her lips. 'Some of us want to know how this thing ends,' she said, with a roll of her eyes.

In the café afterwards Jacob offered to buy us a coffee, but I said I'd prefer chips and a milkshake.

'You've got a really sophisticated palate,' he said as he sat down and handed me my offerings. He took a sip of his over-priced cup of foam.

'I know what I like and I like what I know,' I said, drenching the chips in vinegar and salt before cramming four into my mouth at once.

'Each to their own,' he said. 'I've been thinking about China next. Maybe do the Great Wall.'

'Why not just watch a documentary?' I dipped a chip into the froth of my milkshake as Jacob grimaced in horror. 'Don't knock it till you've tried it,' I said.

'Do you honestly think that?' he asked. 'That everything you need is on TV?'

'I don't know. I mean, I just don't get what you gain from . . . *doing stuff*,' I said. 'It just all seems like so much effort. Can't you just read a book or something?'

'Because I want experiences,' he said with an arched eyebrow. 'First hand.'

'What if you just want to stay in one place, or just be still for a while?'

Jacob became more animated, the way boys like him always are if you didn't share their wayfaring ambition. My theory is that they know you're on to something, but can't admit it to themselves.

'But the world is huge. It's endless. Who wouldn't want to

see as much of it as possible?' he asked, taking a chip from my plate as I glared at him for his forwardness.

'Exactly,' I said. 'What's your endgame?'

'Excuse me?'

'You just said it, it's endless. You can never *see* everything. Why bother even starting. You'll only come up short.'

'That's the most tragic thing I've ever heard.'

'Sarah told something once. She said that her dream in life was to have the luxury of doing the same thing, every single day, without having to pay it a second thought. That way, she said, she'd be free to just be herself. I loved that,' I said, thinking back to her admission on the beach, her guard lowered with the fourth sip of stolen vodka and her speech slurred with the fifth. 'That was something she and I had in common, I think. We both found it so hard just to be ourselves that it was like a luxury. I mean,' I said, correcting myself through a mouthful of potato, 'I mean being ourselves was just so fucking complicated at times, like there were so many spinning plates, that simply to stand still was like the best holiday of all.'

'I get that,' Jacob said.

Sarah and I were united in our bemusement at the world at large. So many people, with so much to love about their lives, still made themselves so needlessly mysterious, adding layers of pretence. We, on the other hand, longed to have lives we didn't feel we had to hide from view.

I spend half my time kicking against the current trying to get back to myself.

Trying to reconnect with the parts I know.

Trying to cling on to whatever it is that makes me *me*, even as the riptide pulls me down and out.

I'd give anything to be nothing more than myself.

208

When I told Jacob this he just smiled.

'You were real with me, I think,' he said, before correcting himself. 'I *hope*,' he tried again, and I nodded in agreement. My instinct was to run from the conversation, and yet the truth was I had been grateful to have met Jacob that summer.

'I think I needed you more than I thought I did,' I said and he nodded. 'You were just . . . when I needed someone who'd just let me be, you were *there*.' I was uneasy with my own honesty but keen to say it once and for all. 'You listen. You see me without any of the bullshit I usually give. It's not often you get to just be yourself with somebody. I think I was with you. I think I really needed to be. So thanks. I mean it.'

Jacob nodded and smiled for a moment.

'Claudette, whoever you were with me – and I think it was the "real you", as you put it – I liked it. I like you.' He said. 'And I think . . . well, no, I don't think. I'm *sure* Sarah felt the same way.'

I felt itchy, in the way I always did when someone said something nice about me, and I attempted to downplay his words with a deep eyeball roll.

'Don't do that,' he said, sternly. 'Don't dismiss how important these things are. Sarah was fucked, in every conceivable way. Whatever you did or didn't do I think she had something with you that maybe she didn't have anywhere else. At that point at least. Don't make out like it didn't matter. Because it did. You did a good thing, Claudette. Even if it was just being in the right place at the right time. For a moment you mattered to someone. And that counts.'

I walked home alone that evening. I ducked past shops where posters requesting information on Sarah's whereabouts were smudged and torn with exposure. Scraps of police tape clung in filthy ribbons to the grates of the drains.

Throughout the town, the feeling was that Sarah's moment had either passed or was passing. The cameras grew noticeably less and less. The columns and features in the papers grew smaller. Even in the café Jacob and I heard a couple discussing her in a voice usually reserved for overindulged children.

'Well, I mean, if she only drowned then why are they still going on about it?' said the woman as she flicked through the newspaper. 'Happens all the time. Especially places like this. All those police . . . should be out catching real criminals. Not like anybody had her . . . just another silly girl didn't realise how strong the current was,' she said, as her husband sat in silent agreement.

It seemed like the less morbid her final moments, the more the entire ordeal was just another case of a girl pleading for attention; stamping her foot until all eyes were on her.

The less they cared the more the fire inside of me grew; the one that had to understand why Sarah had died; the one that demanded context for a life that had ended so cold and so alone.

I heard Sarah calling, too. Demanding attention. There was still a place for her, even now.

Her voice played in my head as I walked alone. I imagined how she felt as her body was swallowed by the sea; as she was dragged out, away from wherever she had been, far, far out to where nothing could hurt her again.

I had to try hard to catch my breath, suddenly panicked, when I realised that a stranger's shadow had been tracing my footsteps through the town in the amber haze of the street lamps.

I didn't turn around. Nobody ever does when they're being

followed. Nine times out of ten this would put your mind at ease; your heart would slow, your temperature would rise again.

You'd be safe. It's that one per cent that keeps us ploughing on in a desperate hope of escape. The one per cent that stops us from facing our fears.

I rounded two corners. The shadow followed behind me.

They trod lightly but quickly and the footsteps grew louder until I could feel them right behind me.

A huge pain shot through my right leg and I winced but didn't scream. Somebody had kicked me. Not as hard as I'd ever been kicked before, but certainly enough to stop me in my tracks and force me to slow my pace. Then I turned, thinking that if I was forced to fight I'd rather do so with my fists than my elbows.

It was the little girl from the photographs, the one I'd seen at the re-enactment, just hours earlier.

'You little bitch,' I said angrily, glaring down at her. She was staring at me with the fury of a thunderstorm. 'What did you do that for? I should kick your stupid head in!' I bent down and rubbed my calf, as the girl continued to stare at me in her hand-me-down tracksuit, her unkempt hair matted to the side of her head.

'You're a thief,' she said.

'Who are you?' I said. 'And no. I'm not.'

'That's not yours!' she said angrily, grabbing my wrist and holding it up as high as her arm would allow, highlighting Sarah's bracelet. '*It's not yours!*' She kicked me again in the shin before bursting into tears.

PART FOUR

Another Place

18

A Most Peculiar Man

'Roseanna?' Mr Fitzpatrick asked, with a knowing smile, as I sat on his carpet, rolling up my jeans to show the purple welt where she'd kicked my shin.

'Pretty name for the Antichrist,' I muttered as Mr Fitzpatrick chuckled gently to himself. 'It's not funny. That was her second effort too. There was one on my calf as well but that's not as dark. Mostly internal wounds I shouldn't imagine.'

'Well, she's no angel but she's not quite the devil incarnate, either. Somewhere in-between. Like most of us, no doubt. Would you like another biscuit?' he asked, handing me the small saucer on which Mint Viscounts had been artfully arranged.

The answer to this question, for me and any other vaguely sane person, is always 'yes'. Mr Fitzpatrick knew this. For a man who acted so sour in public he shared my insatiable sweet tooth. I still beat him on appetite though; he was often astounded at my inability to reach capacity where food was concerned.

I reached out and took two biscuits and he gave me a quick wink that suddenly made me sad. It was a wink that he never showed anybody. The wink he'd no doubt been saving one day for his own grandchildren. *There's my girl*, it said.

I winked back subtly and he looked as if he'd been given the most elaborate gift of his life.

When the girl – whom I now knew to be Roseanna – started crying, I panicked. Once you've been through an illness that manifests itself through your emotions – extinguishing and augmenting them to unmanageable levels – the idea that a person, even a child, can cry an appropriate amount in an appropriate instance seems entirely alien. A bout of sadness is enough to render me and plenty of people I've met incapacitated for days, weeks, months. That a human can reasonably respond emotionally to their thoughts is a bigger leap for me than most fantasy novels.

So I did what I did best when I didn't know what else to do. I swore and told her to shut up.

'It's me that's just been attacked,' I hissed quietly, as if by lowering my volume I'd lower hers too. 'Come on, stop being such a little tit. Stop crying.'

She heaved for breath in the alleyway, holding her dirty face in her hands as her body throbbed and jerked to her tears, like she was being shot through with electricity.

I got down on my knees (painful, having recently been hoofed repeatedly below the waist) and leant in to her. 'It's OK,' I said. 'It's fine. You won't get in trouble.'

I reached out and placed my arms around her. Hugging does not come easily to me. Nor do children. At first I was rigid; the embrace was not the warm, comforting fabric I'd imagined – rather like a towel left out to dry overnight. I was stiff and uneasy, and rough to the touch.

The girl didn't seem to mind, though, the way some children

don't. She saw the gesture for what it was, and allowed herself to soften into my body, forcing me to fully embrace the hug with the gratitude of someone who has never known true affection in her life.

'God, you stink,' I whispered as she began to calm down, her breathing becoming something that she controlled once more, rather than a violent onslaught of air that caused her bony body to tremor.

'They can't make me bath,' she said as she wiped her nose with the cuff of her sleeve, varnishing the right side of her face in the process. 'She told me not to let them. They try, sometimes, but I won't let them. I'll run away,' she said defiantly.

'Who told you?' I asked.

Roseanna stared at me, evaluating whether I was to be trusted.

'Sarah,' she said eventually, as she began to cry again, this time eschewing my attempt at a consolatory hug before skittering back through the alleyway as quickly as she had arrived; disappearing into the maze of streets before I'd had a chance to follow her.

I looked up at Mr Fitzpatrick.

'So. Are you going to tell me how you knew her then?' I asked.

Mr Fitzpatrick sighed and straightened, as if preparing to make a statement in court.

'I knew them from a while ago,' he said. 'Roseanna and Sarah. They live together in the home. *Lived*,' he corrected himself flatly.

'Why were you there?'

'I helped out. Two days a week. No money in it but they give you bus fare, even though it's only down the road,' he said. 'I was a teacher, once. Art. Worked in schools rougher than you'd know ... I hadn't worked since Robin had gone but I wanted to do something useful with whatever skills I had while I still could. I'd bring art supplies and the children would make things – pictures, collages, jewellery ...'

My eyes lit up as I held up my wrist.

'The bracelet?' I asked.

'Ah yes,' he said and smiled, reaching forward. I gave him my arm and he held it gently in his dry hands, inspecting the handiwork of red rope and shells. 'A Mother's Day present from Roseanna to Sarah. That girl was closest thing she ever had to a parent.'

'Sarah didn't seem like the motherly type,' I said.

'You'd be wrong. She cared, in her own way. She had a good heart – terrible struggle showing it a lot of the time, but a good heart nonetheless. I was there the day they met. Some of the younger boys were trying to make action figures out of salt dough. Poor things looked like snowmen on a summer's day but they seemed to be enjoying themselves all the same,' he said. 'Roseanna was brought in by a couple, a man and a woman, who had a small bag for her and a clipboard. She went straight into the kitchen and sat down on a seat at the head of the table. She was a seasoned pro, even by her age. She knew that you had to mark your territory from day one. Feisty when it came down to it, but fragile all the same.

'Sarah had been there that day, too. She'd been missing for two nights in a row, but this was the house she'd lived in for longer than she'd ever lived anywhere, she always came back. Only this time, there was a new face at the table.'

He told me that before long they became inseparable and, with Sarah to shield her, Roseanna avoided the plight of being the new kid. The taunting and teasing, the tricks and initiation rituals doled out by the long-termers, never reached a peak. Any instances of unpleasantness were sharply dealt with by Sarah. Usually a threat would suffice, but on occasion brute force would be issued, until Roseanna became untouchable.

'She'd found something she could keep safe,' he said. 'A project. Art was never Sarah's thing. She was never going to channel her mood through a painting or a vase. But in Roseanna ... in Roseanna there was somewhere for her love to go. There was a person she could protect the way nobody had ever protected her. And I don't just mean from the other children.' He shifted in his seat. 'Roseanna slept in Sarah's bed with her, when she was there, which was becoming less and less the older she got.'

He paused, noticing my expression, which was both rapt and incredulous.

'When you hugged her,' he said. 'Did she ... ?'

'Smell?' I offered. 'Yes, like a bin. It was disgusting.'

He smiled. 'Sarah made her promise. Whenever she was gone she wasn't to wash. I only found this out later. Not her teeth nor her face nor her body. Told her to spend her days playing out, running about the beach and the dene. "Get good and muddy. Be the biggest little scruff in the world when I'm gone," she'd told her.'

'But why?' I asked, though I feared that I already knew the answer.

'It's not a good place, Claudette,' Mr Fitzpatrick said solemnly.

'When Sarah wasn't there, nobody could protect Roseanna,' he said. 'And if she didn't wash then nobody would want her. Nobody would touch her.'

'Oh God,' I said and felt my insides churn. 'Why didn't anybody do anything?'

'The staff, not all of them, but some of them ... the children were taken advantage of. Not all of them, but many ...' he tried. 'None of the children ever said anything. They didn't have to. You could see it in their eyes. Those blank stares. People talk about Sarah, about the things she did. About how she lived her life, what she was allowed of it. But she learnt the hard way. She said she was going to take Roseanna away. Said she had big plans. "I'll die before I let anything happen to her" she'd told me the last time we spoke. And then she did ... It's my fault. It is my fault.'

'No,' I said. 'I'm sure you tried to stop it.'

'I told the police. Told the services. Told anybody whose number I could find. But they didn't believe me.'

'Why not?'

'I'm an angry old fool, remember,' he said.

'Doesn't mean you don't deserve to be taken seriously.'

'I was just another timewaster,' he said. 'And I had no proof. Nothing but knowing, deep down, deep inside of my soul, that those children weren't safe.'

'But surely,' I said, 'once she went missing, they would have taken you more seriously.'

Mr Fitzpatrick shook his head

'To rectify a mistake is to acknowledge that they made one in the first place. Girls like Sarah are too easily buried,' he said.

'I tried,' he said, wiping a tear from his eye. 'But 'I didn't try hard enough.'

'We can try again,' I said quietly, staring at my bag on the floor. 'I think together we can make a difference.'

'No,' he said, releasing himself from our embrace. 'No, it's no good. They're not interested. She drowned. Slipped in the water and went under. They don't care about her life.'

'I don't mean just Sarah. I mean the home.' I opened my bag and let the contents spill out on the floor. 'I've got this theory,' I said. 'I think people only care when it's an emergency. When something is so loud that it can't be ignored.' I waded through empty, curled pill packets and tampons before I found what I was looking for. 'I mean, I had to go through a school window before anyone would admit I wasn't just a moody attention-seeker. And Sarah, well ... nobody cared about Sarah until she was past tense. *Here.*' I offered him the journalist's business card, the one who had stopped me my first day back. Nancy, with the name of her newspaper printed at the bottom. 'Let's make it an emergency. Let's make it so loud they can't ignore it.'

'I don't know,' he said, uneasily

'For Sarah,' I said, and he softened. 'And for Roseanna. Before it's too late.'

'Will you be here?' he said eventually, placing the card on the table where his cup of cooling tea sat beside a stack of photo albums. 'When she comes?'

'Of course,' I said. 'We're a team. I'll be here as long as you need me.'

In the end, I made the phone call. Mr Fitzpatrick's phone had a rotary dialler and the apprehension of returning to zero after every digit made even him seem uneasy.

Nancy answered in what sounded like a wind tunnel. Her voice seemed distant and inside out. Somewhere in the background an announcer boomed a train's delayed arrival time. After I told her my name, she demanded that I explained who

I was exactly. When I told her I was the girl who'd sworn at her she said I'd have to be more specific than that. Eventually I reached for the easiest label I could find.

'I'm the girl who didn't want to speak to you about Sarah Banks. The crazy girl.'

'Oh,' she said. 'I assumed you were a dead end.'

'Yeah I get that a lot,' I said. 'Look, I'm with someone who'd like to talk to you. It's important.'

'Is this about Sarah?' she asked in a voice that seemed to be chivvying me off the line. 'That's old news. Nobody's covering that. Try one of the local papers.'

'It's about more than Sarah,' I said, frantically. 'It's important and it's huge. I promise it will be worth your while.'

'Right,' she said, sounding cautiously interested. 'Well, I'm covering an *X Factor* audition over your way on Thursday. I've got half an hour to spare, but that's it.' She rang off the phone quickly, after giving me a time and a place.

'And?' Mr Fitzpatrick asked, looking suddenly older and frailer than I'd ever seen him before.

'We're on,' I said, hoisting my bag over my shoulder. 'And here,' I said removing my bracelet, 'if you see Roseanna tell her I was just keeping it safe.'

'You and old Fitzpatrick seem to be getting on well,' Dad said, once I was back home. Paula had taken over the living room with reams of paper; she was preparing a sign for the church hall about her latest venture (a geriatric dance class) and Dad and I were huddled on the small sofa, trying to catch glimpses of the television over her bobbing head.

'He's nice really. You just need to take time. Actually, I'm worried about him.'

222

'I still haven't forgiven him for the trouble he caused,' Dad said, shaking his head. Dad didn't do grudges or negativity, but when someone questioned his parenting skills – as Mr Fitzpatrick had done frequently – his lip curled, literally and metaphorically.

'Yeah well, that was ages ago. He's had a hard time of it. Everyone acts out when they feel like their pain is being ignored. You've forgiven me enough times. Besides, he's my friend and he's a good man. He's going to do something brilliant soon, something that should have been done a long time ago.'

'Really? What masterpiece might that be?' Dad asked, as Paula swore and jerked her arm at a paper cut.

'You'll see,' I said. 'Just wait. Everything will be fine.'

'Hey!' Dad said, in mock indignation. 'That's my line.'

'Yes it is,' I said. 'And as we both know. You are always right about everything.'

I moved onto the floor and began flicking through the magazine cut-outs and scraps of paper that formed Paula's palette for the evening as she harrumphed and scowled her scissors across a length of pink sugar paper.

'It's only the church hall,' I said as she shook her head and balled up her botched effort, ready to start again. 'I doubt it'll even get read, let alone critiqued on its artistic merit.'

Paula looked up and sighed.

'Help me, Claudette,' she said before releasing a long groan at the sheer magnitude of her task.

'I'm no good at this sort of stuff,' I told her. 'I can't draw. I can't even cut straight.'

'You made me that Mother's Day card once,' she said and I shuddered.

'I was six. And anyway, didn't I spell your name wrong?'

'On purpose,' she said matter-of-factly.

'Just keeping you on your toes.' I skimmed through some of her paperwork and lesson plans, oblivious to whether or not they may have been confidential.

'Hmm,' Paula said as she arranged the letters she'd cut out at the top of the page. 'Looks rubbish, doesn't it?' We both stared down at her efforts. 'There's so much competition to get a space at the hall nowadays, I just want it to pop. I want to create a real buzz.' She looked at me with menace. 'And really stick it to Sheila Jessop and her stupid tea dance.'

'Oh good, a gang war,' I said. 'Is that what this is? You want to be the biggest and the best do-gooder. I know you want a Pride of Britain Award. I saw you on the website when I had mumps last Christmas and had to sleep on the sofa.'

Paula waved me away with her hand

'That was for someone else!' she protested, unconvincingly. 'Either piss or get off the pot, Claudette. I'm stressed enough. All I ask is you bring your famously chipper positivity in my time of need?'

I sighed. 'You want to know what I think?' I said.

'Well, obviously,' said Paula.

'I think that old people don't want jazzercise, or whatever it is you're doing. None of them really need to learn a rudimentary rumba. They dread the lesson part of these things.'

'And you'd know?' she asked.

'Actually, I do,' I said. 'They want cake. They want hot drinks and sweet treats. And they want gossip. They want to tell stories and to hear them in turn. They want company and to enjoy themselves while they still can.'

Paula nodded. 'They're lonely.'

'Yes. They're lonely, that's all, they don't need to extend their lives through gentle exercise. They need to enjoy whatever life they've got left. I bet if you filled that hall with trestle tables and chairs, tea and biscuits, played some chamber music on the lowest setting your ghetto blaster will allow and left them to it, they'd have the time of their lives.'

'What makes you so sure?' she asked, though I could tell she was coming to my state of mind.

'Mr Fitzpatrick, no doubt,' Dad muttered from behind us.

'Exactly.' I said. 'I've seen him, what, half a dozen times in the last three weeks. And do you know? I reckon I've found out more about him in that time than anyone else has in the last twenty years. People are just people. We all want the same thing.'

'Cake and love,' Paula said as she clapped her hands together.

'I'd have gone with sugar and gossip, but potato, po-tah-to, I suppose.'

'We could call it Paula's Pantry,' she said. 'Or Cake and Company.'

'Call it Choux and Me Makes Two,' Dad said excitedly, sitting up bolt upright as each sweet treat known to man passed through the rhyming dictionary of his mind. '... Cake's Progress,' he yelled, suddenly unstoppable. '... *The Rolling Scones*!'

'... I like Big Bundts And I Cannot Lie?' I tried as Dad high fived me for my input.

'Whatever,' I said, standing up. 'I just don't want to have to sit through another eighty-year-old singing "You're The One That I Want" on the back of a cardboard Cabriolet at your Christmas Extravaganza. It's unkind to all involved.'

I could tell I'd already lost Paula, as she opened her giant notepad to a fresh sheet and began drafting ideas.

'This is perfect, Claudette,' she said as she scrawled away. 'You really are a good girl,' she said. 'So thoughtful.'

225

I rolled my eyes and stood up just as Dad was putting his phone back in his pocket. Dad checked his phone on the hour every hour. It had been on silent since the day he had bought it, out of courtesy to the world at large, and the only people who ever texted him were Paula and myself. But still he checked. Just in case.

He caught my eye and gave me a proud smile as I made my way to my room.

'Thank you,' he mouthed.

'Anything to get her out of the house,' I mouthed back.

19

The Haunted Girl

They say that a good argument is supposed to help a relationship in the long run.

Saying things that have long been unsaid will clear the air.

Venting your emotions will wipe the slate clean.

They have obviously never been a seventeen-year-old girl.

All I seemed to be was things unsaid. It's all anyone was, as far as I could see. Donna too. Most people I knew seemed to survive on a healthy diet of seething silence. And yet depression made it harder for me to get by that way. I didn't have the filter that most people had, that allowed them to keep painful things from touching them too deeply. Other people managed to deal with each emotion as it happened, one by one, in time and in turn. I would absorb it all until it was too much to bear and then scream for help.

I don't know how long Donna and I had been building to a fight. I wasn't even sure I was aware that we'd been simmering towards rupture. But when we exploded we did it with style.

When I arrived at her house she wasn't her usual self.

'Hi,' she said bluntly.

No benevolent insult. No jokey reference. Just, hello. She let me in and we made our way to her bedroom.

The music filled our silence and highlighted it at the same time.

'I feel like I never see you any more,' Donna said, after some excruciating small talk. In the kitchen I heard her mum turn off the radio and bid Adam a farewell before she stomped through the hallway in her high heels, locking the door behind her.

I shrugged and sat up on her bed.

'I've been busy. I don't know. It's been a strange summer.'

'I'll say,' she said. 'You don't even text me back any more. It's not just that you don't get in touch; you don't even acknowledge it when I do.'

'Sorry,' I said. 'But what with Jacob and everything else . . .'

'*Ah*,' Donna said, with mock understanding. 'Your great project.'

'What?'

'You're going to solve the mystery of Sarah and cure yourself,' she said slyly. 'Watertight plan, Claudette. A sure-fire winner.'

She stood up and changed the track on her phone so that a slower, angrier tune began playing from the speakers that rested on her windowsill.

'Jacob told me all about your little mission. Sounds like some Famous Five fun.' She sipped the water beside her bed. 'We were worried about you,' she said, and I felt my stomach lurch.

'We?' I said. 'What, you're like a *collective* now?'

Donna shrugged. 'We've been seeing each other on and off,' she said as if it were no big deal.

I felt my face heat in a flash. I was upset, angry, embarrassed, confused. For no good reason whatsoever Jacob felt like mine.

After the hospital, all the while Sarah was gone, I needed the space that Jacob had given me. He had taken me as he found me, with none of the silt and mud from the tsunami of the months before we met.

'I didn't know.'

'Yeah well if you'd have answered your phone maybe you would have.'

'And you talk about me, I suppose?' I said and Donna laughed.

'You're a subject ripe for analysis,' she said. 'What do you *think* people do, Claudette? They talk about their friends. They worry. You're still not well.'

'How would you know?' I spat. 'How would you know anything about what I'm going through.'

'I wouldn't,' she said annoyingly calmly. 'That's the problem. You never tell me anything. So I try. And I try. And then . . .'

I began to cry. She shrugged.

'I'm doing everything I can at the moment to keep my head above the water. Everything I'm doing I'm doing to survive,' I sobbed.

Donna scoffed. 'You really believe that, don't you?' she said. 'You're not even trying to get better. You're just looking for something to blame next time you get ill.'

'That's a horrible thing to say.'

'Yeah, well, I don't think you want to get better. I think you're scared.'

'Scared of what?'

'Scared of yourself. Scared that without the crazy, you'd have to accept that maybe you're just a horrible person.' She laughed. 'You spend so long distracting yourself, Claudette. You make Jacob your audience for this fresh new version of yourself, you turn sleuth to try and solve Sarah, you knock about with Daniel Vesper and that old creep . . .'

'Fuck you,' I barked, and she rolled her eyes.

'I think you're scared that you don't know where it ends and you begin. That's the truth. Sometimes depression comes for you and it's enormous. Sometimes you can't move. Sometimes you can't speak. Sometimes you can't function. But it's not some poltergeist; you can't blame every single thing on it. You're a human being, Claudette, sometimes you really are just an arsehole. It's not a disease. It's you.'

'Can you imagine what it's like for me?' I said.

'No, Claudette, I honestly can't.'

'Everywhere I go, everything I do, I've got this *Jaws* theme tune at the back of my head. This creeping dread and all I can do is try and stave it off for as long as I can. So yeah, sometimes I try to distract myself, but it's a question of necessity. God, Donna!' I yelled. 'Be my friend. I'm so fucking scared right now. I'm in over my head and I need to know someone is there for me. I've messed up, fine. And I don't know what to do and I can't work out if I'm crazy or in trouble.'

'It wouldn't be the first time you'd been both,' Donna said coldly. 'Sometimes I think you're exactly where you want to be, Claudette.' She began to cry herself, gently and reluctantly, the way Donna always did.

'I need to leave,' I said, standing up. 'I can't believe you're being like this.'

'You brought it on yourself. You're not immune to being pulled on your bullshit.'

'Yeah well I certainly feel pulled.'

'You do know he's leaving, don't you?' she said as I made my way out of her room. 'And then where will we be? Then who will you be? You'll be stuck with yourself again, just you, as you are. You're going to need us, Claudette, but I'm not sure how many times you're going to be able to hit pause on everybody you know before we give up completely. You're like this eternal *maybe*. Sometimes we need a solid yes or a no.'

I stumbled towards the door down the hallway. Adam yelled after me, asking if I was coming or going or how I was; the specifics of his words didn't quite make it to my brain. My legs were shaking and my breathing quickened as I steeled myself to focus on each step, one foot in front of the other, one at a time, until I made it down the corridor into the piss-sealed tomb of her tower block's lift.

Donna had been right, I thought, as I sat alone on the prom-enade, staring out at sea. Everything had been accurate, in a roundabout sort of way, but it still didn't mean she'd had the right to say it. As I sat there with tears drying in sharp scratches down my face, I wanted to wade out into the water and slip under, never to return.

The argument had settled in my brain like half-eaten trifle, layers and layers piled up and slipped underneath one another, in an ugly, gluey mess. All I knew was that I felt rotten, and nothing would cheer me up.

As if the universe hadn't thrown enough horror my way that afternoon, Ross was sitting cross-legged on the wall of the block of flats at the bottom of my street by the time I made it home. He looked freezing, with his fists clenched beneath his sweatshirt sleeves, staring at the cracked paving.

'You all right?' he asked, as I tried to walk past him as quickly as I could, even though pretending not to have seen him would have been entirely impossible.

'No. I'm really not in the mood today, Ross,' I said as he stood up and began to follow me.

'Have you been crying?'

'Does it matter?'

'Has something happened?'

'What do you want?' I asked, turning to face him.

'Is your dad home? You said I could come,' he asked nervously.

'Yes. Sorry. Come in,' I said with weary resignation. 'The coast is clear.'

'Can I make you some tea or something?' I asked as we settled on the sofa and Ross gave me a quizzical look.

'Who are you again?' he said and we both laughed.

'I honestly don't know sometimes,' I said, pulling my knees close to my chest and holding myself as tightly as I could, like a locked seatbelt, until my arms began to ache. 'Why didn't you just text me if you wanted to see me?'

'Lost my mobile,' he said. 'Well, haven't been keeping it on me. More hassle than it's worth.'

'That's a bold move, Ross,' I said. 'You can't be Dan's favourite errand boy if he can't pin you down.'

'That's the idea.' He paused. 'I'm staying back home again.' He did not elaborate on where exactly home was this month. 'It's all getting too much.'

'What, the life of a small-time drug baron didn't have the opportunities for internal promotion you'd been hoping for when you joined the company on the ground level? Or was it the staff wellbeing?'

I was too sharp. Ross stood up.

'If you're going to be like that . . .' he said, and I rolled my eyes.

'Sorry,' I said half-heartedly. 'I didn't mean to lash out. Not at you, anyway. It's Dan I hate. You didn't deserve that.'

Ross hovered for a moment before he settled and sat back down next to me.

'Is it about Donna and that Jacob lad?' he asked, staring at the ground. 'I saw them getting off with one another down the pub.'

It took everything in my power to stop myself from shaking.

'They can do whatever they like. He's just a tourist. He doesn't mean anything to me,' I said, instantly regretting it, even though I knew Ross would never remember the lie long enough to relay it.

We were quiet and Ross shifted in his seat.

'Do you know *anybody*, Ross?' I asked. 'I mean really, know them inside out. Know who they are? Know how they think. How they feel. Know what you are to them and what they are to you?'

He looked bemused at first, and then the clouds parted and the question made sense to him.

'I don't think anyone does,' he said. 'Not really. What about you?'

'I don't even know myself half the time,' I said, trying not to cry. 'I just feel like everything I do is wrong. Every thought I have is backwards or inside out.'

'I thought I did,' he said, quite rightly ignoring my wallowing. 'I thought I knew Sarah. I mean, I did, more than most, but I thought I knew what had happened to her, too,' he said.

Ross was hurting, I could see that. But then so was I. As I watched him I felt passing guilt that my first thought on letting him into my house was to try and have sex with him. Not that there would have been much effort involved. Ross was like a kebab. Every girl had had him at least once when they were drunk and there was literally no other option available. Nobody, to the best of my knowledge, had ever woken from the experience feeling anything other than nausea and mild regret. Ross included, probably.

The more I thought about it, the more I realised Ross probably went home with every girl who asked, not because he had some insatiable urge, but because more often than not it meant he had somewhere warm and dry to stay for a length of time.

As for me, it wasn't lust that had made me consider sleeping with him that evening. Between the depression and the recovery and the various tablets I was on, I was as uninterested in sex as I'd ever been. If anything it was vanity. I had felt so lousy for so long. Donna had just itemised my human failings in ugly detail. I wanted to prove that I could bring some happiness or pleasure to a person, bring something more than just pain and regret, even if only for a fleeting moment. But I looked at Ross, sitting on my dad's sofa, and I knew I couldn't sleep with him, just to make myself feel better. I'd known him for as long as I'd known anybody and he didn't need me taking advantage of him on top of everything else.

In the end, maybe the fact that I'd realised that before acting on my impulse, was proof that I wasn't all bad.

'What happened?' I said to Ross once more, moving closer. 'I know you cared about her, you've told me that. But enough now.' I took hold of his arm. 'You tried to help her. You thought she'd gotten away. But she didn't, you know that now. So, why did she disappear that night? Why did she die?'

Ross sighed and looked at me, wiping his mouth into an 'O' shape as he shuddered once. 'You're like a dog with a bone, Claudette,' he said.

I stayed quiet. This time I wanted the truth.

'We were close,' he began carefully. 'Me and her. I loved her. Not in that sort of way. But the way you love someone you know is good inside. I tried to help her that night.'

Ross said that in the days leading up to Sarah's death she was being followed. Her every move was traced by Dan's hired help, who skulked and stalked. Everywhere she walked she cast at least three shadows, whilst Dan and his ghouls searched for their missing stash.

'She started hanging out at Grey's House not long after I did, once she got moved to the home,' Ross said. The thought that a life around Dan Vesper was somehow more inviting than the house where you were supposed to be cared for, broke my heart. 'She needed somewhere to go and Dan had an open door policy when it suited him.'

'How does he do it?' I asked. 'How does he get so many people to work for him?'

'What? Like you, you mean?' he asked.

'Yeah, well I was doing it for a reason,' I said. 'To understand Sarah.'

'Dan recognises damage,' Ross went on. 'He's always got a quick fix for whatever hole you need filling. You might need money. You might want something that'll make you forget who you are for the night. A bed for a while,' he said, rolling his eyes. 'And that's fine. But by the time you've got what you needed your debt is bigger than you could ever imagine. You can never repay Dan, you can only keep him sweet, or hope to.'

'So Sarah got in over her head.'

'Eventually,' he said. 'We all did, in a way. But Sarah wanted out. Got clever, started skimming profits here and there. She knew I wouldn't say anything. She knew I cared about her too much.'

'And Dan found out?' I asked and Ross nodded.

'That night he got the hell in him. Sarah had been to the Mariners because she was due paying.' Ross laughed again. 'She was brazen; I'll give her that. She'd been robbing from him for weeks, but she'd create holy hell if her pay packet was ever delayed.'

'What happened?'

'There was the usual there. A few lads. But Dan was there too. That's when she knew it was bad. Dan never goes to the Mariners. He's at the top of the pile. Keeps himself removed from the heart of the operation. When she saw him she knew. She knew she was going to die that night.'

'But nobody murdered her,' I said. 'She drowned.'

Ross shook his head.

'Dan made us leave the room. Sent us all downstairs. Said he wanted what was his. So we left.'

'What did he do?'

'I don't know. But she got away,' Ross said. 'At first.'

Ross told me how they sat and listened from downstairs, in the creaking, unlit entrance to the Mariners. He told me how they felt rats scurry across their feet as, upstairs, voices got quiet and then loud again, and then louder still. He said there was the sound of a slap, and then another, and then a tussle before glass broke above them and the entire building began to creak and shake.

'That's when Dan came downstairs, doubled over and holding his balls. His fists were red raw and covered in blood and he was furious. She'd gone through the window, climbed down the scaffolding. He sent us after her. Said he didn't care how many parts she came back in, that he wanted her and his money.'

'So you chased her?' I whispered quietly, desperate to hear what Sarah's last hours entailed but keen not to throw Ross off the story's bleak track.

He nodded.

Some men made it into cars and tore along the roads and the back alleys, shining headlights into wheelie bins – checking back yards and boarded-up shops that Sarah had known how to get into.

Others made way on foot, tracing their way down towards the beach, and out towards the lighthouse, but couldn't make the walk due to the ebbing tide.

'I walked down the promenade with another two lads. I went first. They were fat and I know what the rocks are like down there. I can get over them in no time.'

'Sarah could too,' I said, having seen her navigate the patch like a gymnast on more than one occasion.

'They were slipping and yelling all the way. They were well behind by that point. I reached the edge of the rocks and made my way along the beach . . . ' Ross shivered a little. 'I only just saw her. She was walking out, into the water. It was already up to her chest. She went slowly, so nobody would hear her, right underneath the pier. She must have heard me because I saw her turn to look at me one last time before she made it to where she had wanted to go. By the time the other lads caught up, I told them I couldn't see anything. I wasn't lying, either. She was well hidden behind the beams.

'They spent all night up there, keeping an eye on the beach. It must have been raining because when they got back the next morning they were soaked through and grey, like they were dying,' he said. 'She must have held on for hours. She must have been so cold.' Ross stopped, held his face in his hands, and cried. 'I tried to help her,' he said between sobs. 'And I thought she'd gotten away. I thought she was gone.'

I was shaking too. I leant over and hugged Ross until his bony body stopped shaking and his sobs were gentler, more controlled.

'I know you did,' I said. 'I know.'

The police had already announced that they were no longer treating Sarah's death as suspicious. The spotlight was dimmed. The town could relax.

There would be no arrest.

There would be no trial.

There had been no murder.

But Sarah had been killed. She'd been killed over and over again before she was taken by the waves.

I imagined her alone that night, growing cold and then warm, accepting the tiredness that surrounded her as the waves rocked her to sleep, like a mother should have done. I saw her, in my mind's eye, dragged out to sea; rushing on a current until she moved so fast it was like she wasn't moving at all, travelling towards nothing for ever, to some sort of freedom where she could finally sleep.

Then I imagined her body ripped backwards. Her clothes removed by the groping waves. I saw her being pulled back – back through the sea, back from peace, to the harbour and the estuaries where she would have walked when she was alive. Back through the narrow passages to where she was found; naked and stained like church glass, glittering with silt. I saw her cast in clay, stuck to the wall of some riverbank where with dead eyes she watched over the town that had killed her, the town that thought she had slipped away quietly. I imagined her watching every bowed head as the investigation made progress, hoping that they'd get away with what they'd done to her. I imagined her watching every public mourner who'd looked away as she was diminished, day by day, by an unkind life, by people who took from her and took from her until the only way she could live was to risk being killed to get away from it all.

Mr Fitzpatrick and I had done everything we could to see that the children's home got what was coming to them. But no matter what the police reports said we all bore responsibility for Sarah. Nobody could trace where her desperation had started. But it had ended cruelly and unnecessarily at the hands of Dan Vesper. And I owed it to Sarah to let the world know.

'I hate him too, Ross,' I said quietly as he began to calm. 'I hate him so much.'

Ross unfurled from our hug and looked at me.

'But what can you do?' he asked. 'What can anybody do?'

'He can't be caught for killing Sarah but that doesn't mean he can't be trapped.'

'He's stronger than us,' Ross said, shaking his head.

'But we're smarter than him. Trust me,' I said. 'I just need one thing from you, and I'll see to the rest,'

'What?' he asked.

'I need you to tell me what it would it take to get Dan into the Mariners,' I said. 'And I need you to help me do it.'

20

After the Storm

We were the only people sat on the seats outside of the café. The sun shone but not brightly. Both of us wore T-shirts and concentrated hard not to shiver. Neither of us were willing to acknowledge we were too cold for such a continental set-up.

Jacob sat in front of me looking slightly wronged and slightly accusatory at the same time.

'So are we going to talk about it?' he asked meekly, though his face suggested that he wanted to do anything but.

'Haven't you and Donna had adequate time to analyse the situation?' I snapped, tipping teaspoon after teaspoon of sugar into my tea. 'Apparently you make quite the team when it comes to problem-solving.'

Word had reached him via Donna that we'd had a falling out. Or rather that I'd been assassinated with words in the middle of Donna's box bedroom. I ignored seven texts and an unusual midday knock on my front door. I eventually relented the third time he tried to phone me. I knew once the phone rang that he had significant feelings about what had transpired. The only reason anybody our age used their phone as a phone was: a close friend or relative had died and a text would be inappropriate.

They were a drug dealer.

They'd missed the last bus home and needed a lift.

Or, more often than not:

They'd fucked up and needed to sort something out ASAP.

Jacob sighed and put his hand out, gently holding my wrist, to stop the sixth sugar from hitting my cup.

'What exactly is it I've done wrong?' he asked with an arched eyebrow. 'What have we done that's so bad.'

I made an *ugh* sound at the use of 'we' and maintained eye contact as I spooned one last heaped measure of sugar into my coffee.

'Nothing,' I said sharply.

'Really?' he asked. 'Because it doesn't feel like that.'

'No,' I said, sipping my tea, which by that point was mostly syrup. My insides zinged to life with the warm hit of sugar. 'That's not what I meant. It wasn't that you did nothing wrong. Doing nothing was what you *did wrong*.'

'Right,' he said, wearily. 'Glad we cleared that up then.'

I swore at Jacob as I placed a handful of spinning coins on the table for my tea and toast and made my way towards the promenade.

Not many people were out and about that morning. It was too late for the rush hour flow of bodies hurrying for the bus, but too early for most people to be mooching about looking for things to do.

I slid beneath the rusted bars and dropped down to the lower promenade, picking up my pace as Jacob dropped down behind me and attempted to keep up.

'So, what?' he said, trying hard to maintain a steady tone

despite being out of breath. 'You're angry that I made a friend other than you? That a girl might have been interested in me?'

'You know that's not true!' I yelled, spinning around. 'Stop making out like I'm being unreasonable. I don't care what you do and who you do it with. But you and *Donna*? That's different. It feels like a betrayal.'

I stopped short. The word fit so perfectly. Maybe I was being unreasonable. Maybe I was being unfair. Certainly I was being unkind. But I felt betrayed by the situation, though still couldn't explain why. It just turned out he hadn't fit the exact mould I'd cast for him.

'How have we betrayed you?' he asked, his voice beginning to rise. 'By making friends, by getting close at the wrong time?'

'Why didn't you just tell me?' I asked.

'Because you'd have reacted like this.'

'Not if you were honest in the first place.'

'That's not true,' he said. 'You want everything laid out perfectly, Claudette. You want everything in its place but it's not. Life is messy and it's complicated.'

'Oh you're so wise.'

'And you're so dumb. You're smart, yeah. But you're dumb. You're doing things all wrong. You're trying to do so many things at once that you're achieving nothing whatsoever.'

'You've really got me down to a T, haven't you?' I said, turning to leave.

'Well if I'm so annoying then why do you bother, Claudette? Surely I'm not worth the effort. I didn't ask for any of this. You came to me. You pestered me. What exactly is it you expect? What exactly is it you want from me?' he asked.

I spun around, tears of fury and frustration salting the rims of my eyes.

'Everything!' I yelled, so loud even I was shocked. 'I want everything. All at once and for ever. *And fuck you for not giving it to me!*'

This was the truth.

This was my truth.

It was how I felt about Jacob. How I felt about the world.

Jacob had been my opportunity to become a blank page. With him, as with no one else, I found the bare foundations of myself upon which I could build the girl I knew I could be, become the person I wanted to be seen as.

My anger wasn't at him, not really. I was angry at myself. Everybody likes the idea that they are seen by others the way they see themselves. That beautiful. That clever. That able. That unique. Whatever it is. But we're messy creatures, and we're broken goods and we're full of stupid mistakes, and to expect anyone to see you without your errors is unreasonable to the point of stupidity. That I'd even thought this, least of all pinned it on Jacob, was on me. But I was damned if I was going to admit it.

I stood for a moment feeling pathetic, sobbing uncontrollably in the middle of the promenade, my head in my hands, my arms shivering in the shady breeze of the concrete stretch. It wasn't long before Jacob came towards me and wrapped me in a hug.

'Don't,' I said, trying to wriggle from his embrace, for some reason. I began to laugh through my tears and I could feel a smile in his voice as he spoke gently to me.

'You're impossible,' he whispered, holding me tighter as I relented.

'I know,' I said. 'I'm so sorry. I don't know what's wrong with me. I really don't. I don't know who I am.' I said, laughing, 'I don't know what I want. I'm just . . . '

'You're just looking for your place in the world,' he said. 'Like everyone else. Congratulations, Claudette. You're normal.'

'Shut up,' I said, 'I am special and I am different. My pain is unique.'

'Yeah, so's everyone's,' he said, holding me tighter still. 'You'll figure yourself out one day,' he said.

'What about you?'

'Me?' he asked, passing our shared weight from foot to foot so that we rocked gently like a pendulum. 'I'm a lost cause. One of life's eternal travellers. I'll keep moving until I stop for ever,' he said and sighed.

'It just seems like such a waste,' I said quietly, suddenly aware of just how much I'd miss him once he was gone. 'Any one place would be lucky to have you for the duration.'

He laughed and kissed my head.

'I don't know what version of you I got over the last few weeks, but I liked her, for what it's worth.'

'I liked you too,' I said. 'I wish you could stay a bit longer.'

'I know. But I can't. I just wish . . . ' he said, trying to find the right words. 'I just wish we'd met in a place we both wanted to be.'

'I just wish that place existed,' I said flatly, my head pressed against his T-shirt, staring out into the endless grey slab of the sea.

'I think it does. And I won't stop looking until I find it,' he said.

'Text me when you get there?' I asked.

'Deal,' he said.

A car pulled onto the kerb as I made my way towards Donna's block of flats.

It had been following me since I'd left Jacob on the beach and my pace had quickened to a gentle trot.

Hers was the fourth tower along – the farthest from the beach – but her flat was the highest in the building. The penthouse suite, her mum would sometimes joke, as we held our noses against the stench of piss in the corridor.

Two car doors opened and closed behind me and footsteps grew in speed and volume as I skipped the last paces to the doorway of her building and hammered her flat number into the scratched keypad.

'Scuse me, love,' came a voice from behind, as I pressed the buzzer frantically, trying to appear as casual as I could in the pinhole camera.

'Come on now, Claudette.' A second voice. 'Manners cost nothing.' It was said with a laugh and their outlines spread in the glass of the door just as it buzzed open and I hauled myself inside, pressing it shut with my back as two fists pounded to be let in.

I ran towards the lift and pressed my finger on the UP button as it whirred and clanked in its familiar descent. Just as its doors began to open a third voice and a jangling of keys came from the entrance.

'Couldn't help us out mate?' said the blurred figure from the car. 'Only gone and left my keys inside.'

The man laughed obliviously and opened the door as I hammered fourteen and pressed myself against the back of the lift, as the doors closed slowly and sealed shut.

I had no idea who had followed me there, or what exactly they had wanted, but as the lift rose my legs buckled beneath me, and I spent the short journey on the floor, clawing desperately at my own breath as I blinked back tears.

I had only known the outlines of Sarah's world since I'd gotten out of hospital, and already it felt like it was destroying me.

I was amazed she had survived for as long as she did.

Donna's room was cut through with the invisible ripples that always linger after an argument. I'd asked Jacob how she was before I left him and he'd said she didn't hate me. *Nobody*, he said, *gets angry if they don't really care.* It was her concern for me that caused her to lash out.

I wasn't convinced by his logic. I spent half my life getting mad at dumb people and stupid shit that in the grand scheme I didn't care one bit about. And Donna seldom said anything she didn't mean, so there had obviously been some heft to her outburst.

Any attempt at small talk was futile but I was determined to give it a damn good shot regardless.

'I almost had sex with Ross,' I said expectantly, keen to appeal to one of Donna's biggest areas of interest.

She shrugged and turned her back to me.

'You probably should have,' she said. 'I'm worried your business is going to heal over if you leave it much longer.'

'Nah it's safe. I'm always messing around down there.'

There was a silence, and then an audible intake of breath from Donna.

'I do hate you sometimes,' she said. 'No matter what Jacob said to make you feel better. And I mean hate. Not, like, I hate maths or I hate it when you wait ages for a bus and two come along at once. Like, fully blown biblical hate. I want to kick the shit clean out of you sometimes, Claudette. You wind me up so much it's unreal.'

'I know.'

'Yep. It's all your fault. As you know, I'm perfect,' she said, turning with a frown tightly screwed on to her emerging smile.

246

'I know,' I said, allowing myself a small smile. 'I'm sorry. I've played it all wrong, haven't I?'

Donna sighed and shrugged.

She told me how she'd first gone to Jacob when I'd spent so much time avoiding her, with the intention of assassinating him for having stolen me from her. And that she had stayed in touch as he was the only way she got any sort of news about me, and how he'd kept her updated, and she'd acted as a sort of translator for him – explaining my behavioural quirks as best she could as I tangled him in the web of my recovery.

'So maybe you're right,' she said with an arched eyebrow. 'Maybe everything really is all about you.'

'I'm sorry,' I said.

'It's just, I spent so much time with you when you were unwell . . . I felt like I was the one you leaned on. Then Jacob serves you an ice cream or whatever . . . and suddenly he's your BFF. When I did see you, Claudette, I didn't recognise you.'

'Oh Jesus,' I said. 'Really?'

'I just . . . ' she began. 'You're not the only one who needs a friend. I missed you. I still miss you. You go away and then you come back and I'm so happy you do. And I know people change, and you've had all this stuff happen to you that can't *not* change you, but . . . I want a friend and I want that friend to be you and when you don't give me that friendship I feel like shit.' She took a breath and carried on. 'I don't want to have to catch up with you every so often because you feel duty bound to keep up appearances. I want a relationship where we know every detail of every moment so that there's never anything we need to catch up on. I want *us* back,' she said, her voice beginning to wobble. 'You're my bro.'

I groaned.

'Donna,' I said fervently. 'I love you so much. And I will have this discussion completely, but if I don't have a piss in the next thirty seconds, I'm going to wet your bed ...'

I stood up, doubled over with my legs crossed tightly.

'Oh, Claudette. You kill all our special moments,' she said, with a weary sigh of resignation. '*Just go.*'

I ran from the bedroom and flung myself onto the toilet, moaning deep relief as I relaxed my lower region for what felt like the first time in my life.

In my frantic scramble to relieve myself I must have forgotten to lock the door, as Adam burst into the bathroom with a towel draped over his shoulder and yelled in horror when he saw me sat there, red faced and panting in ecstasy. I screamed back in turn, and stood up instinctively, shooting a steady stream of piss down my leg and onto the pink fluff of the toilet mat.

I swore and so did he as he turned to leave but bumped into the door frame.

'Sorry,' he said.

'Sorry,' I said, hurriedly sitting down.

'Sorry,' he said again, closing the door behind him.

I finished and decided to go and bug him further.

'Hey perv,' I said, drying my hands on my jeans as I poked my head through the kitchen door.

Adam was sat at the kitchen table, hands outstretched with the look of a man who has seen things he could not un-see glued to his face. I'd watched videos of returning soldiers looking less haunted than he was at that precise moment.

'Claudette. That was an accident ...' he said with panic in his voice.

'Yeah, I know it's fine. It happens all the time,' I said, shaking my hand. 'I got caught on one of those train toilets once and let me tell you . . . those electric doors close s-l-o-w,' I said, stretching out the word for comic effect.

'Yeah, but just in case you thought . . . '

'What? That you get your kicks by watching me panic and piss down my leg? No, I trust that's not your bag.'

'No!' he said, still shaken. 'It's not.'

'Are you working tomorrow night?' I asked eventually and he nodded, pleased for the change of subject. 'Around town?'

'Yeah,' he said.

'Good,' I said, but was gone before he had a chance to ask why.

'Better?' Donna asked, as I slumped back into the room and lay on the bed, placing my head on her lap.

'Yeah,' I said. 'I think your brother saw my fanny though.'

'You didn't lock the door?' she asked.

'Yeah,' I said. 'But he barged in with one of those door-bashers the riot police use and he was like *Drop your knickers and don't move a muscle.*'

'Classic Adam,' Donna said, pulling a thin strand of my hair gently from my head, until the roots pulled tight at my scalp, before twisting it into a tiny little Princess Leia bun that stung behind my ear.

'He's a monster,' I said.

'You are,' she muttered, rubbing her hand across my arm.

'You are,' I whispered, feeling myself grow sleepy against her warm body.

Once I'd said goodbye to Donna I made my way back as quietly as I could into the kitchen. Adam was still sat there in mute horror, making notes from a crescent of textbooks which he had open on the counter.

'Hi,' I said quietly. 'Hitting those books like they're criminals, I see.'

'Just doing my bit for society,' he said.

'They'd be mad not to have you,' I said, hovering over his studies as he tried in vain to shield his rather childish handwriting. 'Maybe you need to make a splash, get their attention.'

'I don't think the police are really into elaborate gestures,' he said.

'No, but I mean if you caught someone . . .' I tried, as vaguely as I could. 'If you caught someone bad, doing something bad, I don't know, if you did something that should have been done a long time ago, would that make a difference?'

Adam shrugged, half-nodding, looking quite interested in my line of enquiry.

'Why has nobody ever arrested Daniel Vesper?' I asked and Adam laughed once in a knowing sort of way.

'He's not as stupid as he looks,' Adam tried. 'Keeps a safe distance.'

'But the club. The drugs. Everything,' I said as Adam leaned in closer with a growing concern.

'What are you up to, Claudette?' he asked and I shrugged as best I could.

'I just always wondered. He's hiding in plain sight. He's in the club most daytimes. There must be enough in there to get him for something?'

'Nothing is that easy,' said Adam, trying to look me in the eye despite my best attempts to avoid his gaze.

'Adam,' I asked eventually when my awkward lingering had not incurred the offer I'd hoped it would. 'Will you do me a favour and walk me home?' I asked.

For some reason seeing Dad that night made me burst into tears.

I'd been at home alone for a good hour or so. Not really doing anything. Not really minding.

I felt positive enough, having patched things up with Donna, and I was certain I was as solid with Jacob as I was ever going to get. It felt, tonight, as if things were starting to calm down. The fog was settling. I could see things about my life that I hadn't seen clearly before; dozens and dozens of different paths that needed tending to in their own time, at their own pace, rather than one terrifying, unmanageable whole. The thought was soothing to me, albeit long overdue, and all the better that I had Donna back to match my pace and keep me centred.

'How are you, clever girl?' Dad asked as he made his way in the door, his empty Tupperware box making a hollow thud sound as his backpack swung behind him and caught on the doorframe.

'Hi Dad,' I said, though the second syllable was distorted beyond the point of recognition as the tears began to flow.

Dad dropped his bag to the floor and came straight to my assistance.

'Hey now,' he said, rubbing my back and hugging me to silence with shushes and there-there's. 'Hey now. What's all this? What's all this silliness, eh?' he asked, rubbing my back harder and harder until I was still.

'I'm fine,' I said, swallowing hard on tears.

'Clearly,' he said, taking my shoulders as he stared straight into my eyes. 'What's happened? Where's this come from?'

I smiled despite the tears.

'Nowhere. Nothing's happened, Dad. I'm fine. I'm feeling

better. Really I am. I really think something has clicked today. I just had this huge row with Donna and she said some awful things but they were true but . . . ' I said, winding myself up again and again. 'I'm just happy to see you, that's all. I'm happy you're home.'

'Silly girl,' he said, taking me in his arms again. 'I'll always be here no matter what. No matter where you go, no matter what you do. Whatever happens. I'll be here when you get back, and I'll be so, so happy to see you.'

21

Chasing Fire

I kissed both Dad and Paula goodbye after dinner.

We'd had a quiet meal. Quiet by our standards, anyway. Normally Dad would have anecdotes from work, or Paula would be relaying the latest battle within the gilded hierarchy of the community centre. But that night conversation was forced or non-existent. For some reason the meal felt tense, as though we'd all received bad news and were trying to put on a brave face for the sake of one another.

The scrape of our cutlery was interrupted only by the satisfied 'ummmmms' and 'aaaaaahs' of Dad and Paula, who'd been suitably impressed by the new stir-in sauce they'd picked up at the corner shop.

I was preoccupied with a flaking Ross, who I'd been texting, and who was becoming increasingly reluctant to aid me in my mission.

He said that he was certain it wouldn't work.

There was too much chance involved.

What if it went wrong?

What if one of us got hurt?

What is the best possible outcome even if everything went to our admittedly loose plan?

For a long time, the thought of some bleak ending would not have bothered me. It was hard explaining to most people just how little you cared about yourself for a large proportion of your life. If a person hasn't experienced absolute indifference to their own mortality then they could never possibly understand.

But it wasn't the cruel bravado of depression that carried me to the Mariners that night. More and more I was feeling better. I felt connected again, to myself and to the world; a world I sometimes enjoyed, and actually wanted to be a part of. Caution had returned as I grew better and stronger, but my desire to confront Dan hadn't cooled.

I wanted him gone. I wanted him captured. I wanted him to feel helpless and beholden. I wanted him kept in a place that he couldn't escape, like Sarah had been, like all the lost souls who'd gone to him for help and ended up stuck and spinning for ever and ever in the hungry mechanism of his small-town empire. I wanted to give him a taste of his own medicine.

I felt about him the way I sometimes felt about my depression. I wanted to pick him out like a splinter; remove him from his context until it was just him, alone and vulnerable and small. At the very least I wanted to see that someone knew, knew what he had done; knew that he was responsible for the death of a girl. A girl he should have cared for. A girl he could have saved.

I'd made it up and into a bath just as the *Countdown* theme was beginning to play. I dried and dressed myself and sat on my bed as I cooled and calmed before straightening my hair and scraping it back painfully until it was glossed against my head and held tight at the back, the way girls at school always would before starting a fight.

By dinner time I was as ready as I'd ever be.

The night was warmest we'd had all summer. It was the sort of night where it never really grows dark. The sort of night where nobody sleeps and everybody rises the next morning feeling exhausted and leaden; coated in sweat. Even the jeans and the vest top that I wore were clinging to my skin.

Within a moment of finishing my last mouthful, my phone buzzed in my pocket. The clock on the dining room wall struck eight and I knew that the message was from Ross.

'I'm off,' I said, kissing Dad and then Paula on the head.

'Oh,' said Paula, taken aback. 'What was that for?'

I shrugged and knotted the laces of my boots tightly.

'Just because,' I said.

She and Dad shared a glance and then he followed me into the hallway as I tucked my keys into my pocket.

'You are going to be OK tonight, aren't you?' he asked, as I opened the front door. Warm air blasted into the hallway like we were stepping off an aeroplane into some exotic land.

'Yeah, of course. I'm just out with some people from school. I might stay at Donna's.'

'I have a bad feeling about this,' Dad said, taking my hand in his. 'Don't go out, Claudette, not tonight. Stay here. Stay home.'

I smiled and released my hand from his, hugging him as I slid one foot out of the door.

'I'm going to be fine,' I said. 'Really. I'll go and then I'll come back. Trust me.' I attempted to unfurl from our hug only for Dad to hold me tighter and tighter.

'I love you, Claudette,' he said quietly. 'Be safe.'

I made my way out into the night.

'I'll be back,' I said, as I made my way down the street. 'I'll see you in the morning.'

I met Ross two streets back from the Mariners, behind the old newsagents. He was smoking a cigarette and clutching a plastic bottle of cider that was half drunk.

'So cool,' I said, rolling my eyes as he jumped at seeing me. The cigarette shot from his lips and rolled off the kerb and down the drain.

Ross sighed and took a sip from his bottle.

'It's you, you make my nerves bad.'

'Welcome to my world,' I said and took the bottle from him, taking a swig before grimacing.

'What is that?' I asked, as the sugary poison trickled down my throat.

Ross shrugged.

'It was only a quid. Well, would have been if I'd paid. Deep pockets ...' he said with a smile, sliding his hand across the large gap at the front of the hoodie and pushing it outwards from his belly, demonstrating the full scope of his shoplifting abilities.

'Nice,' I said, taking another reluctant sip. 'So much for supporting local trade.'

'Nah, it was from the supermarket. Sticking it to the Big Man, aren't I?'

'*Robin Hoodie*,' I said, taking a third sip before conceding defeat and handing it back to him.

'That was nearly funny.'

'Two more sips and that'd have floored you and you know it,' I said.

Ross checked behind me to make sure the coast was clear. 'What's the plan, then?' he asked.

'I just need some time on my own with him. I want to talk to him.'

'He's not really that chatty.'

'I'm endearing.'

'You're insane,' he said. 'Literally you're mad. Not the way everyone thinks, either. You're fully blown out of this world mad.'

'It's my shtick,' I said, then paused. 'Does he know you're back on the grid?' I asked and Ross nodded.

'We're text friends again,' he said, taking a cheap pay-as-you-go mobile out of his pocket.

'*U OK hun* and all that?' I asked.

'*L-O-L*,' Ross said, somewhat contradicted by the dour look on his face.

'Can you get him here alone?' I asked.

Ross nodded. 'Now?'

'No time like the present,' I said as he began to text.

'You do realise once I send this there's no going back.'

I looked up at sad scaffolding of the Mariners.

'What room did he take Sarah to?' I asked.

'Top floor. There's no real rooms there. All the walls were smashed in. It's open wide like a football field or something.'

'I want you to get him up there. I'll wait.'

'And then what?'

'Then you leave.'

'Leave you on your own with him?' said Ross. 'Are you crazy?'

'We've established that. It's OK, Ross.'

'It's not. He'll come for me,' he said. 'He'll come for me and he won't stop until he finds me.'

'He won't get the chance,' I said. 'Send the message. Let's get this show on the road.'

Ross showed me the professional way into the building. The front was boarded with corrugated iron from the development that never was. It carried torn posters of local club nights and the odd ripped poster inquiring about Sarah's whereabouts. But behind the building, where the scaffolding jutted out like the ribcage of some rotting carcass, there was a cellar door which opened to an expert touch.

'I'll wait here for him,' he said as I slid my way inside, pulling a padlock from my pocket with the key sticking out and handing it to him. Ross had shown me the way in, but he had also shown me the way out.

Other than the front entrance and the cellar door there was only one way to escape the Mariners, should the situation ever call for it: the double fire doors on the top floor, which opened out onto the old metal staircase that spewed down towards the ground. Ross said that at one point it had been secured with a chain and padlock, but they'd both long since been cut through. Ross's only other task that night was to ensure the door was secured.

Dan was to have only two possible points of exits. My plan, however tentative, could not cope with the variable of a third.

'Oh,' I said, just as he was about to seal me inside. 'Can I have a cigarette?'

'I thought you hated smoking?' he said, looking uncertain.

'Yeah well life is short,' I said. 'May as well make it that little bit shorter.'

'Fine,' he said, taking a crooked roll-up from a crinkled box. 'Here.'

'Light?' I said as he rolled his eyes and handed me a packet of matches.

'Thanks,' I said, taking the whole box before he had a chance to object and closing the door behind me. I heard him grumbling as his footsteps clicked sharply up the stone steps and disappeared into the distance.

I stayed pressed against the door until my eyes adjusted to the darkness. Shapes came and went like ghosts until the image of the building settled into itself and I was able to recognise it was a space I could navigate, as opposed to the jumble of dark edges and overhangs that it had been at first.

I made my way through the basement. It was made up of a series of filthy, interlocking, boxy rooms of crumbling walls and carpets of tin and glass.

The stairs to the ground floor were solid, which surprised me. The whole building felt vulnerable, like a daydream that would vanish if you blinked hard enough; as though one overly confident step in the wrong direction could bring it crashing down around your head. To touch something solid, to feel rooted and steady within the disintegrating walls, was an unexpected sensation.

The sound of my footsteps hit the upper levels like light shone on a den of bats. With each tap of my heel on stone I sent creatures scurrying outside.

By the time I reached the ground floor I was alone in the building.

When we were growing up, Donna and had vowed that we'd one day live in the Mariners. The moment it was closed and shut down our future seemed certain. We'd buy it together after acquiring a paper round each, transform it into a palace filled with pizzas and crisps and animals and then use it as a base when we were home from our roles as World Explorer and Professional Cat Burglar (me) and Rich Ex-Wife of A Professional Wrestler (Donna).

Looking around I wasn't quite so certain I'd fully thought this plan through. The building was rotten from the inside in a way that a lick of paint and some strategically placed scatter cushions could never alter. Walls were so broken they wouldn't be strong enough for the supports that mending them would require. The floorboards were patterned with ash and muck and were so frail they barely held themselves upright, let alone the weight of an inhabitant. I felt a twinge of nostalgia for the fading moments of the Mariners' prime that I'd witnessed as a little girl. And, odder still, a brief hit of empathy. The same way I'd had to break completely before I'd had a chance to reform, so the Mariners was beyond the point of return; its only hope was to be torn to the ground and rebuilt from rock bottom.

My ascent to the top floor was brief, but destructive. Everything crumbled to the touch. My hand on the banister caused a snapping of wood that sent a row of slats hanging over the edge of the winding staircase, like the overbite of some cartoon whale. More than once I felt the floor begin to crack beneath my feet and was forced to tiptoe quickly forwards, lest my high school wish came painfully true and the ground did in fact open up and swallow me whole.

The top floor was as sparse as Ross had described it, and it felt less stable than even the rest of the building would have suggested.

The entire length of the building had been opened up to the roof, with windows on either side like a train carriage. The only thing breaking the flat stretch of darkness were the beams that burst from the floors in V shapes and poked through the patchwork roof that opened in places to allow for shards of moonlight.

I sat alone in the dark, flicking matches, sending ignored smoke signals that swirled on the rafters before being swallowed by the night. I was cupping my hand above a flickering flame – daring myself to press an inch closer, trying to ignore the burn and the growing scent of my own flesh when I heard voices downstairs.

Ross's ever eager footsteps shadowed the steadier stomp-stomp-stomp of Dan as their voices made their way through the Mariners. Their voices were shrouded and mumbled but became clearer the higher they climbed, like they were emerging to the surface of a muddy river.

'I heard someone up here,' Ross was saying in pinched tones as he scurried after Dan up the second staircase.

I flicked the flame of the match and wafted the smoke as best I could before ducking behind a thicker beam. With my hand cupping the screen to catch any stray light I opened my messages and texted Donna.

Can u text Adam and send him to the Mariners? I think something might be up, I typed, before hitting send and slipping the phone into the back pocket of my jeans.

'I can't hear anyone,' said Dan.

'Smells like burning,' Ross said bleakly, as they reached the top floor.

'It certainly stinks,' Dan said. 'This isn't a game is it, Ross?' he asked.

Ross took a few seconds to respond. 'I think I heard something downstairs,' he said nervously. 'I'll go and have a look. You check in there.' He scurried away before Dan had a chance to insist otherwise.

I heard Ross stop at the mezzanine. The sound of chains clanking implied that the lock had been secured. The front door and the back door were the only means of escape.

Dan made a long, steam-train exhale that seemed to chill the entire building and turned to leave.

'Hello,' I said, stepping out from the shadows. I hadn't entirely believed our plan would work, let alone planned exactly what I would say to him if it did.

He wasn't startled, but I could tell I'd given him a fright. He turned quickly to see who was there and then squinted the way you do at a person whose image isn't immediately familiar.

'Is this a joke?' he said, walking towards me.

More footsteps from downstairs – quick and light – before the rear door was opened and closed with a sharp click.

'I wanted to give you this,' I said, balling the two notes Dan had paid me for the flyers that never got delivered and throwing them to the floor in front of him. Dan smiled and I found myself taking two steps backwards, brushing my hand across the wooden beam I'd been hiding behind to steady myself as I stepped towards the windows at the front of the building.

'A deal's a deal, Claudette,' he said with a smile. 'Sometimes there's no going back.'

'I get to choose,' I said and he scoffed. 'Not you.'

'Pretty dangerous out here for a lady on her own,' he said as he stepped closer still. I felt a wave of fear judder from my heart right down to my legs but forced myself still.

'I'm no lady,' I said.

'That you aren't.'

'When did Sarah come to you for help?' I asked and he shook his head.

'I think you've got the wrong person,' he said. 'In fact, I'm not sure I recognise you at all. Have we ever me before?' He laughed. 'You look confused. Do you get confused sometimes?' he asked, gently taking my arm in his. His hands were cold and hard. Snags of chewed fingernail scratched at my skin as he inspected my arms.

'Sometimes,' I said, growing cold at his touch.

'Ever think about covering these up?' he asked, stroking his fingers across my scars.

'No.'

'They're hideous. Don't they remind you of the time you nearly died?'

'They remind me that I lived,' I said quietly, snatching my arm away.

'You're a brave little soldier aren't you, Claudette Flint. You think you've got through the worst life has to throw at you, well guess what? You haven't. You haven't survived. You just haven't died yet,' he whispered sharply, his breath a pungent mix of cheap spirits and old tobacco. 'Don't mistake coincidence for achievement.'

'You're a poet,' I whispered, leaning in to meet his face as he jabbed his fist into my stomach, causing me to double over, hitting the floor with my knees so that I was forced to stare up at him as he towered over me.

'You stupid little bitch,' he said. 'What did you think was going to happen here? What difference did you think you could make?'

My insides were screaming and I knew speech would be hard won, but I forced myself to laugh as he walked away.

'You think you're that special?' I asked. 'You think you're that important? You're a sad little man worth nothing. Less than nothing. You only attract kids, whose lives are so bad even your company seems like a positive alternative. You're tiny. And you're weak. And I hate you.'

Dan turned slowly and watched me as I stood up.

'Really?' he asked, lifting the fabric of his jumper to reveal a knife handle sticking from the elastic of his tracksuit bottoms. 'You might want to rethink your attitude.'

'Sarah didn't rethink hers though, did she?' I asked.

'And look where that got her.'

'Thousands of pounds of your money that you still haven't got back,' I said as he lurched towards me and grabbed me around the waist, pressing me towards his body.

'Dead,' he whispered, so loudly that he may as well have yelled it. 'She had big ideas too. And look how that turned out.'

I somehow released myself from Dan and walked back over to the window.

'I've fought worse than you,' I said as he began to circle me, keeping his distance.

'Oh really.'

'You're nothing.'

'I was something the night Sarah died.'

'You killed her.'

'Is that what you want to hear?' he said. 'Some big confession?' I nodded. 'Nah,' he said. 'I didn't kill Sarah.'

'You took every chance she had of a life away from her.'

'Now who's the poet? But the stupid bitch swam out into those waves herself. Shame, really. If I had caught her that night I would have done it.'

'Done what?'

'Killed her.'

'I knew it,' I said.

'So what now?' he asked, raising his arms either side of him

264

up to the ceiling expectantly, as he spun around. 'You record-ing my confession? You going to have me arrested for a crime I would have committed given half the chance? Or are you going to go and tell everyone how brave and strong you are and how bad and weak I am?' he asked as we slowly moved in circles. 'Or, are you going to kill me?'

'No,' I said, stopping beside a window. 'But I will fight you.' I felt my phone vibrate three times in my back pocket.

'Might I remind you, little girl . . . ' he said, taking the knife from its resting place and pointing it towards me, dabbing the air either side of my head like he was knighting me from afar.

'Nah,' I said. 'You'd kill me before I got a punch in. I want to test your strength.' I took the matches from my pocket. 'Your real strength. Have you ever played Chicken?' I took a match and lit it, flicking it in his direction, the same way he had gotten the barman's attention that first day in the club.

'You want to take this outside?'

'No,' I said, as the tip of another match exploded on the sandpaper before I flicked it his way. 'I want to stay here. Right here.' I lit three matches together, lowering their heads until the entire sticks were on fire.

The tips of my fingers began to singe and I moved the matches as quickly as I could without extinguishing the flames, before placing them on a dry patch of the wood surrounding one of the huge windows of the Mariners.

The bone-dry old wood began to singe and smoulder quicker than I imagined, and before long there was a beautiful lick of fire teasing tentatively up the window.

'You're as crazy as everyone says, aren't you?' he asked shak-ing his head as he laughed.

'Maybe,' I said. 'But I bet I can sit this out longer than you.

I bet I can sit here longer than you can. I bet I can watch you run, terrified, before it gets too much.'

'I think you've bitten off more than you can chew,' he said as I moved forward slowly. The flames began to multiply steadily and smoothly, the heat silently pulsing at my back until it became unbearable. 'I think you've underestimated me.'

'And I don't think that's possible,' I said, kneeling down so that I was sat on the floor with my knees bent beneath me.

'I'm a man of pride,' he said, slowly lowering himself to the floor but remaining poised on two bent knees like a praying mantis.

'You're a piece of shit,' I spat.

'I will cut your tongue clean out of your head if you ever speak to me like that again,' he whispered.

'I will fight you,' I said

'You will lose,' he said. 'My army is bigger than yours.'

'Ah,' I said. The flames grew so bright that night had become day inside the cranium of the building. 'Honour amongst thieves and junkies. And bastards.'

'Them's my people,' he smirked.

Outside there was the sound of running towards the building. Inside, the smell of the fire moved from bonfire night to something more sinister. The back wall began to pulse and glow, the flames spreading outwards and upwards.

'How many of them do you think would take a bullet for you? How many would lie for you?'

'Once I pull strings they tend to stay pulled,' he said, glancing up at the flames that were licking towards the ceiling. Even he couldn't hide his concern.

'But what if they had the chance to get out? What if one word and they could be away from you and everything you do.'

'They know where their bread's buttered.'

'Only because you make it that way,' I said. 'You squeeze people out. You stamp on them, stamp them down and down until they feel like they've got nothing to offer the rest of the world.'

'It's not personal,' he said with a shrug. 'It's just business.'

'Not one person you know is friends with you because they care. Not one person you pay wants to accept your money. You got where you are by taking people at their lowest and greasing the pole so they could never get back up.'

'That's how the world works,' he said as flames crept along a beam at the far edge of the wall. 'There's the weak and there's the strong.'

'Then there's the bad,' I said as the sound of someone yelling outside grew over the flames. I coughed into my hand as the smell began to tickle the back of my throat and Dan raised his eyebrows in a smug, expectant arch. I wiped the beading sweat from my top lip on the back of my hand and continued. 'But you're only strong while it's all underground. While it's all hush-hush. Once you've been smoked out . . . once it's out in the open, they'll turn on you like cannibals. Not one of them will save you.'

Dan looked uneasy and made it to his feet.

The air in the room felt like a vice that was crushing in around my throat. 'They'll be coming now,' I said. 'Coming to see the commotion, to see who's here. It's been a long time since you let yourself be seen in HQ, eh?' My voice was raised over the roar of the flames.

'I'm the mastermind.'

'You're an idiot,' I said. 'Don't you see? They've wanted to nail you for so long, Dan, but you were so far removed. Now they have you where they want you. They're coming, like you came for Sarah. The difference is they'll catch you, right in the middle of it all. How much money do you have stashed in here? How many grams are hidden in these walls? Your entire life is on fire and you're too stupid to realise that you can't outrun it. You lost. Sarah won. It's finished.'

In that moment Dan was frightened, and it felt nourishing to see. For the first time ever he seemed to recognise that he was alone.

'Bitch,' he yelled, turning quickly and running from the room.

I made my way as close to the door as I could, savouring the cool air of the corridor, and smiled as I heard him trying the locked fire escape.

He yelled and screamed, kicking his frustration as he flew down flights of stairs only to be met by the loud, authoritative knocking of a truncheon on the corrugated metal of the main entrance.

He slipped down towards the cellar staircase, while I defied every instinct in my body and made my way back into the burning room. I picked up wood, bottles – anything with heft from the floor – and began throwing them through the glass of the rear windows, trying everything I could to alert whoever was outside to the back of the building.

Before long the heat and the smoke grew too much. The room, however sparse, was hazy and obscured. I counted to eight on my fingers and made my way back towards the door from memory, never lifting my feet from the ground lest I tripped, before I arrived in the corridor and collapsed on the floor.

I gifted myself a moment to breathe before jumping back to my feet. The pounding of the front door grew louder and I could hear that the metal was beginning to give way to whatever force was being used on the other side.

I jumped down to the mezzanine level and retrieved the second key from my pocket just as the front door gave way and a stream of footsteps cascaded into the main hall of the Mariners. The chain scratched my hand and drew blood as I unravelled it but eventually I made it out onto the escape staircase and down to terra firma.

Blue lights cast shadows from the back of the building where the sound of Dan being held to the ground by officers played out like sweet music.

I removed my bobble, and drew my hair across the front of my face as I slid beneath the iron fence surrounding the building. Then I was out in the yard of the ice-cream shop next door. This was our meeting place. But Ross was not there.

I whispered his name almost inaudibly, and then again, more frantically this time, as the sound of sirens grew closer.

The old wooden door of the outhouse opened and Ross looked up at me from where he sat on the floor, tears rolling down his face.

'We're safe,' I said, sitting down next to him and closing the door behind me.

'What happened?' he whispered. 'Are you OK?'

'He's gone,' I said, holding on to him in the dark. 'It's over.'

22

Another Place

Once it was all over, and the dust had settled on our little town, Paula and a team of her closest friends and enemies from the community centre organised a memorial service for Sarah. One of the pictures Jacob left for me had been used on the remembrance flyers handed out throughout town.

Between the pier and the lighthouse it seemed as though the entire town had turned out. Even those who would normally venture no further than the pub made an effort to pay their respects. Mobility scooters chugged unsteadily across the sand until their wheels were stuck in the soft ground and spun helplessly, while children ran to the shore, kicking and splashing, celebrating the last moments of light as yet another summer drew to a close. Even people who got two buses to school turned up. Some were in uniform. Most in their Sunday best – they stood patiently in line with their parents, while volunteers handed paper lanterns with marker pens and candles from the trestle tables which had been erected on the dunes above.

It is strange to see your entire world congregate. The only other time I'd seen so many people in one place was on New

Year's Eve, the millennium year, when we'd followed the bangs and the lights as a rogue firework took out a chip shop and a neighbouring kebab shop in thick, oily flames which gave everything the faint odour of scorched fat long into February.

I had worn a dress for the occasion and felt unusually good about myself as I made my way down with Dad and Paula to write messages on our lanterns before we released them into the evening with the others. My confidence was not unfounded, either, as Donna made a lewd gesture from across the beach where she stood with her mum and Adam – who, since catching Dan Vesper, was in training for his role as real life policeman.

What they found in Dan's jacket and car alone would have been enough to have him jailed for so long nobody would ever remember what he had done or who he had been. But the bundles of money and drugs that the firemen had discovered after extinguishing the top floor of the Mariners really stuck the boot in it. Dan would be conducting his business from a cage for as long as anybody could comprehend. The thought of him trapped and unable to get out made me happier than any person's captivity should have.

We made our way towards the front. Paula held tight on to my arm as her ankle went loose in a soft patch of sand.

'That's the last thing I need tonight, to be airlifted out of here and have to call the whole thing off.' She laughed as she gripped my arm tighter. Her duties were done but she still insisted on wearing a hi-vis jacket over the black dress she had picked for the occasion, lest anybody mistake her for a simple reveller and totally overlook her authority and input into the whole affair.

I'd caught her crying in her bedroom that morning, when I'd been running around the house looking for a hairbrush.

'What's the problem?' I asked, my dress only half zipped up at the back and already making me itchy and irritable.

Paula dabbed her eyes as she sat on the bed and looked up at me.

'You look nice,' she said, as another tear rolled down her face.

'You don't. What's wrong? Has one of the volunteers pulled out or something?' I said, sitting down and turning my back to her, holding my hair back from my neck as she politely zipped my dress up without making the grievous error of huffing and puffing at the tenacity of the zip, as Dad often would.

I turned to face her once I was sucked into my garment and she shook her head.

'No – no. All systems very much go!' she said, punching the air in mock enthusiasm. 'It's just ... it's been a funny old summer.'

'You're telling me.'

'And that poor girl,' she said, wiping another tear. 'I just keep thinking about her out there alone, and it's ...'

'It's OK.' I gave her hand a brief squeeze. 'It's over now. Wherever she is it can't be any worse than when she was alive. Sarah died,' I said, removing my hand. 'It was wrong and it was awful. But you have no idea how many people get to live because of that. Just think how many bad things have stopped because of her.'

'Oh I know,' Paula said, rallying and sniffing any emotion from her face. 'I just. It's just a tragedy isn't it?' I nodded. 'So expected and so shocking all at once. I just want to take that little girl in my arms, to keep her safe. I know I'm nobody's mother, but still ...' she said before beginning to tear up again.

I sighed and rolled my head back as though it had been freshly severed.

'Ugh!' I grumbled. 'Fuck that!'

Paula was shocked. 'I beg your pardon?' she said, the angriest I've ever seen her.

'I said, fuck that. You know you're my mother. You're the only one I've ever had and you're the only one I'll ever get. You're my mum, so wear that mantle with pride.'

'Oh,' she said mistily, clutching her fist to her chest.

'I'd never ride you this hard if you were just some random woman my dad was seeing. I'm an arsehole and you have to take it. That's what being a mother is all about. It's your divine right and as much as it kills me to say it you excel in your given role.'

'Oh, Claudette,' she said, wiping a happier tear from her eye this time. 'That's the nicest thing anyone's ever said to me!'

She brought me into a tight hug and made it clear through brute force that it was an embrace that would only end once she was good and ready, and that this would be some time in the distant, distant future.

I wrote a secret message on my lantern and popped the tea light into the holder, prepared for flight.

'Mine's a message to you, my girl,' Dad said, as he readied his vessel and tucked the marker pen into his pocket.

'Well don't tell me what it is or it won't come true,' I said.

'That's birthday wishes, not lanterns,' Paula said.

'I think it's a transferrable rule,' I said, as Dad smiled.

'Whatever happens I'll make it come true,' he said, hugging me. Across the beach, removed from the crowd but close enough to participate, I saw Ross standing alone. He noticed me and winked. I smiled back and gestured for him to join us but with his eyes he politely refused. I shrugged and smiled and carried on watching the water as the sun began to melt into the ocean.

Even I was surprised, after the fire, when there were no knocks on our door. No policeman asking questions I couldn't answer, or hurling accusations that I could not deny. I suppose they got what they wanted. They'd finally snared Dan – after years of him evading them, sacrificing his underlings as he scaled the top of the murky empire he watched over.

Ross and I spent over an hour in the coal shed, feeling the flames above us quench and cool as the fire brigade blasted jets to the rafters. For a long time we hardly said a word. Rather, I hacked and coughed until my lungs felt clean, and Ross dampened his sleeve with drops of leftover cider, carefully wiping streaks of black from my cheeks. Both of us were exhausted from the night before, and from the weeks and months and years before that. Damaged by a life that hadn't always been kind, but safe in the knowledge that somehow, with little more than a box of matches and a stupid plan, something had changed.

Once the coast was clear enough, we made our way out from the yard. I dipped my head and stared at the ground as we passed by the policemen who were taking notes and trying to decipher the static instructions of walkie-talkies. I knew my face was sooty and my edges singed. They would have clocked me in a heartbeat. Ross was not quite so demure.

'What's going on there then?' he asked a policeman, slipping his hand around my waist as he lead me through the scant crowd.

'Never you mind. You'll find out soon enough,' said an unimpressed policeman who was making notes on the bonnet of his car. 'Why?' he asked, standing up, suddenly interested. 'You haven't noticed anything suspicious?'

'There's smoke coming out of that roof,' Ross said, pointing to the top of the building as we walked on. 'Pretty sure that's not always been there.'

The policemen mumbled something patronising to Ross as we made our way across the promenade. Donna had texted with instructions that she was home alone and a warning that if I did not turn up within an hour she would call my dad, the police, the school – just about anybody that could listen.

I turned back briefly towards the Mariners, my hair caught on my face, and saw Adam giving a statement beside a second police car. I hadn't noticed him before but he had clearly spotted me, as his eyes met mine with a look of relief and concern. I nodded once and hoped he'd interpret the look as intended – my apology and my thanks. Mostly I hoped he'd see in it that I was fine. I was alive and that I was well. I'd say it all, in words, one day, no doubt. But for the time being it had to suffice.

We showered and changed at Donna's house as she spat and snarled at our own stupidity. We threw out our clothes down the rubbish chute, rich with smoke, and Donna gifted me a pair of jeans and a jumper and Ross one of Adam's old tracksuits as she snuck brandy from her mum's bottle into the mugs of tea she'd hurriedly poured.

Her fury faded eventually into relief, before she herself dimmed to sleep. After that Ross and I were alone, and we talked quietly to the sound of Donna's rich doze, until the sun bleached the night.

We talked about when we were children. We talked about school and friends and how we came to be here, now, at this point in our lives. Mostly we talked about Sarah. We shared parts of her that neither one of us had known when she was alive and, like eyes adjusting to a strange room in the dark, she suddenly became whole again, and alive again. A rounded story, a beginning and a middle and an ending.

'What are you going to do now?' he asked as the sun began to rise.

'I'm going to do what I always do,' I said. 'Put one foot in front of the other and see where it gets me. What about you?' I asked.

'Dunno,' he said sleepily. 'Maybe I'll just follow you for a bit.'

'I can't guarantee I'm on the best path,' I said.

'We can keep each other right I reckon.'

The investigation of the children's home made the news, but not in the way Sarah's disappearance had. I was at Mr Fitzpatrick's house, drinking tea and regaling him with anecdotes about my life whether he wanted to hear them or not. He turned on the news in time for the local headlines as he did every night. I was mid-sentence. It was only a brief mention, cast in the shadow of a larger investigation, but all the words we wanted to hear were there. There were inquiries, there were arrests – the children were rehomed indefinitely.

Mr Fitzpatrick shed a tear as the camera cut back to the studio, and then segued into a feature on recycling bin wars.

'You did it,' he said, quietly, tapping my shoulder heartily as I sat at his feet, bent-legged and staring at the TV.

'We did it,' I said, looking up at him.

'To Sarah,' he said, reaching down and clinking his teacup against mine. 'For making the world a better place for all those after her.'

'To Sarah,' I whispered, clinking the edge of the china gently to his. 'And all those after her.'

He had moaned like hell when I'd told him about Paula's coffee and conversations mornings every Wednesday at the Community Centre.

'The only reason I'm going is to shut you up,' he told me the day I came to chaperone him to the first meeting. 'And you must stay with me. I don't like spending too much time around old people. They make me feel claustrophobic.'

I'd practically had to carry him there and then spent the entire duration feeling pissed when he ditched me for a pair of merry widows who volunteered at the library two days a week and were thrilled when he was able to elaborate upon the books of Vatican art they evidently got their kicks from.

'How was it?' I asked as we walked home eating a bag of chips that lunchtime.

'Pfff,' he said, picking a piece of batter from the side of the paper cone. 'It was what it was I suppose.'

'So you'll be going back?'

'Only to keep up the numbers,' he said, picking up his pace.

More often than not he was the first one there each Wednesday, tapping his watch and huffing and puffing if Paula was a minute late opening the centre. He'd usually be there until everybody else had left, too, helping us to clear up the tables.

'They do make such a mess, the oldies,' he'd say, scraping icing and cake crumbs into black paper bags.

'Well anything to keep them off the streets,' Paula would say, week on week. He would laugh, week on week, like he hadn't heard the joke before, and return the gesture with the same old joke of his own.

'Cake wasn't up to much this week, Paula. You've a heavy hand.'

'Oh really,' she'd say.

'Icing was a bit dry.'

'Like your attitude. Now hurry up with those bloody forks. They've ju-jitsu in five minutes and if there's one class you don't want to mess with ...' she'd say, raising her eyebrows as he elaborately picked up his pace.

'They say it's meant to be the quietest time of your life, old age,' he'd mock-moan. 'Not for me. Not a moment's peace and quiet.'

'You love it, old boy,' she'd say, giving his arm a reassuring squeeze as she made her way around the hall, collecting stray napkins and wiping spilled drops of coffee.

On the beach everyone lit their tea lights one by one. The crowd expanded as we stepped back to allow room for the heat to enlarge the paper lanterns that pulled lightly towards the sky like winged creatures; only really alive when in flight.

There was a countdown before we released them and slowly a warm glowing wave rose and swelled, blooming above us before dispersing into hundreds and hundreds of low stars, all scribbled with messages of love and remembrance and hope.

The silence on the beach was unusual but felt right in that moment, in its own peaceful way. It was as if for the first time that summer we were all free, and at peace. I leant back into Dad and felt a rush of happiness that I hadn't experienced in a long time. It was happiness that they were there. Happiness that we were in that place, at that time. Happiness, more than anything, that I was there with them, too.

That was what depression was to me; constantly wanting to be somewhere else. An insatiable urge for another place. Some people make a joke of it. You tell them that's how it feels and they laugh and roll their eyes. They want to be in Barbados, they say. Or they want to be anywhere else but the factory line or the checkout counter or the office desk between nine and five every weekday. They usually mean well but if they really understood then they wouldn't be so flippant. If they knew that what you meant was a place outside of yourself, a place that never did and never would exist – a place you'd rip your skin on jagged shards of glass to reach. If only you could step out of yourself, and only for a moment, just to breathe the same clear air that most people took for granted day in, day out.

In that moment on the beach, with Dad behind me and Paula by my side, and Donna and Ross and all the people gathered there, all of that desperation had evaporated. Not for ever, I knew that, but as the tide peeled slowly back and the lanterns filled the sky I felt a rush of calm at the thought that I had come home.

Beyond there was darkness, and beyond and beyond. But in that moment there was only light, and warmth and love. I had been taken and I had been returned. And this would happen again and again, but having lived through it once I knew I was strong enough to weather whatever lay ahead.

I was not Sarah, and I never would be.

There would always be a home to return to. And I would always find the path back there; no matter how long it took.

I'd go away and I'd come back.

And I'd go and I'd come back.

And I'd come back.

I would always come back.

Acknowledgements

Thanks, as always, to my friends and family. Particular thanks to Katie C, whose name I couldn't quite fit anywhere but here, yet who never once mentioned it and maintained a dignified silence on the subject throughout.

Thanks to Broo Doherty, for over a decade of putting up with my endless bullshit.

Thanks to everyone at Atom, whose individual efforts deserve more than this thoughtlessly collective acknowledgement.

And thanks to Sarah Castleton, for making books better.